Also by D.L. Darby

<u>Standalones</u>

Where the Flowers Bloom

<u>Weekend Wonderland Duet</u>

Peppermint Wishes

Starry Night Kisses

<u>Sugar and Scotch Duet</u>

Slice of Temptation

Sweet as Sin

<u>Angels of Désirer Series</u>

Burn With Me

Lie With Me

Play With Me

Die With Me

DOLLS & DAGGERS

WHO SAYS KILLERS CAN'T WEAR PINK?

SERIAL KILLER BOOK CLUB
BOOK ONE

D.L. DARBY

- Accidental cannibalism - I ruined jerky. You're welcome.
- Dismemberment - Let's be honest, they don't need them anymore anyway.
- Talk of SA of a child by a parent - Don't worry, revenge is sought.
- Past family trauma - Mommy issues.
- Detailed sex scenes - To make your kitty purr.
- References to psychological/emotional abuse - And how our babes overcome them.
- Talk of DV - He deserved that rump roast.
- Drink tampering - He fucked around and found out.
- Murder - But make it pink.

- Coloring of dog fur—Not cruelly.
- Mentions of animal cruelty - I'm sorry, I made it brief and not on page.
- Sex near dead bodies - Because that's hot.
- Beating someone to death with a crowbar - Because they couldn't find a hammer.
- Talk of SA by a teacher - Vigilante origin story.
- Dolls - Enough said.

"A Thousand Miles" – Vanessa Carlton

"Oops!...I Did It Again" – Britney Spears

"Juno" – Sabrina Carpenter

"all the good girls go to hell" – Billie Eilish

"Dangerous Woman" – Ariana Grande

"Perfect Day" – Hoku

"I Wanna Be Yours" – Arctic Monkeys

"Gangsta" – Kehlani

"Who's Afraid of Little Old Me?" – Taylor Swift

"Somewhere A Clock is Ticking" – Snow Patrol

For the readers who "feel too much."
You're exactly what the world needs right now.

If I hadn't seen it with my own eyes, I'd never believe it.

Watching it unfold in real time, though, is something else entirely.

She's a glowing neon sign against the pitch-dark night—a beacon of hope for desperate men like me who believe they don't have the strength to carry out the work she's doing.

A fucking vision.

And my once-fucking nightmare, wrapped in a flimsy, sheer nightie.

The pale pink fabric clings to her, drenched from the relentless downpour, turning see-through due to the rain. Her ample breasts heave in a Morse code of pure bliss, dusky nipples hardened to stiff peaks that strain against the delicate fabric. Luscious curves I've spent two months dreaming about—bent over my desk, writhing beneath my hands—tempt me with their dips and arches, trying to lure me from my hiding spot in the shadows of the shrubbery along the fence.

Her head tips back, bubblegum-pink lips curling at the corners, stretching into a smile that pops her dimples—the same lips I've imagined wrapped around my cock far too many times.

Mascara runs down her cheeks in coal-black rivulets, the rain washing away the mask to reveal the truth beneath. A crack of lightning splits the sky, illuminating her flaxen locks, which are sticky with blood. The downpour intensifies, as if the heavens themselves are trying to cleanse her of her sins.

A muffled cry slices through the night, cutting through the rumbling thunder and the deluge of rain, effectively cutting her euphoric moment short as her attention falls to her feet.

I'm too far away to hear her words, but the shape of her lips and the gleam of her perfect white teeth tells me she's speaking to the man cowering in the grass.

My heart hammers against my ribs as I watch the shift—the serene composure giving way to monstrous tenacity.

Never in my wildest dreams would I have guessed that the object of my obsessions—my desires—had been standing right in front of me all along, hidden behind the face of my formally despised work rival.

How could I have ever hated the same woman I'm utterly besotted with?

Whatever the man says, it's enough to send her to her knees. She straddles his waist as she plunges her dagger into his stomach.

Blood arcs through the air, splattering her beautiful face, mixing with the raindrops, pooling in the grass.

His screams pierce the night, a symphony of agony, perfectly harmonized with the treacherous notes of the storm.

She reaches to the side, picks up her discarded mask, and slips it over her head. The doll-like covering is creepy as hell, and the man's cries pitch higher, the sound almost musical as she lifts her arms for another blow.

I can't hear her, but I know she's singing him her lullaby.

Ring around the rosie.

Pierce.

Pocket full of posies.

Slash.

Ashes. Ashes.

Stab.

We all fall down.

Silence descends as swiftly as her dagger, muting him forever.

And as it does, my cock hardens.

The laughter I've fought so hard to hate these past two months creeps into every quiet crevice of the back-yard, into every fractured piece of my soul, fusing it back together like some kind of macabre, golden-laced art.

Abruptly, the laughter ceases.

The baby doll mask turns in my direction. "Come out, Songbird. I know you're there."

Dove Carroway—my arch-nemesis at work and the center of all my affections—is the Baby Doll Killer.

I never stood a fucking chance.

"Do DO DO do do do do."

I snap my head toward Fang, my sweet baby puppers, and point a freshly manicured, watermelon-themed nail at him, doing my best Terry Crews impression.

"And I need you," I belt, harmonizing—badly—with Vanessa Carlton's *A Thousand Miles*.

Fang lets out a long, suffering groan and buries his furry face beneath a paw, wiggling deeper into my tufted blush duvet.

"Aww, baby boy, is my singing that bad?" I croon, abandoning my morning routine at my makeup vanity. Crossing the room, I scoop him up and nuzzle our noses together. "Pep up, buttercup! You're giving Monday moods, and it's Thirsty Thursday!"

His tufted tail wags as he licks the tip of my nose.

"That's more like it, baby boy!" I beam, tucking him against my side as I stride over to my calendar. "We have no work tomorrow, tequila and tacos tonight, and on Saturday…"

I shift Fang slightly, freeing up a hand to tap the neon pink circle marking this weekend.

"…it's meat processing day."

A shimmery sticker of a pink fluffy cat wearing a blue bowtie sits squarely on the eighteenth.

The last day Jefferey Nills will see the beautiful, buttery sun.

Who is Jefferey Nills, you ask?

Only the worst type of man alive—the kind who preys on little girls.

The kind who will writhe in agony as I slowly remove his penis and make him watch while I slice it into strips to dehydrate for my sweet puppy.

"So much fresh meat this week," I sing, grinning as I return Fang to my bed to finish getting ready for work.

Outside, New York is already alive and bustling this brilliant summer morning. Even my early-2000s playlist can't drown out the city's sunrise theme song: impatient taxi horns, people shouting into their mobile phones, footsteps pounding against the pavement in a mad rush to get to work.

Life here is chaotic, and I love it.

After all, chaos is my middle name.

No, seriously. My parents hated me.

Allow me to introduce myself.

I'm Dove Chaos Carroway, Senior Investigative Journalist—S.I.J., for short—at *Metro Media*. I'm five feet even, obsessed with the color pink, and spend my weekends luring men into hotel rooms under the guise of being an underage girl so I can brutally mutilate them and turn their privates into jerky for Fang.

Also known as the Baby Doll Killer.

Shh. Don't tell anyone.

Anyway. Back to the fresh meat.

Metro Media is bringing in a new S.I.J.—someone with impressive references, apparently. Am I happy about some newbie stomping all over my turf? Hard no.

Even harder no because it's a dude.

Don't get me wrong—I'm not one of those women who hate men. But *Metro Media* always gets the hottest scoops on the Baby Doll Killer. For good reason, obviously—I write the stories. Everyone at the agency knows those are mine.

If this guy starts poking around?

That might get... tricky for *moi*.

And it would be such a shame if I had to remove an innocent bystander because he couldn't keep his nose out of my business.

I'm not above deleting someone from existence if they become a problem.

Swiping on some glittery lip gloss, I add one more coat of black mascara to my already-fluffy lashes before pulling the rollers from my hair. Once it's fluffed and sprayed to perfection, I dress, make sure Fang has food, and gather my things.

Pausing at the mirror by the front door, I check my reflection.

Every part of me is a carefully constructed facade. A mask. A porcelain veneer painted in pink and blonde and bubblegum sweetness.

A living doll… from your worst nightmares.

Slowly, I press my painted lips into a smile, mentally preparing for another outstanding performance given by yours truly.

"Showtime," I whisper.

"Book Club this weekend?" Bunny Jones, my best friend and fellow serial killer, asks over the phone as I make my way through the crowded streets.

We've been friends since the night we crossed paths going after the same man—to kill, not to fuck.

I specialize in eliminating men who prey on children. Bunny prefers those who abuse women. This particular target happened to do both.

After enduring a brutal marriage to a man who used her as a punching bag, Bunny snapped. One night, all that pent-up feminine rage erupted in a series of lethal blows—delivered with a frozen rump roast straight to her husband's face until he was nothing but a pile of unrecognizable meat.

And because she's all of five-two and cute as a button, the authorities chalked it up to a burglary gone wrong. An intruder, they claimed, must have been after whatever her husband had stashed in the safe upstairs.

Conveniently, it turned out to be a fuck ton of money. Plus, he had insane life insurance. Bunny is set for life and doesn't have to work at all—though she chose to return to what she did before she met him, working as an investigative assistant for the Metro Police Department.

Lucky us.

"Yes, but you'll have to help me dehydrate. It's a culling weekend," I singsong into the speaker, waiting for the little man to light up the crosswalk sign.

"Sounds good. You know me, I love jerky." Her

voice carries a telltale lilt, hinting at a smile. Bunny lives for talking shop in front of her clueless coworkers. "Excited to meet the new guy?"

"Absolutely not," I reply, grinning as I step into my building and make a beeline for the coffee shop on the ground floor.

Ted, the handsome barista who's worked here longer than I have, already has my morning mocha ready. Without breaking my call, I scan my employee card. He hands me the cup, and I slip him a five-dollar bill with a wink before heading upstairs.

Like all *Tailor Industries* buildings, this one boasts top-tier amenities—gourmet food court, a high-end gym, and fully stocked locker rooms. It's part of why I chose *Metro Media* as my home base. Employees just scan their card, and any charges get deducted from their paycheck at a super reduced rate.

Happy employees make for lucrative business ventures. And no one is happier than those working under the *Tailor Industries* umbrella.

"Gotta go—getting in the elevator now." I press in with the early-arriving masses. "Love you." I make a kissing noise, waiting for Bunny's return farewell before hanging up and slipping my phone into my pink Dolce & Gabbana Devotion knockoff.

I sip my iced mocha, savoring the unexpected

cinnamon syrup Ted added. The spicy sweetness bursts on my tongue as my thoughts drift to the new guy.

Maybe I'm overthinking it. Maybe he's not here to cover the Baby Doll Killer. Maybe he's just a nice, standup guy looking to cover other crime avenues. I haven't written about Bunny's alias in a while. Perhaps Joe—my boss—wants someone to cover both killers separately to keep site traffic up.

"Morning, Dove," the man himself greets me as I step off the elevator. His bald head gleams under the office lights, and his bushy gray mustache twitches with the strain of his smile.

"Morning, Joe!" I flash him a wide, toothy grin. "Are you excited about the new guy? I heard he comes highly recommended." My voice drips with honey as we weave through the maze of cubicles toward my small office.

Multiple people smile and greet me as we pass. To an outsider, it probably looks like I'm the boss and Joe's my assistant. *Metro Media* was failing, and the big bosses were threatening to close it down when I swooped in and revived it like a phoenix from the ashes.

My stories on the Baby Doll Killer captivated a new, obsessed audience. True crime junkies live for my exclusives. Since I have the inside scoop, I put us on the map as far as online media goes.

"Well, that's what I wanted to talk to you about," Joe starts hesitantly. "See, he was originally hired to cover the Shadow Siren, but—"

"Joe." My tone stays impossibly cheerful. "If you say the Baby Doll Killer, I'm going to have to pretend I didn't hear you."

Dove Carroway is always a bright, pink bundle of joy. No matter her mood.

Sweat glistens on Joe's pasty forehead. He dabs at it with a blue handkerchief dotted with red hearts as we reach my office. "I know, I know. I told him that's your area of expertise, but... well, he's very insistent."

Leaning in just enough to invade his personal space, I turn the knob and push open my office door. "You're the boss, Joe. Just tell him no."

"Here's the thing, Miss Carroway—"

A smooth baritone rolls through my office. "I really hate the word 'no.'"

Startled—and irritated because nothing startles me —I swing my gaze to the man sitting behind my desk.

I blink.

Uh, excuse me? The audacity!

He smiles, and it's completely devilish. The kind of grin that probably knocks most women flat on their backs.

It does nothing for me.

Rising from my chair, he moves toward us with a

slow, calculated gait, extending a hand. He's tall. Like, really tall. Then again, everyone is tall to me—even with four-inch heels.

"Wrenley Campbell." His dark brown eyes rake over me, assessing. Judging. I know what he sees—a joke of a woman whose job he'll have no problem stealing. "Looking forward to working together."

Oh, Songbird, we won't be working together at all.

He's got that lethal combination of sun-kissed skin, dirty blond hair cropped on the sides while the top is styled to perfection, and rich brown eyes with high chiseled cheekbones that would usually make my panties wet. He looks like he belongs on the cover of a high-end magazine. And he knows it.

Confidence drips off him in waves as he sizes me up like he's the Big Bad Wolf and I'm Little Pink Riding Hood.

I flash him my best smile—the one I use to lure victims to their gruesome deaths.

I shake his hand weakly. Let him underestimate me. Let him believe he can take my job.

It'll make my victory so much sweeter when he realizes I'm not a woman to be messed with. "Dove Carroway."

Soon to be your worst nightmare.

Disgust.

Pure, unadulterated disgust floods my veins the moment I lay eyes on the beautiful woman before me.

It's irrational but lethal—poisonous. Suffocating. Her azure eyes, so eerily familiar, pierce me with a quiet madness, dragging me straight back to that room, to a time when I was younger. Helpless.

She has the same bouncy blonde hair. The same pretty blue eyes that sparkle with lies, hiding a darkness no one else sees. Long, thick lashes and a heart-shaped face painted to perfection. The only notable difference is the outfit—head-to-toe pink. A color *she* detests.

It's not the same. Stop it, Wren.

Dove's enticing smile never falters as dark thoughts echo through my mind. Delicate fingers, with nails painted like watermelon slices, slip from mine and settle on her hip, drawing my attention to her white skirt—too short to be office-appropriate.

Judging by the way my new boss watches her, like he beats his dick to the image of her prancing around in outfits like this, I'd say she gets away with whatever she wants.

She doesn't return my polite sentiment about looking forward to working together. I mask my amusement with charm and flattery. "I'm a big fan. I've followed your work since the Baby Doll Killer started sending in the nursery rhyme videos. It's amazing how much you can glean from an otherwise silent serial killer."

Her cheeks flush. The backhanded compliment and insinuation that she makes a bunch of shit up for her articles sails over her head as she giggles and waves me off. "Oh, there's nothing silent about her, Song-bird. You just have to stop yappin' to hear what she has to say."

Okay, so the insult didn't go over her head.

My fabricated smile drops. My blood turns crystalline at the nickname. Heat sears my lungs, stealing my breath.

Joe seems oblivious to my discomfort. Dove tilts her head to the side as she scrunches her button nose. "It's okay," she says, her tone too cheery, like a kindergarten teacher explaining a simple word to one of her students. "I'll teach you how to listen."

"Well then." Joe coughs, lightly touching Dove's back as he motions between us. "Looks like you two are off to a good start. Dove, would you mind showing Wrenley to his office?"

My chest remains tight, but I force a tense smile and nod. Dove's head swings toward him, breaking our stare, and my lungs finally expand. She places a hand on his shoulder, locking eyes with him. "Of course, Joe. Don't worry. I've got this."

Somehow, her assurance is anything but reassuring.

As he leaves, Dove turns back to me, her smile somehow even larger. She rounds my frame, setting her things on a table in the corner. "So, you want to cover the Baby Doll Killer, huh?"

Fighting the urge to rub the ache in my chest, I watch her unpack—a pink tufted satchel, then her purse—meticulously placing her laptop, phone, and notepad on the desk before glancing at her keyboard. Her big blue eyes flick to mine for a split second before she adjusts it slightly *then* gives me her full attention, choosing not to speak on the fact that I disturbed her desk when I sat there.

Was it a bold move? Probably. Nothing screams, *hey, I'm coming for your job* like acting as though it's already mine. I could do without the light pink walls and cream crown molding—though, on closer inspection, they might actually be wallpaper.

But I can daydream about renovations later.

Feigning contemplation, I buy time to calm down. There's no possible way she could know what that nickname does to me. It's the literal meaning of my name. I fight the urge to growl when she uses it again, this time impatient for my answer.

"Sing, Songbird. Why her and not the Shadow Siren? You are aware she's my area of expertise? If you're such a fan of my work and all."

Somehow, though she's chastising me, she makes it sound like praise. Her voice—a raspy blend of sex and bubblegum pop—is as paradoxical as her appearance, as the darkness lurking beneath her milk-and-honey complexion.

Stop comparing them.

"Because even though they're both basically vigilantes, the Shadow Siren isn't nearly as interesting as the Baby Doll Killer. She's basic in her form and not nearly as intricate as the Doll."

Dove's eyebrows shoot toward her hairline. "Oh?"

I don't mention my obsession with the Baby Doll Killer. That I've been consumed by her ever since her first video was leaked online. Dove doesn't need to know my fixation runs deeper than the Mariana Trench.

I swear the corner of her mouth twitches like she's trying to fight her amusement. "Is that so?"

Charm filters back into my timbre. "Do you not agree?"

"It's just interesting to hear you basically compliment a serial killer who murders men." She laughs, tilting her head. The sunlight filters in through the window behind her, bathing her in a glow that makes her seem almost ethereal.

"Bad men who prey on innocent children." I don't mask the bite in my tone, and it seems to placate her.

"Well, how about this? Why don't you start by working on something about the Shadow Siren, and I'll take a look before—"

"Are you my boss, or is Joe?" I cut her off.

Dove bites her bottom lip, pearly white teeth that are too straight to be natural peek out before she lets the plump flesh go and rounds the desk. Perky breasts strain against her pale pink silk blouse, every inch of her swathed in a cotton candy color scheme from her sparkly eyeshadow to her platform heels.

When she reaches me, I can't help but acknowledge how our vast height difference turns me on. For a moment, I allow myself to imagine what she'd feel like beneath me. Those big blue eyes looking up at me while she struggles to take my cock. Soft curves reddening from the strike of my palm. My height kink flares. Without her shoes, she's even shorter, which, unfortunately for me, really makes me want to bend her over her desk and bury myself inside her until she can taste me.

I don't remember the last time I had such a strong reaction to a woman.

It worries me that it's possibly because she looks so much like *her*, which, in my mind, is completely unacceptable.

She hums as though she knows where my mind has gone, stepping into me until our chests nearly brush. "Would you like me to be your boss?" Her sultry question hits me right between my legs, causing a swell of revulsion to splash against my insides.

"I'd like you to show me to my office," I reply, breathier than I mean to.

What the fuck is wrong with you, Wren? Stop acting like a fucking teenager.

Dove steps back, and whatever just passed between us dissipates. "I think you're really gonna like it here," she chirps, motioning for me to follow, her bright and bubbly demeanor back in place. "Nadia will be by later to take you through orientation and give you the rundown on how this place works. You're more than welcome to work on something for the Doll, but at the end of the day, we decide on the spread as a team."

She leaves the unspoken fact that they'll have her

back before mine hanging between us—a silent warning to stay in my lane and out of her way.

Something slithers through me as I follow the petite blonde—my new work rival. As I trail after Dove, only half listening to her annoyingly chipper voice, I drown in her thick scent of cookies and warm vanilla—like walking into an ice cream shop. By the time we reach my office, my stomach churns from the sugar-spun greetings she's scattered across the office.

People adore her, and she knows it—uses it to her advantage.

A monster dressed in pink who will make you love her while she plots to ruin your life.

It's been a long time since a woman caught my attention, though not for their lack of trying. I'm not stupid—I know what I look like. *She* never missed an opportunity to groom me to perfection, telling me how handsome I was until I learned that my looks and charm could get me whatever I wanted.

However, the only thing I seem to want, I can't have. No matter how hard I try.

My days are spent chasing the identity of the Baby Doll Killer and following up on leads. My nights could easily be filled with meaningless hookups and half-hearted promises to call the next day, but there's only one woman who occupies my thoughts. And she's a stone-cold killer.

Five minutes in Dove's presence, and I feel like that's about to change.

She grabs the frame of what I assume is my office and swings into the room, twirling with her arms out as she announces, "This is you. You can decorate it however you want, though you have to run paint choices by Joe."

I refrain from pointing out that if she can have an office that looks like it belongs to a rich little girl, then adding my own personal touches—like my murder board and thumbnail posters from the videos the Baby Doll Killer sends to the police—shouldn't be a problem. Men like Joe are all the same. If they bend for the women, a few well-placed words and a threat or two will make them break for the men.

"I'd be happy to show you around at lunch, if you'd like," she sings sweetly, as though we didn't get off on the wrong foot. As though I didn't waltz into her office and loudly declare that I want her job.

Keep your enemies close and all that.

"That won't be necessary, thanks." I hold her gaze as I step around her and sink into the chair behind the mahogany desk.

Dove smirks, perching on the edge of it. My eyes work overtime to ensure they don't drift to the strip of thigh I can see from my peripheral vision.

"Do you have a problem with me, little Songbird?"

"Don't call me that. And trust me, sweetheart, there's nothing little about me." A smirk curls over my lips. I shouldn't goad her. Shouldn't feel the flicker of satisfaction as her eyes widen a fraction, curiosity darkening her gaze when I finally meet it. And I certainly should not be picturing her small frame trapped beneath me, writhing as I plow into her with a force that could split her in half.

She sucks in a sharp breath, lips pressing into a thin line as her eyebrows arch toward her hairline. "You know, I could report you to HR for that. What a way to start your first day," she taunts, singsong and saccharine. "I won't." Leaning over my desk, her blouse dips low, offering a glimpse of lace-encased breasts as she whispers, "But I could."

With a wink and a giggle, she hops off the glossy wooden surface with a flourish, placing her hands on her hips with a shrug as she steps just out of my line of sight.

"I make a better friend than I do an enemy, Wren. Your choice." Her voice lilts in the space between us, carrying its own rhythm—a song only she can hear. But if I listen hard enough, I'm starting to pick up the beat.

"It's Wrenley," I growl through clenched teeth, fixing her with a hard, sidelong glare from beneath my lashes. It's a petty move—something a woman would do—but I refuse to turn my head and give her my full attention.

Dove's smile stretches so wide I half expect her cheeks to split and pour glitter-speckled blood all over my Oxfords. With another shrug, she spins away, and the hem of her skirt flutters around her perky ass, teasing the promise of a peek at the supple skin beneath if I keep staring long enough.

"I think I'll stick to Songbird." Her words drift behind her on a sugary cloud as she sashays back to her office.

My fist tightens, and my cock hardens behind my slacks like a poorly trained puppy, eager to return to its master despite the inevitable punishment.

Yes, please, beat me. I'd prefer her to do it, but at this point, I'll settle for a good palming session in the bathroom on break.

"Fuck you," I mutter to the rock-hard flesh between my legs.

Breathing deep through my nose, I scrub a hand over my face, trying to discreetly adjust myself under the desk.

So much for an easy first fucking day.

"Okay, I know you're doing recon tonight, but I need you," I plead, layering my voice with as much persuasion as possible.

"Love Dove, I hate tacos and tequila night. Detective Dick will be there with all his little buddies, and it's so Jersey Shore it's disgusting. Why don't you just join me?" Bunny's tone is flat, completely unconvinced.

I don't blame her.

She and Detective Dick—aka Hunter Remington—have been at each other's throats since she rejoined the department. And as much as I try to get her to admit it, she refuses to acknowledge it's because they want to hump like her namesake.

"New guy is going, and I can't let him try to steal anyone in the office from me." I glance around the break room as I whisper my mission into my phone, ensuring no one overhears. Wrenley has already charmed half the floor—the female half—and it's only lunchtime. Who knows what will happen by tonight? "He's definitely playing dirty. I saw him bringing Sharon a coffee and Cecilia a blueberry muffin, and you know that bitch loves her muffins."

He's after my job, and I can't let him win.

Besides, who can do a better job of writing about me than me?

"Is he that hot?" Bunny actually sounds interested.

Even though she can't see me, I point my yogurt spoon in warning. "Don't even think about it."

"Oh, honey. I'm thinking about it for *you*. When was the last time you got laid? And a rival? The tension? Swoon." She croons the last word like a damn romance narrator.

Monotonously, I reply, "You realize how ironic that is, right?"

"I-I... That isn't... It's not the same!" I can practically see the blush staining her freckled cheeks as she vehemently denies her attraction to Hunter.

"Uh-huh, sure." I pop a spoonful of strawberry yogurt in my mouth just as Wren enters the break room. I don't even have to turn around to know it's him. Whenever we end up in the same space, my body tingles like it has a Spidey sense, hyper-aware of the songbird cooing at all the little chickadees in the office.

"I have to go. Think about tonight. Please?" I say quietly, tossing the foil top from my yogurt and turning to head back to my office before I have to interact with grumpy Mr. I Wanna Steal Your Job.

Wrenley is painstakingly handsome, I'll give him that, but his earlier rudeness will surface at some point, and no amount of good looks can make up for the fact that he's a dickfa—

"Hello, Dove. I dropped something off for you on your desk. Feel free to go over it before passing it along to the rest of the team." Wrenley's smooth, deep voice drips over me like ice cream on a hot summer day.

Sticky. Sugary. Messy.

His presence at my back is suffocating, and I tilt my head up to see him looming over me. He grins at me from upside down. Or is he right side up, and I'm the one bending backward to get a better whiff of his cologne?

What is that? Cinnamon, citrus, and... sunshine?

Sunshine doesn't have a smell, Dove. Get away from him. Now. Before he fucks up your other senses.

"Holy shit, is that him?" Bunny perks up. "He sounds sexy as hell. Count me in for tonight. I'll take one for the team."

My eye twitches, causing Wrenley's to crinkle with

mirth. I spin out from under him, my mask firmly in place as I face him and cheerfully exclaim, "I'm sure it's riveting, Songbird. I'll take it home to read before bed. I need something new to help me sleep."

He tenses at the moniker. It's what his name means, so I don't see the issue, especially if it keeps cracking his chiseled armor.

"I look forward to your notes," he grits out between clenched teeth, shoving his hands into the pockets of his navy Alain Dupetit.

I know a cheap suit when I see one.

"Whoa... A hundred bucks says you two fuck by the end of the night," Bunny laughs, reminding me she's still on the phone. "You've convinced me. I'll meet you at your place at six."

"Easiest money I'll ever make." I don't bother saying goodbye, holding Wren's glare with wide eyes and a saccharine smile as I hang up.

"Betting against me already?" His eyes narrow, and his pouty lips split into a smirk that makes my stomach flutter.

Only for a second.

Once that stupid measure of time passes, my palm twitches with the urge to smack the smarmy grin right off his gorgeous face.

Instead, I smile sweetly and shift my phone to the hand holding my yogurt. Stepping into him, I trail my free palm from the top of his left lapel to the bottom, relishing the way his eyes darken a fraction and his tongue darts out to lick his lips.

"You know what they say about betting, Songbird?" I lay my palm flat against his chest. Or maybe his abs. Either way, he's rock solid, and I have to fight the urge to fist his shirt and climb him like a tree.

I really do need to get laid.

"What's that?" His biceps flex like he's also fighting his body's impulses, but his hands remain in his pockets, even as he leans in ever so slightly.

"They say in a bet, there's a fool and a thief. You may think you're the thief, Wrenley, but I assure you, I'm no fool."

"I'm not the one betting, Dove." His rich tone drops to a hush as he leans down, his breath warm against my ear, sending electric zaps down my spine, like touching one of those fly swatter contraptions—not quite painful, but not pleasant either.

Yet, the proximity, combined with his heady scent, sends a rush of warmth between my legs. My lips part as he draws back slowly, nearly brushing his cheek against mine.

"But if I were, I'd gamble everything and side with whoever was on the other end of the line—as long as it's against you."

He straightens and turns, walking away without so

much as a glance in any direction other than his office, leaving me to gape after him.

If only he knew what he just bet all his chips on.

"OF COURSE, he's friends with Detective Dick," Bunny groans before slamming back a shot of cheap tequila.

"And, of course, he's a good writer." I toss back two in a row, forgoing the lime as I signal our favorite bartender for another round.

Wrenley's piece on the Baby Doll Killer was impressive, I have to admit. I wasn't sure what to expect, but the way he writes about her—*me?*—is almost poetic. His article didn't just praise her; it read like a love letter to the woman herself.

Yourself. Like he was spouting Shakespeare directly to you.

My articles are written in a way that endears my alter ego to the public, painting her as a vigilante, exposing the filth of her victims. Wrenley, though— he writes like he wants the world to fall in love with her.

"It's not fair that he comes in and ruins our lives in less than twelve hours. Alex!" Bunny slaps her hand on the bar as the bartender refills our shot glasses. "We need a time machine so we can go back to tomorrow—"

"Yesterday," I chime in.

"Yesterday, before the *California Dreamin'* hottie stole my bestie." She leans over and wraps her arms around my shoulders, her long raven hair cascading over me like a cloak.

I look at her incredulously. "Wait. What? No, no, no. No one has stolen me."

"He has!" she cries dramatically, flinging the back of her hand to her forehead with mock derision. "He's tucked you under his wings and flown the coop!"

"I can't tell if you're joking, and that's saying something," Alex interjects, his icy blues narrowing as he pours a shot for me only. "Tacos for you, missy. Or no more alcohol."

"Hey!" she protests, sitting up straight, all evidence of theatrics vanishing from her hazel eyes. "Jesus fucking Christ, I was just kidding. Give me another, please. And three of the cola-braised beef." She turns to me. "You eating?"

"Yeah, I'll have the same." A round of cheers from across the bar snags my attention. Wrenley is with Hunter and his cop buddies, plus a few women from work.

Fucking Cecilia. I knew he'd get her with that damn muffin.

"How do he and Detective Dick even know each other? I thought you said he just moved from California," Bunny asks with a more sober tone than she had a minute ago. She glares at them, the motion crinkling the teal foil stars stuck to her cheek—a mask for the scar left by her husband.

My best friend's mood swings on a dime, and sometimes, even I can't tell if she's tipsy, stone-cold sober, or just a divine actress. Years of hiding her true feelings, of keeping her tongue in check to avoid her husband's wrath, left their mark. Even now, two years after his death, some habits die hard.

"Apparently, he lived here as a kid. They were childhood friends before his family moved to the West Coast for reasons I couldn't dig up." I tear my gaze from the corner and find Bunny watching me, a slow, predatory smile curving her lips. "What?"

"You're into him." Not a question. Not even an observation. Just cold, hard truth, according to Bunny.

"I'm... intrigued," I admit. Anyone who can watch the videos I send to the police of me dismembering men and gleefully stabbing them to death, then turn around and still wax poetic about my appearance and intent? That's bound to pique my interest.

My eyes stray back to the corner, only to find Wrenley watching me intently. For a moment, everyone else in the bar fades away until it's just us. I've never had such a visceral reaction to someone I just met.

Disgust? Sure. But immediately wanting to jump someone's bones all because of his looks and overall disdain for my person?

I guess there's a first for everything.

"Why are they coming over here?" Bunny's voice tugs me back, and I blink.

Wrenley and Hunter are indeed making their way toward us, empty beer glasses in hand despite the full pitcher at their table. I feel Bunny tense beside me. Her body language shifts—rigid, twitchy, like Hunter has caught her in a snare.

If I didn't know better, I'd say she was afraid of the detective.

But I do know better, and if there's anything Bunny's afraid of where Hunter is concerned, it's only her feelings for him.

"Well, if it isn't Detective Dick? I see you picked up a stray. Better keep an eye on this one." My voice jingles with feigned merriment. "He thinks he's a thief."

"Oh, so it's not just me then?" Wrenley laughs, signaling Alex for another beer before flashing Hunter a smirk. "She's this cheerful with everyone."

He's shed his suit jacket, the sleeves of his white dress shirt rolled up, revealing toned forearms.

Hunter laughs, ignoring Bunny entirely as he locks his amber gaze on me. "You know, Dove. If you're not careful, one of these days, some guy is going to mistake your antagonism for foreplay."

Heat flashes in Wrenley's eyes as they slide back to mine. The type of fire you can't figure out if it's meant to consume you or burn you to ash. I hold my smile, cocking my head, silently daring him to add to Hunter's comment.

"Maybe *I* should go to HR," he muses with a full grin before turning to Bunny. "I take it you were the one on the phone earlier? The one I'm betting with? Hi, I'm Wrenley."

He sticks out his hand, arm crossing in front of Hunter, who steps back, irritation flashing across his handsome features as he looks between his friend and mine.

Bunny shakes Wrenley's hand meekly to make herself appear weaker—just like I did when I met him this morning—then gifts him with a dazzling smile. "Bunny. And I'd be careful betting against Dove. I'll survive because I'm her best friend." Her gaze drops, eyes settling between his legs. Her grin turns feline. "You, however, are going to be eaten alive."

My brows flatten at the innuendo, and I shoot her a deadpan look.

Hunter smirks, taking a sip of the new beer Alex

sets in front of him before giving Bunny and me our tacos. "Eh, I think Wren can hold his own. Dove isn't so scary once you get to know her. Right, doll?" He winks at me, and I'm almost positive he's trying to get under Bunny's skin.

Wrenley glares at him for the affectionate term, his lips curling in distaste for a hot second before his features shift back to pretty-boy charm. He turns that devastating grin on me. "I fully intend to prove that Dove and I can work well together. I'm not trying to take her job. I'll be happy to work under her."

My eyes narrow. Liar. If that were true, he wouldn't have spent all day schmoozing. He would have been busy trying to endear himself to *me*.

Bunny chokes on her taco. Bits of beef and cabbage go flying across the bar top as she exclaims, "Oh, I'm sure that'll happen. Under, over, side by side. She likes to be in control so—"

"That isn't what I meant," Wrenley cuts her off sharply.

She shrugs. "Then you're not on my side of the bet."

Wrenley looks at her quizzically while my lips curve up in a grin that denotes my victory for today's verbal spar. "Wanna tell him what you bet me?"

"I don't really care. I told you I'm not a betting man. It was a joke, Dove," he sneers.

"Well, that's good. Because I bet her you two'd be fucking by the end of the night." Bunny's abrasive delivery causes Wrenley to cough into his drink, foam and golden liquid spewing from between his lips to join the remnants of her taco on the smooth, glossy walnut.

"Not happening," he manages between sputters as Hunter pounds his back, not even looking mildly concerned.

I extend my hand out, palm up, curling my fingers a few times as Bunny reaches into her purse, grumbling about how much she hates to lose.

"So then, Songbird, I'll ask again—who's the fool?"

WRENLEY

Hunter grips the bag tighter, his feet sliding back a few inches from the force of my hit. A smarmy smirk twists his lips as he raises his brows in amusement.

"What's got you in a tizzy? Lover's quarrel again?"

"We." *Punch.* "Aren't." *Punch.* "Lovers." *Punch, punch.*

Even though he hit the proverbial nail on the head. My first official week of work has been hell.

From my suggestions getting shot down in every meeting to my articles being siphoned into a folder on Dove's desktop, I've been reduced to churning out mediocre reports about shit I couldn't care less about while Dove's work still takes center stage.

Charming the office hasn't helped either, because the one person I actually need to impress is the one person immune to my dazzling smile and good looks. If anything, the infuriating woman is completely unaffected.

A fact I find most irritating—though, for the life of me, I can't fathom why.

Dove Carroway is an enigma. A riddle I can't crack. On principle, I don't want to be attracted to her, but every time she's in my general vicinity, I can't fucking look away. It's like our eyes have a magnetic pull, drawn together no matter how hard I try to resist.

"It's kinda creepy how much she looks like—"

"Don't fucking finish that sentence, Hunt."

The bite in my tone echoes through the gym. I wipe the sweat from my brow with the inside of my arm as we switch places.

Hunter studies me, unconvinced. "Is that your issue with her? Because I've never seen that woman dislike anyone. And for as long as I've known her, I can't think of a single soul who has a problem with her. She's like bubblegum personified—sweet, sugary, and addicting... if you know what I mean." He shrugs casually, but I know he's baiting me.

He's been doing it all week. Every time he sees me and her together, because for whatever reason, he sees something between us too. A force yanking us closer, even when we try to stay apart.

"What about Bunny?" I counter. *Two can play this*

game, asshole. "She's more my type. I like the whole rocker chick thing she's got going on—sexy without meaning to be, you know? Maybe we should do a double date."

The more I talk, the harder my best friend hits the bag, each strike forcing me to use more strength to keep my feet firmly planted. "Funny," he quips. "Come near my girl, and you won't have eyes left to look at Dove with."

"Oh, Bunny's *your* girl? Does she know that? Last time I checked, she hates you."

I let go of the bag just as Hunter lands a blow, stepping back to remove my gloves and take a sip from my water bottle.

"Ha. Ha." He deadpans. "She just pretends to hate me. Just like you with Dove." He levels me with a knowing stare. "I'm serious, Wren. I've never seen you like this with a woman before. You're not one to go out of your way to be snarky, so what gives? If it's not her looks, is it just because she won't publish your articles? If that's the case, give it time. You just started there. She probably feels threatened because you're a man, and statistically, it's a male-dominated field. She pulled that place out of the gutters. Show a little respect."

The thing is, Hunter's right. *Tailor Industries* was this close to cutting *Metro Media* before Dove came in and revived it. I don't know why I felt the need to start on a sour note with her.

Fuck a sour note. You basically emo-screamed an anthem about being THE MAN in all caps, Wren. No wonder she hates you.

And I'm learning quickly that when Dove dislikes someone, she doesn't make a show of it. No. She delivers her displeasure on a rose-gold platter, laced with cotton candy and glittery sugar sprinkles—making you think she's treating you special while she's really poisoning you from the inside out.

My ringtone cuts through the silence.

The gym is quiet for a Sunday, or at least that's what the attendant at the front said. We usually go to Hunter's gym, closer to Metro P.D. headquarters, but since I have access to the one in the *Metro Media* building, we decided to try it out and haven't returned to his since. The air here smells crisp and clean, not like a pit of sweat-drenched misery, and there's a cooler with free imported water and top-tier sports drinks just outside the locker rooms—which are fully stocked with the best hair and skin products money can buy.

We hadn't even made it out of the locker room before Hunter announced he was going to be my permanent plus one.

He chugs his water, giving me a sidelong glance as I swipe my screen and send the call to voicemail.

"Everything okay?" he asks, the question heavy with a familiar delicacy that rattles the marrow in my bones.

Even after all this time, my best friend still hasn't given up hope that I'll eventually talk about what happened back then. Why I had to leave New York and finish high school across the country in California—confirm his part in that decision.

Lighten up, Songbird. Life isn't as serious as you make it out to be. Dove's parting words from Friday echo in my head just as my screen lights up with a voicemail notification.

"How *is* your mother?"

Hunter's eyes are glued to my screen as I lift my tired gaze to his. His lips are tight, his skin a little paler than it was seconds ago, and his amber eyes are dark with the same shadows as the last time he asked that question.

"She's fine," I clip, swallowing the bile rising in my throat as we head to the locker room.

Hunter inhales sharply, another prying question no doubt on the tip of his tongue, but his phone buzzes, stealing his attention.

"Shit." He breathes the word out, quiet but firm.

"What is it?"

"The Doll struck again." His voice is grim. "She sent in another video."

A zip of adrenaline shoots down my spine.

Finally.

"Does that mean you have to go in?"

Hunter sighs, knowing full well I'm going to hold him to his promise this time. So far, I've had to wait until they scan her videos for any clues to her identity, but he guaranteed me a seat at the table when the next one dropped.

"Do you have your press badge?" He pinches the bridge of his nose, already typing out a message.

"Always."

I can't stop the way my voice shakes with excitement.

Hunter gives me a dry look. "Only you would be happy to hear she took another victim," he mutters. It's followed by something else, but I don't hear it over the blood rushing in my ears.

Because my excitement isn't just about the Baby Doll Killer taking another life.

It's that I get to see the video before a certain pastel-pink princess does.

<u>Dove</u>

Oops!...I Did It Again blares over the speakers as I thinly slice the last remnants of Jefferey Nills' penis. I sing along, swaying my hips as I lay out the meat, preparing it for the dehydrator.

Fang gnaws contentedly on the final piece from the previous batch, stretched out in his oversized pink bed between the kitchen and small dining room. "Is that good, baby?" I coo.

A jingle of keys makes his ears perk up, and seconds later, Bunny's dogs—a black Pomeranian named Yasha and a white one named Maru, after one of her favorite animes—come bounding in.

The kitchen fills with excited yips as the dogs greet each other before Yasha and Maru snatch up Fang's jerky, immediately tussling over it. My sweet little sharer decides to let them have it, jumping up on Bunny as she walks in, a bottle of watermelon vodka and our book of the month clutched to her chest.

"Hey, Love Dove," she sings. "Excellent song choice. Very appropriate." She sets the alcohol on the counter and scoops Fang into her arms. "Hey, my man."

"How was your weekend?" I ask, popping the trays into the machine. "Everything go well?"

A smirk curls her lips before she kisses the top of Fang's head and sets him down. He joins her pups, who've already broken the jerky into smaller pieces, settling beside them with his portion. "Everything went great. Kent Peterson won't be bothering anyone ever again."

"Did you make him suffer?" I retrieve our usual drinkware—blush-colored vintage goblets we found at a flea market last year—and start mixing our drinks.

Bunny hops onto a stool, plopping her black leather bag beside her, digging through it for the ring light she uses when we take our book club photos. "I busted each of his knuckles, slowly, one at a time, and the bastard had the audacity to pass out after the fourth one," she says with mock astonishment.

"What a weakling." I laugh, retrieving the rose-shaped ice cube molds from the freezer and popping out the pretty chunks of ice, each containing frozen raspberries and mint leaves.

We share a grin before she continues, adjusting her phone and pulling the book closer to play with lighting. "I know, right? Anyway, I used smelling salts to wake the asshole up and continued on my merry way. He's currently stewing on his evil ways in my basement with crushed hands and feet. I'll finish him off tonight." Her voice is light, almost cheerful, as she snaps a few photos of the pretty pink book.

"Ooh, drawing this one out?" We clink glasses, taking small sips before setting up the shot.

Tailor Tech, a division of *Tailor Industries*, is preparing to launch a new social media app called

Iconic. Employees are getting the opportunity to test it before the public launch, and so far, Bunny and I are enjoying it. We've already built quite a following for our Cereal Killer Book Club.

Bunny pulls a mini box of Lucky Charms from her bag, pouring it into the cream ceramic bowl with little bunnies on it—the one I keep here just for her. Bunny's favorite food group is cereal, hence our book club name. Not to mention the play on words.

We think it's hilarious.

"He's a fucking douchebag," she says, sloshing oat milk into her bowl after I hand her the carton. "Put his wife in the hospital twice this month alone. And she made up good excuses for both trips, which tells me she's used to it." She takes a photo of her setup before shoveling a spoonful into her mouth. "He deserves to suffer."

"Hey." I reach over, laying my hand on hers. "You don't have to convince me, Buns."

Her anger softens, shoulders relaxing as she chews her sugary bite before washing it down with the watermelon cocktail. "I know." She checks her watch. "Let's get this posted before we have to go. What should I put as the caption?"

She types as I dictate. "Found this beautiful gem in a cute, pink bookstore in Brooklyn. It's like *Gilmore Girls* meets *Practical Magic* with a hot, swoony guy, kitty familiars, and an FMC with pink hair... say less! Lucky Charms are the vibes with this magical read. QOTD: Are you reading along with us this month? #weloveindieauthors #supportlocal #jessicahoffaauthor #cerealkillerbookclub.”

Once it’s posted, I round the counter, sitting next to her. Golden sunlight beams through the dining room window, casting its glow over her features, turning the shiny white scar on her cheek a silvery shade. It’s rare for her to go out without covering it with a foil sticker, but she never leaves home without a pack of them in her bag.

“When is the video going through?”

“At three. I’m pretty sure Hunter told Wrenley he could sit in on the viewing this time,” she says, finishing her cereal. “How have things been at work between you two?”

“Interesting, to say the least.” I prop my chin in my hand. “I’m starting to wonder why he wants to work for M.M. He could go anywhere and have his articles published. He’s a great writer, and if he weren’t so infuriating, I’d probably fall for him with how he writes about me... well, the Doll.”

“Why *won’t* you publish his articles?”

“Because he romanticizes her. At the end of the day, the Baby Doll Killer still does just that—kills. When I write about it, I make sure the public knows how awful the alleged victims were. When he writes, he makes murder seem sexy and the Doll alluring. He's enamored with her, and the last thing we need is the public seeing her that way. She's a vigilante, not a sex symbol." I sigh. "I wear fuzzy slippers and sing lullabies, for crying out loud. Wrenley will start a movement where civilians start going out and taking matters into their own hands. That will draw bad attention to *Metro Media.* Not to mention, it'll paint our alter egos in an extremely bad light if the public starts romanticizing us. We still have the press on our side. I'd like to keep it that way."

Maybe I should just explain that to Wrenley—without giving myself away, of course. But I'd be lying if I said I wasn't stringing him along for my own personal reasons. He'll stick around if I keep telling him he just has to work harder before I publish something of his.

And for whatever reason, I don't want the songbird to fly away just yet. Something about him captivates me. Or maybe I'm obsessed with how he sees me as the Doll. It's fascinating—his resentment for me versus his infatuation with her.

A part of me wonders if he's attracted to the *idea* of the Doll. Of a masked woman sneaking in, tying him up, and using his body for her pleasure. It's a normal fantasy for women about men, so why can't men feel the same?

Even more intriguing? The idea doesn't seem so bad to me. I've often daydreamed about having Wrenley completely at my mercy—not to torture or kill, but to fuck. His tall frame quivering beneath me, hands bound so he's unable to touch. His heated gaze taking in every naked inch of me as I writhe above him, riding his generously sized cock until he fills me—and it is quite large. I glimpsed its impressive outline at the gym the other day. The thought of making it fit had me so wet I had to cut my treadmill session short before anyone noticed.

But back to my daydream. Right when he comes, I'll remove my mask, letting him see it's me milking him dry. Me he's allowing to tie him up and fuck him silly.

What would he do then if I untied him? Would he fuck me like he hates me? Pour all his aggression into a sweaty, furious bed session, only to go back to sneering at me in the office?

A shiver runs through me, goosebumps prickling my skin.

"Do I want to know where you just went in your head?" Bunny's voice snaps me out of my trance. My cheeks heat as I avoid her knowing gaze and devilish smirk. "Seriously, Dove, I don't think I've ever seen you in love."

"I'm not in love!" The squeak in my voice betrays me.

"Uh-huh. Sure." She sips her drink. "Just don't let him leave. Maybe throw him a bone every once in a while. Play a little nicer. Because when you put it that way, you're right, and the last thing we need is him spreading that shit elsewhere."

She's right. But something tells me that once I let my guard down around the songbird, he'll prove far more dangerous than he lets on.

Just like I wear a mask to hide who I truly am, Wrenley wears one of his own, hiding his true intentions behind a charming disguise.

I just need to figure out what his secret is.

"YOU HAVE TO BE JOKING." I don't even bother hiding my annoyance as Bunny strolls into the conference room, Dove hot on her heels—a flare of pink in a sea of dark, monochrome civilian clothing and police uniforms.

Her long blonde locks are tied up halfway with a giant white bow, her face painted to perfection. Her light pink ruffled dress hugs her curves yet somehow still looks professional, even paired with her signature four-inch platform heels.

Multiple pairs of appreciative eyes follow her as she trails Bunny toward where I sit at the back of the room. From what I can tell, Dove and I are the only press in attendance, but we're still relegated to the back because this isn't a time for questions—only silent observance.

"Play nice," Hunter murmurs, though I'm unsure if he's warning me or talking to himself. He looks at Bunny with so much yearning I almost feel bad for him. Because as much as he wants her, she returns his longing stare with a disgusted curl of her lip.

"Hunter," she greets flatly, crossing her arms as she turns toward the front of the room and leans against the table.

My eyes hone in on Dove, who lingers a few feet behind. She's laughing, engaged in conversation with an officer who looks at her like the sun shines out of her ass and he needs a hefty dose of Vitamin D.

"Bunny," Hunter returns in the same flat tone, mirroring her posture.

The officer leans down, and my body jerks instinctively—as if preparing to rise and intervene—when Dove slants into him slightly, hanging on his every word. Irrational rage washes through me, laced with irritation and a feral need to plant myself between them.

I hate how my body reacts to her.

Hate the number of times I've imagined her pouty pink lips wrapped around my cock over the last week. Her petite frame beneath me as I bend her over my desk.

Dove reaches out and touches the officer's arm.

"I'll see you Thursday," she says before walking our way.

I bristle as she sits, beaming like she's actually happy to see me. "Beautiful Sunday, isn't it, Songbird?"

Ignoring her, I continue trying to set the officer she was speaking to on fire with my nonexistent brain powers. It's not until she puts herself directly in my line of sight that I refocus on her sparkling blue eyes.

"What are you doing here?" *Same as you, idiot. What kind of question is that?*

Her face scrunches up, mirroring my thoughts. "Same as you, silly. How was your weekend?"

Dove begins unpacking her bag, setting a pink pencil with a white fluffy puffball on the end next to her pastel notebook. A picture of a sunbathing llama graces the cover with the words No Drama Llama. She also pulls out an old-fashioned tape recorder, painted pink, and arranges everything in a neat line before turning toward me, ducking her head to catch my gaze.

"Everything okay with you today? You seem... off. Are you nervous?" Her head tilts in mock sympathy. "Watching her videos can be quite gruesome. Do you need a barf bag?"

She looks like she's trying to hold back a smile, drawing my attention to her bubblegum-glossed lips as the corner of her mouth twitches. My cock jumps in response, and for a moment, I imagine what she'd do if I hauled her out of here right now and shoved her to her knees in the alley out back.

The thought of ruining her pristine image, of being the reason her smooth knees are bruised and cut from gravel, the cause of her mascara running down her cheeks as she gags on me, nearly has me coming in my pants.

"I'm fine." I nod at the man behind her. "Who's the guy?"

Smooth, Wren. That'll surely make her swoon and lift her skirt for you.

Dove glances over her shoulder, and I take the opportunity to ensure no one is looking before I discreetly adjust myself. I don't miss Hunter's snicker, even though his back is still turned.

"Ryan? He's a sporadic pillow partner." Dove shrugs, waving a hand dismissively.

If I had water in my mouth, I would have spit it all over Hunter's back. Instead, the saliva gets caught in my throat, and I choke on a cough.

Pillow partner?

That means he knows what she looks like naked. Probably knows what she looks like on her knees and doesn't just have to imagine it. It means he fucking knows what it feels like to be inside her.

A dangerous feeling slithers through my veins like a

viper about to strike its prey, coiled and tense, ready to kill.

The lights dim before Hunter and Bunny scoot to their respective sides of our table so that we have a clear view of the screen at the front. Someone begins speaking, likely explaining the video, but all I hear is Dove's breath hitching, all I see is the way her eyes light up like she's watching a parade of fluffy white kittens.

Fuck, she's pretty.

I hate admitting how far she's burrowed under my skin like a shiny pink tick. I know she's bad for me, but the longer I stare, the more I want her.

Dove glances over and catches me watching her. Even in the dimly lit room, I see the blush staining her cheeks as her big blue eyes flick down to my lips before lifting back to meet my gaze. It feels like I'm having an out-of-body experience, watching the trainwreck that's about to happen as she leans closer.

My fingers twitch, itching to sink into her hair just to find out if it's as soft as it looks, but I'm frozen as she draws near enough for me to feel her warm breath on my lips.

"Careful, Songbird," she murmurs, low and throaty, the words ghosting over my cheek as she tilts her mouth closer to my ear. "Keep staring, and I'll think you're beginning to like me."

Dove pulls back quickly, not sparing me another

glance as she turns her attention to the screen. I release the breath I'd been holding, my eyes darting up to catch Bunny's amused, wolfish grin just as she turns her head.

Everyone quiets as the video begins in its usual fashion. The words *message incoming* glitch across the screen in broken red letters. Then the Doll's laughter resonates throughout the room—broken and distorted from the modulator behind her mask.

A man sits bound in a chair, sobbing. *"Please, I have a wife. I have children."*

There's a click of a tongue, and a sarcastic, *"Aww."* Then: *"Tell them, Jefferey. Tell them what a bad boy you've been."* Slowly, she comes into view, cocking her head as she circles him.

There's not enough of the room to recognize, and even if there were, the film has been edited to appear as if it were taken on a video recorder from the eighties. Broken lines and fuzzy glitches distort the scene, making her look even more frightening. The full cheeks of the white mask are painted red while the empty eye sockets have been decorated with baby doll lashes around them. Pitch-black stares from between the painted sockets—contacts used to hide the killer's eyes.

The ruby lips on the mask are upturned, but I imagine the ones behind it are as well. She dances her fingers across his shoulder, giggling as he lurches forward and screams, *"Let me go, you fucking lunatic!"*

The scene shifts. My pulse thunders.

"Now, now. That isn't very nice!" She moves to the side, kicking her foot up to rest between his legs. Her babydoll flutters around the tops of her thighs, revealing a frilly garter securing a sheathed dagger.

My chest aches with the need to breathe as she retrieves the dagger and flips it around, plunging it directly down into his crotch. Numerous cries of abject horror rise from the males in the room as the victim releases longer and higher-pitched screams than before.

She stares at her handiwork, looking so childlike standing there in pink fuzzy slippers and her sky-blue nightie. In every video she's sent in so far, she's wearing a different babydoll, along with different colored hair. But the mask, slippers, and contacts are always the same.

Neon pink locks pulled up in pigtails bounce as she yanks her weapon from his flesh and reaches for his belt. *"Should we show them what happens to men who touch little kids inappropriately?"*

Some of the officers look away when she reaches for a pair of black gloves and slides them over her long, black-tipped nails. They might see a demon playing with her food, but all I see is a beautiful craft.

There's art in suffering. And the Doll is an artist.

All of her victims hurt children. Why shouldn't they suffer before their demise? Children should be safe from adults. They should feel secure in their own homes, around their families. And when they find the courage to say something isn't right, people should listen.

Adults should be better at reading the signs.

"You fucking bitc—" His words are cut off by the sharp crack of her backhand, delivered with a pair of needle-nose pliers.

"Ring around the rosie," she sings, prying the pliers open before clamping them onto his mangled flesh.

"What are you doing?" he gasps, his breath coming in ragged, frantic wheezes.

"Pocket full of posies," she continues, voice bright with glee as she reaches for her dagger.

"No! No! I swear—I'll never touch anyone ever again!"

An officer gags as she starts sawing. The grotesque sounds blend with the Doll's lilting lullaby and the man's screams—until his body slumps, unconscious from the agony.

"Ashes, ashes," she croons, spinning on her heel as he bleeds out, his severed dick gripped in one hand, dagger in the other. *"We all fall down."*

The screen flickers. A series of images flash:

—His I.D.

—Him with his family at church.

—A candid shot at the elementary school where he teaches second grade.

—Emails between him and the Doll, arranging their meeting—because he thought she was an eight-year-old looking for someone to talk to.

Each image is interrupted by her spinning and humming. Over and over again. A chaotic, frenzied loop.

Unhinged.

And so fucking admirable.

I wish I had her strength. Wish I could do what she does.

The courage it must take to stand against an abuser, to end their reign of terror. The euphoria she must feel, knowing the predators will never hurt a child again.

"I can't believe such a tiny woman can cause so much chaos," a man speaks up from somewhere in the room.

"Maybe men should step back and learn a thing or two," Dove mutters under her breath.

"What a monster," someone murmurs.

"Her? Or him?" another voice counters, dripping with disdain.

"Don't get me wrong, he's despicable, but look at

her." A man gestures at the screen, where the Doll now stares directly into the camera. "You gotta be pretty fucked up in the head to do that shit."

"Sometimes monsters are just broken people, hiding their scars from a world that has hurt them," Dove speaks louder this time.

Bunny hums in quiet agreement. Hunter and I exchange a look—brows furrowed, lips pressed into matching frowns.

I look back to the woman beside me. She's hunched over her notebook, scribbling like her life depends on it, the puffball on her pen swaying with each furious stroke. As the lights return to normal, she absently reaches for her bag. The screen remains frozen on the Doll's unsettling image with blood splattered across her skin and the powdery white mask.

With a sigh, Dove closes her book and sets down her pencil, rummaging through her purse until she pulls out a caramel. Bunny and Hunter drift toward different groups, leaving us alone.

"It must be nice," she murmurs.

"What?" I can't help but watch the way she unwraps the sweet, how her lips part as she pops it into her mouth.

"To have the power to make a difference. To change the world in such a big way." She begins packing up her things. "I get why you think she's perfect."

"Nearly perfect." The words slip out before I can stop them.

Dove scrunches her nose, zipping her recorder into its case. "*Nearly?*"

The urge to drape my arm around the back of her chair in a show of possessiveness burns through me as my gaze lifts past her, locking onto Ryan who's watching us curiously.

"Her only flaw," I say, jaw tight, "is that she only goes after men."

Dove's breath hitches, carrying her question on a confectionary cloud. "What do you mean?"

I grit my teeth, eyes sliding back to the screen. "Men aren't the only ones who abuse children."

I REPLAY Wrenley's words as I brush through one of my wigs.

What he said... it wasn't just an offhanded comment. There was a reason for it. It takes one to know one.

Is it possible that Wren is like me? Did he trust someone who should have cared about him, only to end up hurt?

The soft tap of Fang's nails against the hardwood pulls me from my thoughts as he appears at the doorway of my second bedroom, ears perked. "Are you ready for bed, baby?"

He sneezes, shaking out his mane of white fur before trotting into our room. Moments later, he reappears, his favorite sweater dangling from his mouth.

"Are you cold, sweet boy? Mommy's sorry, she'll turn down the A/C."

At the peak of summer, the city has been blistering. But I'd rather sleep naked than let my precious pup shiver. After all, the poor thing barely has any hair.

Once he's dressed and curled up in his little fort in the corner of my room, I settle at my vanity, rolling my hair for heatless curls. My thoughts drift back to Wrenley.

While the video played, I'd been watching his reaction. I didn't need to see what was on the screen—I'd been there, in the thick of it, making sure that vile man got what he deserved. But Wren... Watching him, the way he stared, almost longingly. Devoutly. As if the Doll were to tell him she was his goddess, he'd fall to his knees and worship her words as gospel.

Yet he looks at me like he can't decide whether he wants to fuck me or kill me. I'd be down for the former. And he can *try* the latter.

I wonder if he even realizes how often he stares when he thinks I won't notice. How many times I've caught him in my periphery. He let me get so close I could have kissed him, and for a moment, I believe he thought I might.

Groaning, I reach for my pack of Black & Milds.

Fang lets out a soft growl.

I glance over. He's watching me, head raised, eyes sharp with judgment.

"I know, I know! But hey, at least I've cut it down to only when I'm stressed!"

His gaze sharpens, and we have a standoff. I glare back as I move toward the window. He looks away when I light up, waving the heady smoke through the small crack. It burns my throat, but my lungs welcome the warmth, even as the rest of my body seizes in protest.

"What is your deal, Songbird?" I ask quietly into the night.

The city sprawls before me, glittering. The chaos in the streets below hums like a lullaby. The cigar lingers on my tongue, familiar and bitter.

Men aren't the only ones who abuse children. The memory of Wren's words echoes in my mind.

"Are you speaking from experience," I murmur, "or did someone you know go through it?"

A painful clench tightens in my chest. And for one fleeting second, I wonder—if he's gone through it too, will he understand me better? Understand my need for control. Why I keep up this relentlessly chipper personality.

Maybe he won't hate you so much if you show him who you really are.

But the thought vanishes as quickly as it came.

Because there's no way in hell he'll ever understand who I am or what I've been through.

We're opposites.

And this is one case where opposites won't attract.

A RESOUNDING CRASH cuts through the din of the bar, the shattering of glass drawing attention to the blonde whose shoulders slump in defeat as she stares at the mess.

"Dude, Alex, your new girl sucks." Bunny snickers before tossing back a shot of tequila. She sucks on a lime wedge, her oversized leather jacket slipping off one golden shoulder, exposing the iris-colored crop top beneath.

"You think you can do better?" Alex snaps, yanking a tap handle down with unnecessary force. "Why are you even here, Bunny? Thought you hated tacos and tequila night." He mimics her voice in a high-pitched falsetto, shaking his head with exaggerated sass.

He's not wrong. Typically, I have to beg Bunny to come along, mostly because Hunter is usually here too. But something must have happened between them, because tonight, she's dressed to impress—and Hunter can't take his eyes off her from across the room.

Vixey—the new waitress in question—inches up to Alex, her honey doe eyes downcast. "Sorry, Alex," she murmurs.

"It's fine," he grumbles. "I was planning on ordering new glasses anyway."

Bunny erupts in another laugh, and I immediately reach over to push her next shot out of reach. "Okay, I think that's enough for you."

It's rare for Bunny to be rude to other women, but she hasn't forgiven Vixey for spilling a rum and coke on her earlier. Never mind that she's wearing black vinyl leggings, and the mess was easy to clean up.

Vixey shoots me a grateful, fleeting smile before turning away. She's cute, with a '90s style aesthetic— tall, lean, and unsure. Desperate to prove herself. Clumsy as hell. She's spilled multiple drinks on customers and broken just as many glasses, and it's only her first night.

Bunny huffs, and I follow her gaze to where Hunter and Wrenley are playing pool with a few women I don't recognize. It irritates me for only a second before I grab my best friend by the shoulders, forcing her mossy eyes to meet mine. "Wanna get out of here? They have karaoke down at The Lounge. Personally, I'm feeling a little Alanis Morissette."

I ask Alex for our bill, glancing away just long enough to sign the credit card slip he hands me. By the time I'm done adding the tip and total, Bunny is strutting toward the guys in her Tamer Manolo pumps, her glare sharp enough to rival Stone Cold Steve Austin's.

"Buns!" I shout, hopping off my stool to go after her—but before I can take a step, a pair of warm hands circle my waist and pull me back against a solid chest.

My senses are flooded with Ryan's spiced, woodsy cologne. I glance over my shoulder to see him grinning at me. "Hey, babe."

My heart thumps against my ribs as I whip my head around, locking eyes with Wrenley, who has frozen mid-jump shot to stare at us. I don't know why I care. The weird tension between us isn't simmering down anytime soon, but it isn't romantic.

Maybe getting laid and expelling my sexual energy is exactly what I need.

Spinning in Ryan's arms, I flash him my best smile. "Well, hi yourself, handsome. I thought you weren't coming."

He ducks his head, pressing a kiss to my cheek before whispering in my ear, "Not without you, I'm not."

I giggle as expected, dragging my hands up his huge biceps to clutch the sleeves of his Henley. "Well, aren't I a lucky lady tonight?"

It feels forced. Normally, I'd be thrilled to ride Ryan until sunrise, leaving him worn out and satisfied.

He loves going down on me, never overstays his welcome, and even brings Fang treats sometimes.

Unfortunately, just the thought of going home with him tonight makes my lower body as dry as the Sahara. Where my clit would normally pulse and swell with need, it's currently tucking itself further under my hood and peeking around for a certain songbird to pay it attention.

God-fucking-dammit.

I'm going to have to fuck Wrenley out of my system, aren't I?

Just once. Maybe I'll tell him I'll accept one of his pieces on the Baby Doll Killer, and then he'll bend me over my desk in glee.

Just once.

That's all I need.

Once.

"Well, I was just talking to Bunny about getting out of here, but," I glance over my shoulder, where she looks like she's having a heated discussion with Hunter, "I think she might have found something else to do."

Ryan looks over my head at them and laughs. "Those two, I swear. Always going at it. They're fucking, aren't they? I don't know what she sees in that asshole."

"Not yet, they aren't." At least, I don't think so. It

honestly wouldn't surprise me, but I'm pretty sure she'd tell me when it finally happens. Bunny and I tell each other everything.

"Just stay here, then. Let me have a drink or two, and then we can go back to your place." Ryan kisses the side of my neck before signaling Alex for a beer.

We've been doing this for months, but tonight, it feels... different. More intimate. Serious.

Steady.

Things I want no part of, because the closer people get, the bigger the chance of getting caught.

"What's up with Hunter's friend?" Ryan murmurs in my ear. "The dude's been glaring at me since I walked in."

I peek over. Wrenley is still staring, openly, not even trying to hide his narrowed eyes or the downturn of his pillowy lips. "Oh, we work together. Don't worry, handsome, it's me, not you. We can't stand each other."

A few of Ryan's friends walk through the door, and he lifts his arm, curling his hand around his mouth as his words rise above the patrons and the calamity that is Vixey as she spills an entire tray of martinis. "Yo! Guys! Over here!"

He walks their way, meeting them with those half-armed hugs men do. I watch him curiously, wondering why my body isn't lighting up like it usually does in his presence.

I just need to get laid. Does it really matter by who?

Anything to get Wrenley off my mind.

A familiar smooth timbre sounds at my back. "You can do better."

Startled, I whip around, craning my neck to meet the gaze of the man who won't leave my thoughts. "I'm sorry, Songbird, what was that? Did you just pay me a compliment? No!" I place my hand on my chest in mock astonishment. "It couldn't be!"

Wrenley laughs. Genuinely laughs as he braces his forearms on the back of the stool Bunny previously occupied. "Tell me, is he as stupid as he looks?"

"Now, now. No need to be rude." I climb back onto my stool, not missing the way Wrenley's eyes drop to my exposed thighs and linger. "Eyes up here, Songbird. Unless you're offering to take Ryan's place tonight?"

His dark brown gaze snaps to mine, darkening as he scans my face. "Take his place to do what, Dove?"

Heat blooms across my cheeks, traveling south as it puddles between my legs. I shift forward, letting the tension thicken. "Fuck me like you hate me."

I imagine what sex with Wrenley would be like. I like to be in control... but with him? I can see myself compromising. Willing to switch, as long as he lets me dominate him in return.

His eyes widen a fraction. I shift to the edge of my stool, pleased when he straightens and steps closer. Our significant height difference still makes it so I have to crane my neck to look at him. My voice drops to a sultry purr. "I don't hear you saying no."

He huffs, the corner of his mouth lifting slightly in a dry smirk before curling downward once more. I jump when the warm pads of his fingers grasp my thigh. His hand is obscured from everyone's view, settled between me and the bar as he drags his fingers up toward the hem of my skirt.

Ryan could return at any moment, but I couldn't care less. Wren's touch lights me on fire, and every nerve ending south of my navel is electrified, begging for his attention to venture where I want it the most.

"Is that what you want?" Wrenley peeks around the bar before hunching slightly over me, slipping his fingers higher until half his hand is beneath my skirt. The air between us is charged and heated—stifling as it steals my breath and suffocates me with his cinnamon-orange scent. His impressive outline strains against his slacks. My mouth waters, and I nearly reach out to run my fingers over it.

I clench my fists and snap my eyes up to his. "It's clear we *both* want to. So let's just screw and get it over with. Get all the tension out of our system. What do you say?"

Unabashedly, I scoot as far as I can to the edge of my seat, relishing the way his fingers dig into my skin. I tighten my legs slightly, caging him in.

Wrenley smiles, and admittedly, it throws me off. He slides his hand up to the top of my thigh, long fingers grazing the edge of my underwear while his thumb slides between my legs. The nail pierces into my flesh, so fucking close to the most intimate part of me. I shift, raising my hips ever so slightly in an attempt to get him closer to where I want him.

I nearly say *fuck it* and throw myself at him as his other arm snakes around my hip, before he lowers his mouth to my ear. "I wouldn't have taken you for such a wanton slut, Dove. But it's good to know that you want me."

Shock spears through me like a harpoon. *Did I hear him correctly?* Wrenley steps back, and I bristle, nearly falling off the stool as he walks away without so much as a glance back.

A wanton slut?

Oh, he thinks he's clever. Thinks he can rile me up and swoop in when my defenses are down.

Well, he has another thing coming.

No one makes a fool out of me and gets away with it.

<u>Wrenley</u>

You absolute fucking idiot.

You had her. She was offering herself up on a candy-coated platter!

I resist the urge to shake my head in disgust and head for the men's room to deal with my raging hard-on.

What the fuck is wrong with me?

Dove just handed me the perfect opportunity to screw her out of my system. One time—that's all it would take. I'd be over it. Over her. Over those goddamn mesmerizing blue eyes.

And the best part? She admitted she wants me, too.

So why the fuck did I just insult her, and walk away like it was nothing? It's like I can't help myself around her.

Because you're pushing her away. You don't want her too close. The resemblance is too uncanny, and if you look too hard, you won't be able to separate the two. What happens if you take her to bed?

I groan as I enter a stall, sinking onto the toilet. Elbows on my knees, I clasp my hands behind my neck. One-night stands are one thing. But sleeping with Dove? That's mixing business with pleasure, and something tells me once won't be enough. No matter how much I try to convince myself otherwise.

Once I get a taste of her, letting go will be impossible.

But so will letting her get too close. If she knew me —the real me—she'd probably laugh in disgust.

The self-loathing does its job. My cock softens just in time for the bathroom door to slam open. I hear the irritatingly rough tenor belonging to Ryan ricocheting off the walls.

"All I gotta do is bring her dog some treats and the bitch drops to her knees and blows me like it's an Olympic sport, and she's going for gold."

My head snaps up in shock. *Did he really just say what I think he did?*

A second voice snickers. "She's fucking hot, though, man. I'd be locking that shit down like a felon on a life sentence. Ain't a man out there who doesn't wanna fuck her, myself included."

"I'm sure she'd be down for a little group action," Ryan laughs. "She likes getting filled in all her holes, if you know what I mean."

Before I can even process what I'm doing, I slam the stall door open and rise to my full height. The sudden noise makes Ryan flinch as he hastily tucks himself back in his pants. Then he smirks when he sees me.

"What's up? Wren, right? Hunter's friend?"

I know he's a cop. I know you don't put your hands on cops. I know that if he wants to, my ass will be in jail for this.

None of that stops me from grabbing him by the front of his shirt and shoving him against the tiled wall. His back smacks against the gleaming cream ceramic with a satisfying thud.

"Stay the fuck away from her."

In hindsight, he could have been talking about anyone. I didn't specifically hear him or his friend, who's staring in stunned surprise, say Dove's name outright. I made a snap judgment and may have to answer for it.

However, none of that matters.

A slow, twisted grin stretches across Ryan's face. "What's the deal, man? She says you two can't stand each other. So, what's it to you?"

"Because Dove deserves better than a piece of shit like you. Don't fucking talk about her. Don't look at her. Don't fucking come near her again. Do you understand?" I tower over him, grinding his shoulder blades into the wall, nearly lifting him off the ground. "I said, do you understand?" I growl through clenched teeth.

"Dude, let him go." His friend sounds concerned

but not enough to step in, which tells me he's not a cop.

"Yeah, Wren. Let me go. Why the fuck are you defending the honor of a girl who can't stand you?" Ryan taunts, as if he's not seconds away from losing his teeth.

She practically just begged me to fuck her. She can stand me enough to want my cock inside her.

I nearly say the words out loud, but that private—yet erotically public—moment belongs to Dove and me. No one else.

Ryan switches tactics, tightening his grip on my wrists. "What are you gonna do about it?"

"Oh, I'm sure Hunter knows people who dislike your kind." I smirk, knowing full well Hunter's going to be pissed I'm using him as leverage. I don't clarify what I mean by "your kind," letting Ryan fill in the blanks. Could be someone who hates cops. Could be someone who hates cocky assholes who treat women like garbage.

Didn't you just talk shit to Dove and treat her like crap?

It's not the same.

I'm self-preserving.

This guy is just a fucking douche.

Ryan's face drains of color. I hit a nerve. Everyone knows he and Hunter can't stand each other. It's a miracle—for him—Hunter even let him near Dove. Since she's Bunny's best friend, I would've thought she fell under his protection.

"Whatever. Count yourself lucky you can hide behind your little guard dog," Ryan sneers. "But you better hope I never catch you alone. Putting hands on a cop? Bad move."

We lock eyes as I release him roughly. He adjusts his shirt, flaring his nostrils before turning to his friend with a shake of his head. "Let's go."

I follow them out, watching as Ryan storms through the bar and disappears into the night.

Slowly, I make my way back to the pool tables, scanning the crowd for a flash of pink. Bunny and Dove are gone.

It's just as well. At least this way, Dove will have time to cool off before work on Monday.

I BALK at the draft of my article Dove just sent over. Red splatters across the entire thing like someone flicked a paintbrush over my screen. Dove's comments litter the margins, entire passages are crossed out, and a big red note at the bottom reads: *It's been long enough. You should know what we're looking for by now. Better luck next week.*

"Fuck!" My fist hovers over the desk, ready to slam down, but at the last second, I pull back, scrubbing my hand down my face instead.

So much for Dove cooling off over the weekend.

"Rein it the fuck in, Wren," I mutter under my breath. This woman has me tied in knots, and I keep tripping and falling flat on my face.

I tab over to my email, skimming Joe's latest message about why he's siding with Dove—again.

Sighing, I open another email, this one approving my piece on the company owner's wife opening another family center—this time in the Bronx—and how the neighborhood had been skeptical at first, but public approval has skyrocketed as the grand opening nears.

A note at the bottom reads: *Show me more of this.*

I let out a disgusted snort. This isn't what I was hired for. I made it perfectly clear what I wanted to write about when I applied for this job.

Grabbing my phone, I open my message thread with Hunter, ready to complain—until I remember he's still pissed at me. There's no love lost between him and Ryan, but using his name to threaten a cop could have put his job at risk if Ryan had filed a formal complaint. It would have been his and his buddy's word against mine, and we all know how that would've turned out.

My phone rings in my hand as if *she* can sense my weakened state from nearly three thousand miles away. Her name flashes across the screen like a warning signal. I hesitate, finger hovering over the accept button.

A soft clicking sound enters my office, pulling my attention away from the device. My gaze flicks to the open door, but no one's there. Still, the clicking persists. Setting my phone down, I lean over my desk and—

What the hell?

The ugliest rat... dog... ratdog...? known to mankind stares up at me.

"What the fuck are you?" I drawl with disgusted curiosity, watching the creature as it rounds my desk to continue its unblinking scrutiny.

Its body is hairless, mottled brown and white skin exposed, while tufts of fluffy white fur cover its paws, tail, and head like some bizarre lion. A gauzy pink scarf is wrapped around its neck, and a darker pink fuzzy headband—complete with a puffball—sits atop its head, pushing hair into its eyes.

This has to belong to Dove.

The creature lets out a low noise, somewhere between a growl and a soft bark, tail wagging as it rears back and launches itself into my lap before I can react. My hands fly up, unsure if this thing has fleas, rabies, or some other disease I might catch.

It's not that I hate dogs—it's that I'm one hundred percent positive this thing is part New York sewer rat.

"Why are you in here, little dude?" I ask as it circles once before curling up on my lap. "No." I wave a hand in a shooing motion. "Go away."

It yawns, body shuddering with the movement, a tiny squeak escaping its maw before it settles, completely unbothered. A thick, bejeweled collar rattles against an attached tag I hadn't noticed before.

"Fang," I read aloud, letting the glittery skull-and-crossbones ID plate slip from my fingers. "Seriously? She named you *Fang*? Aren't dogs with that name supposed to be scary?"

Fang huffs in agreement before closing his eyes, perfectly content. A notification dings from my laptop. I glance at the sender—Mrs. Tailor's office with information on the new family center—before turning back to work.

I barely notice how much time passes before I hear Dove's frantic voice breaking through the office hum. "Fang!" Even in alarm, her voice is bright and chipper.

The heavy clack of her platforms echoes down the hall. A smirk tugs at my lips. Even if she looks in, she'll never see her precious pup curled up in my lap.

No! Fuck! Why do you keep doing this to yourself? Play nice!

My proverbial angel groans in exasperation, but I flick him away like an annoying gnat. Dove appears just outside the glass separating my office from the rest of the floor, wide blue eyes scanning for her dog while others abandon their cubicles to help.

I glance down, smirking as Fang doesn't move an inch. In fact—yep—he's snoring.

Dove hesitates at my open door, unwilling to look inside. Instead, she calls for her dog again and starts toward the break room.

This time, the little bastard perks up, and he responds with a sharp yip.

Her head snaps around, fury ablaze in her sparking eyes. Yes, I mean sparking, not sparkling. If looks could kill, I'd be a pile of ashes on my chair. She stomps into my office.

"Fang!" she calls sharply.

Like something out of a cartoon, his head pops up over my desk, and he barks.

"What are you doing in here, you silly boy?" She ducks her head back out. "Found him!" Then, turning back to me, she narrows her eyes.

"Hey! He came in here. It's not like I stole him. Maybe keep your ratdog on a leash if he runs off on you."

"Ex—excuse me? *Ratdog*?" Dove sputters. "His name is Fang! He's a Chinese Crested and the cutest thing in all the city!" She coos at him as she scoops him up.

As she collects him, her fingers brush my thigh, and I go rigid. Instant arousal hits me like a truck. She doesn't notice, too preoccupied tucking him into her arms like a baby.

"Maybe if you didn't dress him in pink and glitter, he wouldn't have run off," I say derisively, leaning on my armrest, amusement curling my lips.

Inwardly, I berate myself. *Shut. The. Fuck. Up.*

Both the angel and devil on my shoulders take turns slapping me upside the head as they shout at me. One with his halo, the other his pitchfork, as I keep royally screwing myself six ways from Sunday with this woman.

To my surprise, she giggles. It's terrifying. Especially considering she's shown no form of retaliation for calling her such a nasty name—just aggressive edits and condescending notes in the margins of my work, but that's really nothing new.

"Oh, Songbird," she sighs, smirking. "What am I going to do with you?" She clucks her tongue and shakes her head, her big blonde hair bouncing with the movement and falling over her bare shoulders.

Shamelessly, I drag my gaze suggestively down her body. Her outfit today consists of a bubblegum-pink button-down, collared, short-sleeved top with a matching skirt. For being so short, she has legs for days, made to look even longer by her heels. I flick my eyes back up, licking my lips. "I can think of a few things, but I'd really like it if you'd," I pause, letting my overly sarcastic charm fall flat when I continue, "publish my damn articles about the Doll!"

Dove's thick lashes flutter innocently as she leans in. "Well, Songbird! If you wrote something worth publishing, we would. I've been giving you my notes for over two weeks now. Be a team player and take some direction. Or," she whispers conspiratorially, sugar cookie breath wafting my way, "stick to writing what you're good at."

With a wink, she spins away, pausing briefly when she sees my board of crime scene photos from the Baby Doll Killer videos before sashaying out of my office.

I won't deny it—I watch her ass the entire way, and even then, I close my eyes and lean back in my chair, envisioning how the rounded globes of her breasts spilled over the top of her lacy bra when she bent over.

"Infuriating woman," I whisper through clenched teeth.

Rubbing my brow, I exhale long and slow before pushing to my feet. If I'm going to finish this article before day's end, I need coffee.

Stepping out of my office, I glance down the hall toward Dove's. Her door is open. She's perched behind her desk, fussing over Fang as she feeds him a treat. As if sensing my gaze, she looks up. For a second, I almost go to her, almost apologize for the other night at the bar. I haven't felt this much turmoil over a woman since...

Cotton candy pink lips stretch into a wide grin as she lifts a hand, wiggling her French-tipped nails in my direction before tapping her delicate rose-gold watch— a silent reminder that I'm on deadline.

Shoving my hands into my pockets, I head for the

elevator. The building is eerily quiet for a Monday. Even the coffee shop on the ground level lacks its usual chaotic energy. No impatient employees tapping their feet, no irritable customers storming in off the street. But that's par for the course in a *Tailor Industry* building. Sometimes, I forget that not all of New York operates the same.

"Hey, Wren," Ted, the barista, greets me with a nod. "Your usual?" he asks as he scans my employee card.

"Yes, please. Thanks."

As he starts my latte, my gaze snags on a cup sitting on the counter—Dove's name scrawled across it in bold marker.

Ted follows my line of sight. "She busy up there? She usually doesn't forget her afternoon Americano."

"She lost her dog in the office. Probably forgot she ordered it." With a sigh, I slide the iced drink closer to me. "I'll bring it up."

Condensation drips over my fingers as Ted chuckles. "Oh, Fang? He's such a little cutie. Glad she found him. He never leaves her side. Wonder what caught his attention?"

I preen a little at that—because for whatever reason, the ratdog sought me out and deemed my presence nap-worthy. Not that I tell Ted.

"Mind adding a sprinkle of sugar to her drink?"

Ted asks, already turning away to pump vanilla syrup into another cup. "She always does it herself in the afternoon."

I narrow my eyes at his back before reluctantly stepping toward the condiment bar, where neatly arranged sugars, syrups, and milks await.

Grabbing the crystal container of sweet, addicting white granules, I drag the edge over the ice, scrawling a bold F and U before snapping the lid back on. By the time I get upstairs, the sugar will have dissolved. She'll be none the wiser.

Licking a stray dusting of sugar off my thumb, I immediately recoil, grimacing.

Salt.

Gagging, I spin to tell Ted—then stop. Slowly, I turn back to where Dove's drink sits innocently on the counter, looking completely unsabotaged.

If I had horns, they'd curl mischievously.

Smirking, I collect my own drink and head back upstairs, leaving Ted blissfully unaware that someone swapped the sugar for salt.

Dove sees me from halfway down the hall. Her gaze locks onto the cup in my hand, realization flickering across her pretty features. Fang yips, his tail wagging wildly as I step into her office and set the drink on her desk.

"Ted wanted me to make sure you got this." I

don't give her time to reply before making a beeline for my office.

"Thank you," she snarks, dripping with sarcasm, as though it's my job to caffeinate her.

Three... two... one...

The sound of gagging and spluttering tears through the hall.

"WREN!"

Grinning, I shut and lock my office door just as people start standing from their desks, craning their necks to investigate the commotion.

My angel shakes his head. *You just can't leave well enough alone, can you?*

My devil smirks. *It's his own form of foreplay.*

I should have slept with her when I had the chance.

Now, she'll never want to fuck me.

Now, she's just gonna want to kill me.

"STUPID, STUPID SONGBIRD!" Each word is punctuated by a deep stab, blood splattering my mask. The man beneath me is long dead, and this is entirely outside my usual M.O., but tonight isn't about precision—it's about releasing my feminine rage, not putting on a show for the Metro Police Department.

"Love Dove, if you keep going, we'll have a harder time cleaning this mess up. He's looking worse than Nathaniel did when I got through with him." Bunny sighs, scowling as she scrolls on her phone.

My chest heaves with heavy breaths as I stare down. The man's torso really is starting to resemble Bunny's late husband's face. Sniffing, I wipe my arm against the forehead of my mask, smearing blood across the material.

"I have to get him back, Buns." I press my hands

against the corpse's stomach. The wet squelch of blood and torn flesh echoes through the basement as I push up to my feet. Peeling off my gloves, I toss them and my dagger onto the lifeless body before yanking off my mask and striding toward the stainless steel tray lined with tools.

Usually, we work alone. I prefer meeting my victims in seedy hotels on the outskirts of the city or slipping into their homes while their families are away. Bunny lures her prey down here with the promise of indulging their twisted fantasies before turning the tables. But every so often, we find a man who fits both our victim profiles.

And sometimes you just need to bond with your girlfriend by murdering someone together.

"You need to just fuck him and get him out of your system," Bunny murmurs.

"I don't *want* to sleep with him," I lie, knowing full well she won't believe me. "And if fucking Ryan wouldn't have ghosted me, I wouldn't be so sexually frustrated."

It's odd that Ryan disappeared the other night and isn't answering my messages. Very unlike him, especially since he seemed eager to take things to the next level in our situationship earlier that evening. Not that I would have agreed—but still, a woman has needs, and Ryan was dependable in that department.

A flash of red catches my eye. Blood has slipped past a tear in the disposable suit I have over my white dress. "Aww, fuck! This was one of my favorites, too," I pout, tugging at the plastic. "Oh well." I shrug. "That's what I get for wearing white to a massacre."

Bunny hums noncommittally, still glaring at her screen. She's already ditched her suit and sits cross-legged on a barrel full of liquid against the wall, utterly unbothered that her black leather skirt has ridden up to reveal electric blue underwear.

"What's got your attention, Buns?" I hop onto a barrel beside hers, peering at her phone. She's flipping through a popular social media app, eyeing some random girl's photos. "Who's that?"

"Some fucking badge bunny who's been sniffing around Hunter," she bites out.

"Ah. Well, I feel sorry for her then." I settle against the wall, my gaze drifting to the dead body on the floor. "Someone should tell her Hunter only has plans to trap one very specific bunny, and it ain't her."

She snorts, then sneers. "Well, she tagged him in a photo last night. He took her to dinner."

"Shut up! He did not!" I snatch the phone and tap the picture in question. The woman's manicured hand is delicately holding a wine glass, candlelight flickering in the background. A man sits across from her, but he's out of focus. "Oh, Buns, that could be anyone."

"She *tagged* him! Why would he allow a tag if it wasn't him?" she argues.

"To get your attention. And look, it's working. You didn't even enjoy our friend tonight." I gesture to the body on the floor before giving her phone back. "This is supposed to be girl time."

"You're right." She sighs, setting the device on the barrel before flicking her raven hair behind her shoulders. "I'm sorry. You have my undivided attention. How are you going to retaliate against Wrenley?"

Just hearing his name sends my blood to a roaring boil. "I don't know, but it's gotta be good."

Bunny inhales sharply and faces me wide-eyed. Her plum eyeliner makes her hazel orbs pop, and the glittery gold star stickers covering the scar on her cheek catch the light as a mischievous grin spreads across her face. "What if we send Ginny Tailor flowers and sign the card from him? You said her husband wasn't thrilled about them having lunch."

"Oh my god, Bunny. I'm trying to prank him, not get him fired and run out of Manhattan." I met Jackson Tailor once, and once was more than enough. The man is the epitome of charm and intimidation wrapped in a gorgeously sculpted package, but he only has eyes for his wife and assumes every woman who so much as looks at him wants him. "I tried getting a quote from Jackson once about *Iconic*, and he said, and I quote, *'Sweetheart, I'm flattered, but I'm married.'* Then he just walked off. Joe introduced me to him and his wife later that night, and there was no apology whatsoever. Just an unamused nod before he led his ridiculously beautiful wife away."

"Daaamn, he's brutal... it's perfect!" Bunny cries.

I shake my head vehemently. "No, Buns."

"Boo. You're no fun." She cocks her head, sighing. "We could collect the dog's poop and hide it around his office?"

I wrinkle my nose in disgust. "One: gross. I don't want the entire floor smelling like poo. Two: remind me never to get on your bad side." An idea sparks. "What if we get pink toilet paper and TP his office?"

"What are you, five?" she asks derisively.

"Like your suggestion was any better."

Then her eyes light up, and she grabs my shoulders. "I got it! He's always making fun of your obsession with pink."

She's not wrong. Wren loves giving me backhanded compliments about my outfits and office decor, but... "I'm not following."

"His hair is blond." She nods like I should be connecting the dots. When I don't, she sighs dramatically and continues as if she's explaining it to a toddler. "It would be a shame if someone put color in his shampoo bottle at the gym. Doesn't he go during lunch?"

My brows flatten as I deadpan, "Did you really expect me to follow that train of thought?"

She hops off her barrel, adjusting her skirt as she heads for the door leading to the rest of the basement. "Come on. Who's working security tonight?"

"Whoa! Wait! What about him?" I hitch my thumb over my shoulder.

Bunny just waves me off. "Eh, he's fine. It's not like he's going anywhere."

<h3 style="text-align:center"><u>Wrenley</u></h3>

The spray of warm water soothes my aching muscles. I went harder on the bag than usual today, releasing my pent-up frustration over Dove, the Doll, and work.

Waiting for Dove to retaliate has me more wound up than an old fucking clock. Her little digs and quips are starting to piss me off, and now more than ever, I'm questioning what the fuck I'm even doing here.

My hands ball into fists at my sides as I let the water run down my body, replaying our last conversation.

"I heard someone had a rather awkward lunch with the Tailors today. Sounds like big daddy Tailor got a

little jealous of his wife going to lunch with a handsome young reporter."

"Oh yeah? And where did you hear that from?" News travels fucking fast if she already knows. I thought Jackson Tailor was going to happily snap my neck when he crashed my work lunch with his wife, all because we were talking about the new center she's opening.

Dove giggles. "A lady never reveals her sources. And it sounds like you lost your best one there, Songbird."

"Fuck!" I slam my fist against the tile, wincing as the skin on my knuckles splits.

The swell of red washes away instantly, pink droplets falling to my hardened cock before swirling down the drain.

Violence, Dove, and jerking off all seem to go hand in hand lately—pun intended. Thinking about her pisses me off, which makes me hard, and before I know it, I'm coming to the image of her with my hands wrapped around her throat, imprinted on the back of my eyelids.

Ignoring my erection, I grab my shampoo and close my eyes, lathering my hair and letting the suds wash away any and all dirty thoughts pertaining to Dove. Instead, my mind drifts to the Doll. I don't know why I thought working here might bring me closer to finding her. To figuring out who she is. To getting the chance to crawl inside her mind and cocoon myself there until I can emerge as strong as her —strong enough to face my demons.

I thought maybe Dove had an in. A source, or something, *anything*, to help with her articles. But I can't bring myself to follow her, to try and discover how she knows so much about the vigilante serial killer. I can't bring myself to spend more time with her than necessary—even if she wants me to, if last weekend at the bar was anything to go by. Turning her down gave me a fleeting sense of control, but the aftermath has left nothing but a bigger itch I want to scratch while simultaneously pushing Dove further away.

Even before that night, she clearly didn't want to work together. But who can blame her?

Would things be different if I'd played nice on my first day here? In all honesty, I thought I was. I thought Dove could be charmed, swayed by my good looks like everyone usually is. I saw her office and expected a meek, albeit smart, woman who would happily share the workload.

How fucking wrong I was.

I wash my hair again, keeping my eyes closed as I rotate under the spray, soaking up the warmth before begrudgingly grabbing my towel to dry off. As I wrap it around my waist, I notice a neon pink stain on the soft, white Egyptian cotton.

"What the fuck?" I turn the towel over, scanning the shower for any sign of what could have caused the color, only to see the suds from my shampoo are bright pink.

Adrenaline courses through my veins like a hit—but instead of euphoria, it burns like acid, eating away at my insides.

Quickly, I wrap the towel around my waist and dart out to the vanities, ignoring the odd looks from the other guys in the locker room. I'm sure I look like a cartoon character, comically sliding in my shower flip-flops as I reach the mirrors.

"Are you *fucking* kidding me?" The question reverberates off the walls, met with a few snickers as I rake my fingers through my ruined strands.

Pink!

Bright. Fucking. Neon. Fucking. *Pink*.

If my hair were any darker, it wouldn't matter. But my dirty blond locks are *just* light enough that I know I'll need professional help to fix this shit.

How the actual fuck did she pull this off?

She would have had to bribe a guard to get in after hours—but how did she even know which locker was mine?

"Goddammit, Dove," I seethe through clenched teeth before taking a deep breath, my mind already reeling with ideas for retribution. I grab one of the mini blow dryers from a wicker basket under the vanity.

It's so much worse dry. The lighter strands from my days on the California beaches look like someone took a pink highlighter to them, while the rest of my hair is a muted shade of raspberry.

"Someone pranked you good, huh, man?" Some guy claps me on the shoulder sympathetically as he sets his Dopp kit down beside mine. "Want some advice? Don't let them see you're pissed about it. Wear it loud and proud, my man. Besides," he throws me a wink, "it's not a bad color on you."

"Thanks," I mutter, fully intent on not taking his advice.

However, by the time I make it back to the office, one encounter abruptly changes my mind.

"Oh my goodness! Look at you!" Sharon squeals, clapping a hand over her mouth. "It looks like Dove's gone and publicly marked you as hers."

"For Christ's sake, Sharon, it's not like she owns the color pink," Cecilia sneers in her colleague's direction. "*I* think it looks great, Wren."

I give them a brief nod, hyper-focused on what Sharon said about Dove *marking* me.

Take the in, Wren. And the guy's advice. Don't show Dove you're upset. Let her stew in fear of your vengeance.

Passing her office, I see she's not there. Instead, I

find her in the break room, sipping her coffee while she reads a book.

Nonchalantly, I stroll past her table, hands in my pockets. "What are you reading, Dove?"

"To Kill a Songbird—I mean, Mockingbird." Her sickeningly sweet tone and facetious reply set my nerves on edge, but outwardly, I remain the picture-perfect image of calm as I head to the fridge.

I grab one of her yogurt containers and a spoon, spinning around to see she hasn't even looked up from her book. "Interesting," I prod. "I wouldn't have taken you for a true literary lover."

She snorts, bright blue eyes flicking up for a second to register the yogurt in my hands before returning to her book. "I expect you to replace that."

"Sure, Dove. Why don't we go down to the corner bodega together, and you can pick out whatever flavor you'd like?" I smirk, shoving a spoonful of the strawberry snack between my lips.

She starts to retort, but the words die in her throat as she looks up sharply. This time, she tries to hide a snort behind her hand. "Oh, Songbird. What *have* you done?"

Before I can answer, George from *Sports and Recreation* appears in the doorway, promptly stopping to stare. "Good lord, Wrenley. What happened to your hair?"

Dove fails miserably at containing her cackling, avoiding my gaze as she gathers her things.

"Well, George. You know how boys tease girls on the playground when they like them?"

Dove pauses briefly, eyes darting up to meet mine before turning to leave.

George scratches his head. "Uh, yeah?"

"I think someone just has a crush and keeps picking on me because they're obsessed." I toss the empty yogurt container in the trash and shove my hands into my pockets, my words landing just as Dove crosses the threshold.

She stops, turning halfway, presenting me with a glowing smile. "Careful, Songbird. That kind of thinking goes both ways."

WRENLEY

A SOFT RAP on my office door drags my attention from my computer screen, and I glare at my arch-nemesis. Berry-painted lips curl into a slight smirk as she takes in my still-pink-stained hair before meeting my gaze.

"Have you finished that piece on the Shadow Siren?" Dove asks, bubbly enough to be a glass of Dom. She leans against the doorframe, arms crossed over her chest, phone in one hand as she taps her nails against her bicep with the other. She's absolutely insufferable, yet I find myself unable to look away.

My slacks tighten at the sight of her. The mini ruffled skirt and matching top she's wearing today are white with pink floral designs, trimmed in lace, and entirely inappropriate for work. Yet, despite my best efforts, I appreciate the view, no matter how much I try to convince myself I want to gouge my eyes out from all the pink.

Her white platforms click against the hardwood as she approaches my desk, hands clasped behind her, inadvertently—or vertently... is that a word? I should know whether that's a word or not... *advertently*—pushing her chest out. "Kitty got your tongue, Songbird?"

Snapping out of my daydream—one where she's sprawled across my desk in nothing but those heels—I return my gaze to my computer and nod. "Yeah, I'm almost finished."

I expect her to leave, but Dove rounds my desk and hops onto it like she belongs there. She sets her phone down and swings her feet gently, her sugar cookie scent making my stomach ache. My erection is impossible to ignore, and I shift in my seat, desperate to hide it.

"How many more salon sessions is it gonna take?" she asks.

"At least two more," I reply dryly, retyping the last sentence before hitting send. "And you'll be getting the bill."

Her laugh warbles like she's trying to hold it in, but softens as she reaches out. From my peripheral, I see her hand—and I'd be lying if I said it doesn't shock me when her fingers run through the top of my strands, nails dragging lightly against my scalp.

"I don't know," she teases. "I think pink suits you."

Her hand falls as I look at her, my expression clearly shocked. The seriousness of her action quickly sobers her, and our eyes lock.

Fuck. I'm an idiot.

Dove showed her cards when she said we needed to sleep together to get it out of our systems. And I foolishly folded—not because I wanted to play it safe, but because the longer I spend around her, the more I realize one time won't be enough to get her out of my head.

We both jolt when her phone rings, vibrating against my desk and ruining the moment. The name "*Mom*" flashes across the screen. She declines the call and hops down.

"I have to take Fang to his grooming appointment. When I get back, I'll look over your article."

"You get your rat groomed?" I ask, exhaling as she moves away. The further she gets, the better I can breathe, despite the way my chest clenches at the distance. She's become an integral part of my day—to the point where I'm starting to miss our banter on the weekends. I've taken to stalking her social media just to feel some sort of connection to her. I know what book she's reading in book club with Bunny, what she ate for dinner Sunday night, and what route she likes to take Fang for his walks. I'm becoming obsessed in a way I know will only end in disaster.

But what my body and head want are vastly different from my heart. Even though it's been weeks, I still can't disassociate her looks from the one person who caused me so much trauma that I can't have a functioning relationship.

"Don't call him a rat," she scolds. "You'll hurt his feelings." She grabs the doorframe and swings herself into the hall. "I just have to drop him off. I should be back in twenty."

"He has no hair! What's the point of sending him to the groomer? Why don't you just bathe him yourself?"

She turns and sticks her tongue out before disappearing down the hall.

The stupid, dopey smile lingering on my face doesn't fade even when she walks by a few minutes later. Fang is wearing a hooded sweater, nestled in an oversized pink purse hanging off her shoulder, his tiny head poking out.

"Why don't you just bleach your hair at home yourself?" she quips.

I open my mouth to reply, but she cuts me off.

"Exactly. It's better when a professional does it."

Fang yips and wiggles in his pink prison as if trying to escape and say hi, but Dove turns and heads toward the elevators. Not that I've forgotten, but being reminded of my current hair situation breathes life into a way to get back at her.

Knowing she keeps a large calendar of her meetings and personal appointments in her office, I wait until her elevator is three floors gone before slinking down the hall, trying not to draw attention to myself.

No one so much as looks up at me while I duck into her pink-and-cream monstrosity of a workspace. Everything on her desk is lined up in pristine rows. If I've learned anything about Dove, it's that she's a perfectionist who needs all her tools to be precisely in order before she can get any work done. The calendar in question hangs on the wall behind her desk, littered with neon pink sticky notes in her perfect cursive, and cat stickers.

As I assumed, Fang's groomer is listed, complete with a time and a sticker of a chihuahua wrapped in a towel. I glance behind me before pulling out my phone, ensuring no one has noticed me. Pressing call on the number under the listing, I hold my breath while waiting for someone to answer, debating whether to go through with this.

The rat didn't hurt anyone. Technically, this won't hurt the rat either, but I can't wait to see the look on Dove's face when she goes to pick up her little dog and–

"Good afternoon! Thank you for calling *Fluff N' Puff*. How may I assist you today?" an overly chipper woman greets.

"Hi, my girlfriend is about to drop off our dog for an appointment—Fang. I want to do something special for our little guy's birthday, but I want it to be a surprise for Dove. Can I count on your discretion?" I try to sound normal, so there's no question whether I'm telling the truth, but I'm surprised by how easily the lie slips off my tongue.

Easy there. You're calling her your girlfriend and *talking about the rat like he's your kid?*

The woman squeals so loudly I have to hold the phone away from my ear so it doesn't bust a drum. "Oh my gosh! I love this for her. I didn't know Dove was dating anyone! You can absolutely count on my discretion, sir. We love Fang and would be more than happy to help. What did you have in mind?"

"Well, she recently convinced me to dye *my* hair pink, so I was thinking—" On second thought, maybe this is a stupid idea. Dove loves pink. Coloring her precious dog's stringy mane will probably be the high-light of her week.

"I *totally* catch your drift. Oh! She's walking in now. Don't worry," her voice drops to a whisper, "it'll be our secret."

Before I can tell her to forget it, the line goes

dead, and I'm left standing in Dove's office with a sense of dread sliding down my spine like thick, frozen sludge.

"Fuck. She's gonna kill me."

I browse the rest of her calendar absentmindedly, searching for anything that might tip me off about her source on the Baby Doll Killer. Since I'm here, I might as well go all in.

Every Saturday, the initials C.W. are scrawled in ink, encased in a heart, accompanied by a sticker of a cat wearing sunglasses. I pull up the Notes app on my phone and type in the initials with a question mark, my mind racing faster than Usain Bolt.

Why the fuck is there a heart around them?

Who else is a *sporadic pillow partner* besides Ryan?

Why does this jackass have a standing date with her every Saturday?

Why the fuck do I care?

Why the fuck do *I care?*

I fall into her chair with a sigh, straightening as I sink into the pink leather and realize—it's not a standard office chair. Gripping the arms, I bounce slightly on the squishy seat before settling against the surprisingly luxurious backrest.

Why is her chair so much nicer than mine?

Pulling it in, I sprawl my legs out, deliberately nudging her keyboard a fraction of an inch before flicking her fluffy pen across the glossy, cream-colored farmhouse-style desk.

"If I were Dove's notebook, where would I be?"

One of the large drawers holds a pile of folders, but the smaller ones contain only office supplies and stationery, all in shades of pink and cream. Another drawer on the opposite side reveals a few toys I assume belong to Fang, some granola bars, and a bag of... meat?

I turn the plastic bag over. Although there isn't a label, the snack inside is clearly jerky. It seems like such an odd snack choice for Dove. Now that I think about it, I'm pretty sure the only things I've ever seen her consume—besides yogurt and coffee—are tacos and tequila. If anything, I'd expect her desk drawers to be stuffed with sunshine, rainbows, and a hoard of sugary treats.

I open the bag and take a sniff.

Hmm. Smells edible.

Removing a piece, I find it pleasantly pliable—softer than the usual jaw-breaking variety. I pop a small portion into my mouth. Not bad. Kinda... salty? With a hint of something I can't quite place. It doesn't taste like any jerky I've had before, though.

"Hey, Dove—oh! Wrenley. What are you doing in Dove's office?"

Cecilia's high-pitched voice filters through the

open door, freezing me mid-chew like a kid caught raiding the cookie jar. She scans the room, as if expecting to find Dove with her nose in the corner, before her sharp features curl into a pleased smile when she realizes we're alone.

"Is that from Dove's snack stash? Ooh, you're so bad. Come on now, share with the rest of us. It smells good!"

Before I can react, she crosses the room and snatches the bag from my hand. I know for a fact Dove keeps her office door open nearly all the time, so there's no justifiable reason for Cecilia to take the snack to the door and shout down the hall like she's discovered the gateway to a holy land.

In seconds, the bag is passed around and completely obliterated.

All I can think about is how my retaliation prank has now become a two-for-one special, and Dove is going to murder me when she returns.

Was everyone raised in a barn?

Who steals someone's snack and eats the entire fucking bag?

"What the heck is going on in here?" Dove's curious, sunlit voice drifts above the chatter, reaching me where I still lounge in her chair.

Everyone scatters like cockroaches under a flashlight. Cecilia and Sharon let out simultaneous squeaks, practically fighting over who will be caught holding the evidence.

Dove, however... She's staring at the empty bag.

Her expression? Wide-eyed horror.

"Where did you get that?" she snaps, her gaze locked onto the offenders.

Cecilia and Sharon throw me under the bus with a silent, unified glance before bolting back to their cubicles.

Dove's head swings toward me, her big blue eyes darting between me, her desk, the open drawer, and back again.

"Did you feed everyone Fang's jerky?" Her voice is high-pitched as her expression twists in sheer disgust.

"*Fang's* jerky?"

A slow, creeping nausea rolls through my gut, my stomach roiling in horror.

Our gazes lock. We both gag in unison.

"Oh my god, that's fucking disgusting." I scrub a hand over my face, hovering it over my mouth.

Dove laughs behind her hand, pressing it against her pouty lips.

Giggle. *Gag.* Giggle. *Gag.*

I inhale deeply, exhaling through my mouth, trying desperately to dislodge the taste of the dried meat without actually tasting it again.

"Do I even want to know what kind of animal it was?"

Dove seems to recover faster than I do. She leans against the doorframe, her giggles escalating into full-on guffaws that shake her entire petite frame.

"I can't breathe!" she wheezes between gasping, maniacal-sounding cackles, completely ignoring my question. She clutches her chest, walking further inside, dropping her purse onto the cabinet behind her desk. "Serves you right. What are you doing in here?" she asks, sobering a little as she runs her eyes down my body, taking in the fact that I'm still sitting in her chair.

I think quickly, running my hands along the arms as I lean back, even though I still feel like throwing up into her pink, glittery trash can.

"Wanted to see how the other half lives," I mutter. "Why is your chair so much nicer than mine?"

"Because I had it custom-made and paid for it myself, Songbird."

She steps closer, her voice dipping into something silky. "Now scoot... unless you want me to sit on your lap while we review your article?"

I don't remind her that she's not my boss.

Mostly because Joe lets Dove do whatever she wants. And most of the time, she acts like she's in charge because no one questions her.

She isn't feared, though. She's respected.

I don't want to respect her, though.

I want to disrespect the fuck out of her.

I want to leave her a quivering mess, covered in my cum.

Her whispered words snap me out of my thoughts. "Keep telling yourself you don't want me, Songbird."

My breath catches. I barely register her leaning over me, hands braced on the arms of the chair, her lips near my ear.

Shit.

Did I say that out loud?

She pulls back slightly, gaze drifting downward.

To my lap.

Where I'm hard as granite, seconds from pulling her onto me, despite the open door and the very real risk of someone walking by and seeing us.

"I don't think Junior here gets the memo."

TWO HOURS LATER, I'm pacing the downstairs lobby, checking my watch every few seconds. I called the groomer earlier to ask when Fang would be ready —apparently, they bring him back to Dove. Talk about good customer service. That gives me the perfect opportunity to intercept them and return him to his mother myself.

"You must be Wrenley!" a chipper voice calls from behind me.

I turn, and the sight that greets me feels like a punch to the gut. Fang's once-pristine white fur isn't *just* pink—it's an explosion of color. His head, ears, paws, and tail are dyed in bright swirls of pink, purple, green, yellow, and orange. The poor rat looks like he was dragged straight out of a '90s rainbow art fever dream.

"Oh, fuck. She's going to kill me."

The girl freezes, eyeing me suspiciously.

"Sorry," I recover quickly. "Yes, hi. I'm Wrenley. Come here, little dude."

Fang wriggles furiously, his little tail wagging like a propeller as he squirms free of her grasp and launches himself at me.

I don't know what I did to deserve his approval, but I'm grateful for it at this particular moment.

The girl's frown melts into a smile. "You know, Dove's been bringing Fang in since he was a pup. She's never asked for creative coloring, so we went with a semi-permanent dye—just in case."

"I don't know what any of that means, but I trust your judgment. Thanks again for your discretion."

Fang licks my cheek, stretching his tiny neck as if

he can't get close enough. I've never wanted a pet before, but I can't deny that the warm familiarity of the rat's affection makes me think it wouldn't be such a bad idea.

As I step off on our floor, Joe catches another elevator. His eyes widen comically when he sees Fang, and just before the doors close, he asks, utterly dead-pan, "Oh, Wrenley. What did you do?"

"About to get myself into a whole lot of trouble," I mutter, heading for Dove's office.

The tension between us earlier while reviewing my article had been thick enough to cut with a knife. Now, standing outside her door with this damn neon-colored dog in my arms, I regret every decision that led me here.

What we've been doing so far? Foreplay.

But this? *This* is the start of a war.

I attempt to tuck Fang inside my suit jacket, but the closer we get, the more determined he is to pop his head out. I hear Dove's voice drifting through the hall, bright and bubbly as she laughs about something that happened at a restaurant during a work lunch.

Her gaze meets mine briefly when I step inside and immediately turn to shut the door behind me. The office walls are almost soundproof—but not quite. And I have a feeling they'll be tested in the next few seconds.

"I have to call you back," she says slowly.

I hear the soft click of the phone settling into the cradle of the receiver and I inhale deeply before turning around.

Fang yips, scrambling to free himself from my arms and into hers. I brace for impact—for the explosion of fiery, razor-sharp words I know she's about to unleash.

I expect her to yell.

I expect her to tear me apart, her pretty pink lips forming the kind of scathing retort that'll haunt me for weeks.

I expect her to make me think of that angry little chick meme—because she's so short and I'm constantly reminded of it when we stand next to each other.

What I *don't* expect is for her eyes to go glassy as she reaches for her dog, cradling him to her chest like he's been wounded.

"Oh my god," she whispers with a watery rasp. "Baby, what happened to you?"

My heart clenches, skipping a beat as she lifts her gaze to mine.

"Why would you do something like this?"

She's actually crying now, and *fuck*—why do I feel so bad?

"It's just a prank, Dove. You dyed my hair, I just—"

"He's an innocent animal!" she cries.

Her face crumples as she buries it in Fang's rainbow-colored fur. "I'm so sorry you got dragged into this," she whispers to him, voice breaking.

Her sobs are deep, ragged, and gut-wrenching. Fang whines, his little tongue swiping across her cheek as if to reassure her.

If I felt terrible before, now I feel downright fucking awful.

I hate seeing her cry. It doesn't just make me uncomfortable—it makes me angry. Angry at myself for being the cause of her tears.

A woman like her shouldn't be crying because of a bastard like me.

"Dove, I'm sorry."

"Sorry?" Her head snaps up, eyes blazing as they lock onto mine. "You're *sorry*? He's an innocent animal!" she repeats, voice rising. "What kind of monster are you?"

Her breathing turns erratic, her chest rising and falling too quickly. She's shaking, struggling to get air. My stomach drops.

Shit.

She's either about to pass out or have a full-blown panic attack.

Alarmed, I gently take Fang from her arms and set him on the floor before gripping her shoulders.

"Breathe, Dove. It's okay. It's animal-safe dye—otherwise, they wouldn't have used it. It'll wash out."

She doesn't respond.

I guide her backward, one hand steady on her hip, pushing a chair out of the way before lifting her onto the desk. Smoothing her hair from her damp cheeks, I grip her face gently, forcing her to look at me.

"Dove. He's okay. You need to breathe. Can you do that for me?"

She stares at me, eyes wild.

I inhale deeply, demonstrating. "In. Out. In. Out."

Slowly, her breathing evens out. I wipe away her tears, wondering what the hell just happened.

I expected anger.

Not this.

Something about this triggered her, and I want to know why.

"Shh. It's okay. He's okay," I soothe, pulling back as soon as she's breathing normally.

Seconds later, her fist flies straight into my nose.

Pain explodes across my face. My vision blurs, eyes watering as a metallic tang fills my mouth. I glance down. Blood drips onto my lip, pooling in my hands.

Fang barks as Dove hops off the desk, roughly wiping her tear-streaked mascara from her face.

"You can do whatever to me, but do *not* bring my

dog into it!" she snarls with a vengeance I'd never guess her capable of.

I blink through the pain.

Okay.

I deserved that.

"Mark my words, Wren," she seethes, stepping toward the door and yanking it open. "You will regret this. Now get out."

"For what it's worth, I'm sorry," I say again, knowing full well I fucked up.

She glares, lips curling into something almost cruel.

"Not yet, you aren't," she promises, voice soft and lethal.

Then, with an almost wicked smile, she delivers the final blow.

"But trust me, Songbird—you're gonna be."

BUNNY GAGS, pressing the back of her hand to her mouth as I recount the tale of Wren feeding our coworkers dick jerky. "Oh my god. Is that even safe for human consumption?"

"I mean... it was processed like normal jerky. It was cooked!" She dry heaves again as I turn my back to her and motion for her to secure my full-body PVC catsuit. "It's fine!" I draw out the "i" as she pulls the zipper up. "Look at all the shows with cannibalism."

"Keyword: shows, Dove."

"Okay, Miss 'I used a rump roast to kill my husband.'"

"I didn't eat it afterward! Or him!"

"Po-tay-to, po-tah-to."

Bunny clicks her tongue, patting my back. "What am I gonna do with you, woman? Are you sure this is a good idea? It's completely unlike the Doll to do something like this. Aren't you afraid it will only heighten his fascination with her? Or that he might recognize you?"

I turn and pick up the dagger sheath attached to my leg garter, removing the lacy fabric and securing my weapon to my thigh. "That's what the catsuit is for. Once the wig is on, he won't see an inch of skin. There's no way he'll know it's me."

I don't have to look at Bunny to know she's rolling her eyes. I can hear it in her voice. "I don't know. He's pretty obsessed with you. That program I got from the guys at Tailor Tech to see who's been looking at your socials works just as well as they said it would. Wrenley stalks your profiles constantly."

"Ah. Only half as often as Hunter stalks yours, then?" I grin at my best friend.

She smirks back, the motion causing the scar on her cheek to pucker. "Con-stan-tly," she sounds out. "I think you two lovebirds are a match made in heaven."

"He desecrated my dog. There will be no love matching." I frown and turn toward my wall of wigs, choosing a dusty rose one. The long curls will hide the part of my neck that sticks out of the suit.

"Don't say he desecrated Fang. That sounds gross, and now I'm fighting mental images no one should have to think about." She scratches behind Fang's ears as he lies in her lap, and he groans as if in agreement. I'm still pissed his fur is the color of a Skittles mix. Even though I did it to Wren first, the songbird crossed a line.

After packing my wig, contacts, and mask, I sit next to Bunny and pull on my platform boots. Designed to look like part of the suit, they help disguise my height and the ridiculously high heels. "Are you going to stay here or go home?"

Bunny's pups are slumbering in Fang's dog bed on the floor, a pile of white and black fur resembling a yin-yang symbol. It makes me think of her and me and how well we fit together as friends. It's nice having someone who understands my motives for doing the things I do. Our friendship is the literal sense of 'we listen, and we don't judge.' We just ask where to show up with our shovels and often wait for each other after a kill to be a shoulder to lean on.

She stretches before standing and places Fang on the couch. "I'm gonna go home. You don't need me, right? I can stay if you do." A wicked smile stretches across her face. "But something tells me you might be out late."

"I'll let you know as soon as I get back." I don't entertain her insinuation. All I'm doing is scaring Wren. Showing him that the Doll isn't someone to idolize—and that I am no one to mess with, even if he doesn't know it's me.

She grabs a pack of black nail stickers off the crafting table and tosses them at me with a nod toward my manicure. "Don't forget these."

"What would I do without you?"

"Oh, I don't know, perish from boredom? Yasha, Maru, come on, boys." She pats her legs and opens the door wider as her dogs bound past her into the hall. With a flip of her hair and a wink over her shoulder, she leaves, her mischievous lilt floating behind her. "Have fun, Love Dove."

"I'm not going to have fun! I'm going to scare the living daylights out of him!"

WREN LIVES in a small one-bedroom apartment in Murray Hill, on a busy street teeming with nightlife. It's loud and chaotic, which surprises me because Wren doesn't seem like the nightlife type.

Sure, he spends time at The Tipsy Taco, but we all do. Tuesdays and Thursdays are paramount for networking with new contacts and sources, and that's just been the place to go for the last year and a half.

The clamor makes it easy to blend in. No one looks twice at the long trench covering my outfit or gives me a suspicious side-eye as I slip into the tiny alley between the buildings. I spent all day mapping out the route—pinpointing exactly which window to enter and where to stash my bag and coat—so I can get in quickly and slip away just as efficiently.

"Though she be but little, she is fierce," I chant quietly as I hoist myself onto the top of a dumpster and begin climbing the rickety, old fire escape. The building is a four-story walk-up, so I take my time, careful not to rattle the metal too much. The last thing I need is someone swinging a baseball bat out their window, thinking I'm a burglar.

Don't worry, residents of Wren's apartment building. I'm not a burglar—just a serial killer here to scare the shit out of my annoyingly gorgeous work rival.

A soft glow spills from the hall outside Wren's bedroom. Thankfully, the fire escape leads directly to his room, not the living quarters. Otherwise, this would be a much more complicated feat, and I'd have to wait until much later.

"Ten out of ten do not recommend," I murmur, prepping myself. Having barely three feet to situate my bag, fasten my wig, and put in my contacts—in the dark, I might add, not an easy thing to do—is less than ideal.

Oh, the things we do for pure, unadulterated loathing.

I manage because I'm a pro.

Once my mask is in place, I slide open the window and slip inside, silent as a grave.

I am darkness. I am shadow. I am an angel of death.

From what I can see of Wren's room in the dark, it's spotless, with only a bed and a dresser to fill the space. On the wall is a board mirroring the one he has at work—tracking the Doll and all her accomplishments. Nothing personal. Nothing to make it feel homey.

It's cold and sad. My big ol' heart clenches with empathy.

It's fine, Dove. He just moved back and probably hasn't had time to go shopping.

Taking a steadying breath, I stand at the doorway and listen. The aroma of garlic fills the space, and now and then, the occasional scrape of a utensil against a plate mixes with the rhythmic clicking of a keyboard.

Busy, busy boy. What are you working on, Songbird? Another article I'll have to stow away? More flowery words about how the Doll is perfect in every way for me to get myself off to in the privacy of my apartment?

Don't judge me. I have a thing for words, okay?

Gradually, I make my way down the short hall. So fucking slowly, so my boots don't make a sound. My fingers tighten around my dagger, knuckles likely white beneath my fingerless gloves. My heart beats in my chest with such violent thumps it'll be a miracle Wren doesn't hear it first.

At the hall's end, his apartment opens into a living room on the left and a tiny kitchen on the right. He's sitting on one of those sectionals that got super popular a few years ago for small apartment living—the kind that pulls out into a bed but isn't more than three cushions wide, with the third being a storage chaise.

A small coffee table holds his dinner—a bowl of pasta that smells fucking amazing—and a bottle of imported beer. He's relaxed, laptop on his thighs, thin wire-framed reading glasses perched on his nose.

How did I not know he wears glasses? And why the fuck does it up his hotness factor by a thousand? The glasses, combined with his gray sweats and messily tousled hair, are enough to send my body into over-drive. He's a goddamn booby trap of desire.

I want to stomp my foot and throw a tantrum but settle for an annoyed huff, momentarily forgetting my mission.

Wren's fingers still over the keyboard, his entire body freezing like a scared chicken.

Worst serial killer ever.

His gaze lifts to mine. He blinks once. Twice. Then

shakes his head. Moving his laptop to the cushion beside him, he removes his glasses, rubbing his eyes. "Wow, Wren. You're even imagining her in your apartment now. You seriously need therapy."

I cock my head, waiting for him to realize this isn't a dream. I'm very real, and he should be very scared.

As he looks back up, his eyes widen slightly before he laughs wryly. "Okay, who the fuck are you, and how did you get in here? Did Hunter put you up to this?" Wren looks around like Hunter might be hiding somewhere. "Ha. Ha. You dick." His gaze returns to me. "Seriously, it's not funny. I don't know you. I don't appreciate a stranger in my house."

If I were a burglar, this guy would definitely be dead by now.

Refraining from shaking my head at Wren's apparent lack of danger intuition, I step forward, snapping a sharp, "Sit down!" as he tries to stand.

My voice modulator does the trick, transforming my usually chipper tone into a sultry, distorted rasp. His expression morphs into disbelief. As I approach, his wide-eyed gaze locks onto mine.

"It *is* you," he whispers.

"A little birdie told me you have an obsession." I twirl my dagger between my fingers, ensuring he sees I'm armed and mean business. The glow from the kitchen catches the blade, his eyes snapping to it before meeting mine again. "Do you know what happens when we obsess over things, Wrenley Campbell?"

He swallows hard, Adam's apple bobbing as I step between the coffee table and the couch. A pretty pink flush blooms on his cheeks as he stares up at me, equal parts mesmerized and fearful, and shakes his head slowly while I wait for him to answer.

Placing a knee on the cushion between his legs, I lean forward and drag the flat of my blade down his chest. "Obsessions poison our minds. They make us weak." My blade glides lower over his sinfully perfect abs. I grab the back of the couch to anchor myself as I continue pressing closer into his space. "You convince yourself they aren't bad for you." Wren's breath comes in short, sharp bursts. "But in the end," my mask brushes his face as I whisper in his ear, "most obsessions will kill you."

I expect my dagger to meet the space between his legs and send terror through the man currently at my mercy. However, my blade meets a mass of steel instead. Wren is hard as stone. Completely turned on. And that discovery sends a flood of warmth pooling in my lower belly.

Warm hands encircle my hips and drag me down abruptly, sliding to my thighs to part my legs around his waist. The hand holding my dagger flies out to join the other against the back of the couch, keeping me steady. He straightens, still towering over me even while sitting, his lips nearly brushing the ones painted on my mask as he murmurs, "I'm already dead inside." His hips thrust up, his cock meeting my center through our clothes. "But you can show me a piece of heaven before dragging me to hell."

The moan that escapes me sounds oddly erotic through the modulator. Wren keeps thrusting, slow and deep, his grip firm on my waist. As much as I'm enjoying this turn of events, the victorious glint in his eye reminds me why I came in the first place—and it isn't to get off from dry-humping on his couch.

I shove him back, pressing the dagger to his throat. The movement traps his cock between us, the crown sliding against my clit, and I can't stop my hips from rolling against him. "What kind of sick fuck gets off on a serial killer threatening his life?"

Wren whimpers as I dig the tip of the blade into his skin, a bead of blood welling up. His fingers slide around to grip my ass, guiding my movements, urging me to ride him faster, harder. "You won't hurt me," he moans.

Sweat slicks my skin beneath my catsuit. It's like he's started a fire in my bones, burning me from the inside out. "And why do you think that?"

The need to rip off my mask and watch him unravel beneath me is infuriating. I want to lean forward and lick his skin, taste his blood like I'm a goddamn vampire, and savor the flavor, knowing he's bleeding for me—*because of me.*

"You only hurt men who are guilty," he grits out, lifting a hand to grasp my wrist. He slows our movements, and somehow, it's a thousand times more sensual as we share the air in the sliver of space between us. Eyes locked, he slides his thumb beneath the band of my glove, stroking over my pulse point. "And the only thing I'm guilty of is being utterly enchanted by you."

Pleasure coils low in my belly, fueled by his pretty words and the soft, breathy moans spilling from his lips. I've never been with such a vocal man before, and it's unlocking something primal inside me, a door my ovaries seem determined to launch themselves through.

Attempting to regain control, I twist my wrist free, press up on my knees, and sheath my dagger before dropping back down, rubbing against him with sharp jerks of my hips.

"Oh fuck," he whimpers, head falling back, eyes squeezing shut.

"That's right." My hands run up his chest, fingers curling over his shoulders, fucking him dry and wishing there weren't any barriers between us. "Come for mommy."

My eyes snap open, fingers tightening. The skin around her eyes pinches, almost like she's in pain, effectively stopping my movements just as I'm about to come.

Instinct takes over. My hands shove outward, flinging the Doll off my lap and onto the coffee table. It holds her weight—though my beer ricochets across the room.

"What the fuck?" she demands. The modulator makes the question sound comical, though there's nothing funny about the situation.

"I-I'm sorry... I..." Words fail me. My heart stutters in my chest, and it's painful to breathe. The ache, though, is nothing compared to the sheer humiliation throbbing through my rapidly deflating cock.

It wasn't the Doll I was thinking of. Even though I've imagined this scenario a million times—dreamed of having this moment with her—it was Dove who had occupied my mind.

Dove's big blue eyes and bouncy blonde hair. The image of her in the Doll's place, head thrown back as she took her pleasure from me. And right when I was about to fucking come in my pants to thoughts of a woman who utterly annoys the fuck out of me, the second I heard the word *mommy*...

It was like the world slammed to a halt.

Dove and that vile fucking word *cannot* become synonymous. It's already bad enough that their appearances are so similar.

Embarrassed and ashamed, I force myself to look into the dark depths behind the Doll's mask. A real-life serial killer just rode me to near completion, and I shoved her off like she had cooties.

Wordlessly, she stands. I reach for her, but she pulls away, rounding the table and fleeing down the hall.

Pushing to my feet, I rush after her, adrenaline pumping through my veins at the lost chance to make a connection. "Wait!"

But by the time I reach my room and lean out the open window, she's already gone. I scour the fire escape, looking for any clue she was there at all. A dropped dagger, a scrap of material from her bodysuit —fuck, even a hair from her wig, but she's left no trace behind.

A shrill ring sounds from the living room as my phone goes off. In a stupor, I retrieve it, only to see it's my mother... again. You'd think she'd get the point that I don't want to speak to her. But anytime even an inkling of a thought pertaining to her flutters across my mind, it's like it shoots her a fucking signal. Fury builds in my chest. One second, my phone is clenched in my hand; the next, it's across the room, hitting the wall with a crack.

I had a chance, and I ruined it.

The opportunity to finally get my questions answered stared me right in the face, and instead, I let my attraction get in the way.

And why the fuck was I thinking of Dove?

Bile rises up my throat. I barely make it to the bathroom before retching up my dinner—and part of lunch—as a new swarm of questions floods my mind.

How does the Doll know about me? Why did she let me pull her onto my lap? Will she come back?

You basically edged her and threw her off you. If she comes again, it'll be to put that dagger through your neck for real.

I flush the toilet and slump against the cool porcelain tiles. Maybe Dove is right—partially, anyway. I obviously have too much pent-up sexual frustration.

I need to expel it. And since doing it with Dove will more than likely open a door I don't want to walk through, I need to find someone else to fuck.

NEARLY A WEEK PASSES before I can bring myself to so much as look at Wren. Not that he's sought me out either, but I have a feeling his reasons are different.

The goal was to scare him. Instead, he could have unzipped my catsuit, and I would have let him crawl inside both it and me.

I stare at the blank screen of my laptop while I pick at a cup of yogurt in the break room. My article was due an hour ago, and it's still unfinished because all I've done is wax nostalgic about Wren's moans and how badly I want to hear them again. I'm not even mad about Fang anymore. Especially after I called the groomer and they assured me the dye was safe and non-toxic—which I already knew but needed to hear anyway.

Someone walks by, and the unmistakable sound of

Wren's laughter snaps my gaze to his back as he heads for the fridge. He's on his phone. It's new—his old one was dark, and this one is light gray—and I hate that I notice this stupid detail.

He grabs a takeout container and slides it into the microwave before turning around. The pouty lips I've spent way too much time fantasizing about curve downward as our eyes lock. My chest pinches, my thighs pressing together at the memory of him so hard beneath me.

Wren's eyes darken with a heat he tries hard to disguise. It's want and need all rolled into one delectable look. But the moment I decide to try talking to him, he whips around, snatches his lunch, and retreats without a second glance, speaking quietly to whoever is on the other end of his call.

My phone lights up with a text from Bunny, asking if we're going to the bar tonight. It's Thursday. She knows that's where I'll be, so it's a little strange she's even asking, but I bet it has something to do with Hunter. I respond in the affirmative. Collecting my things, I return to my office and shut the door, intent on finishing my work before I leave for the day.

I never get distracted. Never allow myself to veer from my path. But it's rare that I find obstacles in my way—especially ones that pull my attention like a magnet. With us not talking all week, this should have been the perfect time to get back on track. Instead, I find myself bored. Filling the silence with thoughts of him. Wondering if I should visit him as the Doll again.

He let her in quicker than an egg fries on a hot pan. I want to know why. Need to know what his obsession is with her.

I'm already dead inside. His words from that night have been on repeat every waking moment of every day since.

What happened to you, Songbird?

I think it's time to find out.

"Wow. You're mighty dressed up for tacos and tequila," Bunny teases, reaching for my hand and spinning me in a twirl. "I like the dress, though, and that's saying a lot because you know how I feel about pink."

"Isn't it cute? I know you hate pink, but you love me, and I think you'd love the store. We should go this weekend." I smooth my hands down the crushed velvet of my spaghetti-strap mini dress, a vintage designer find from SoHo. It's so soft I want to keep petting myself.

"I do love you. And so will Wrenley when he sees you in that get-up." She winks, hazel eyes sparkling as she laughs when I rush forward to clasp a hand over her mouth.

Glancing around, I ensure no one from work is within earshot before scolding, "Would you hush? The last thing I need is someone overhearing and thinking I got all dressed up for him."

She pulls my hand down with a grin that crinkles the red foil hearts over her scar. "You *are* all dressed up for him," she jests, walking backward toward our usual spot at the bar just as Vixey rounds the corner with a tray full of drinks.

"Watch out!" I shout.

My friend braces for impact, but to my delighted surprise, Vixey spins gracefully out of the way without spilling a single drop of alcohol. The blonde tips of her long ponytail whip around her head as she throws a smirk over her shoulder. "I swear, you're just trying to run into me now."

Bunny clutches her chest in mock horror. "Who? Me? Never!"

"You better not be, Buns," Alex calls from behind the bar as he fills a pitcher of beer. "You're not getting any more free drinks from me."

"Aww, shucks." Bunny pouts, snapping her fingers in a dramatic swoop that sends her leather jacket slipping off one shoulder. "All right, all right. She's getting better. I'll give her that."

I'm vaguely aware of her ordering our drinks as I scan the bar for Wren and Hunter. Crushing disappointment floods my veins when I spot them at a pool table with two women. Ironically, one is blonde, and the other is brunette. I bristle as the darker-haired one latches onto Wren's arm.

He smiles at her. That charming, panty-melting, all-teeth, full-lips smile that he's only ever bestowed upon me when we first met. The brunette looks ready to climb onto the pool table and spread her legs right here in the middle of the bar. I've never killed a woman before, never harmed an innocent person whose only crime was occupying the attention of the man I'm lusting over, but there's a first time for everything, right?

As if he feels my stare, Wren turns his head mid-sentence, his eyes meeting mine almost immediately. Twin pools of dark chocolate drag down my body, and just like earlier, they darken, his jaw clenching with such force I can see it from across the room.

He moves like he's about to come over—but then stops. His gaze shifts to the entrance. I follow his line of sight and find Ryan stepping inside.

It's the first time we've seen each other since he ghosted me at the bar weeks ago. He doesn't notice Wren glaring at him, but when his gaze lands on me, he pauses.

"Hey," I offer, still standing near the bar where Bunny has a stool saved for me.

"Hey," he replies gruffly, pushing past without another word.

My brows knit. What the hell did I do to piss him off so badly that he won't even speak to me?

"That was weird. What happened between you two?" Bunny asks.

"I have no idea." I glance back toward Wren, only to find his focus once again on the brunette. My chest tightens. Shaking my head, I slide onto my stool and down two shots in quick succession. "I honestly don't understand men."

"Men don't even understand men," Bunny supplies with a sigh.

"Any progress with Hunter?"

"Why would there be progress with Hunter?" She shakes her head like she can't believe I'd even ask such a question.

I flash her a knowing look, propping my elbows on the bar top and fixing my attention on the group across the way. "Do you know who those women are?"

Bunny snorts. "Nope. And I don't care. Detective Dick can do whatever he wants with whomever he wants."

"As long as it's whatever *you* want and it's with *you*, right?" I don't miss Hunter's eyes darting to my friend, as if daring her to go over like she did last time. The game they keep playing with each other is confusing as hell—the longest foreplay I've ever witnessed between two people who want each other as badly as they do. He has to have the bluest balls ever.

She flips her blowout over one shoulder and shrugs, making eyes at a random guy sitting catty-corner from us—one who looks like he wants to eat her alive. She'll give Hunter a dose of his own medicine without a second thought. It makes me wonder. If I do the same, will Wren come to intervene?

Or should I just go over and assert myself? What would he do if I stepped between them and staked a claim I have no right to?

After four shots of tequila, two tacos, and far too many fake-ass giggles from the brunette, I decide I'm ready to find out. Bunny is ignoring me anyway, half-sitting in the random dude's lap while she keeps shooting Hunter glances, playing him at his own game—and winning. Hunter looks about ready to charge the guy with a crime he didn't commit.

"Whoa, Love Dove." Bunny grabs my arm as I slide off my stool and head toward the pool tables. "What are you doing?"

"What I do best." I sharply turn back to the bar and down one more shot for good measure. "Taking control."

Everything that happens next feels like something straight out of a cheesy early-2000s movie. I watch the train wreck unfold as if I'm having an out-of-body experience, secondhand embarrassment creeping up my spine.

Hunter sees me first, jerking his chin in my direction and murmuring something that makes Wren turn. Ignoring the woman standing too close to him, I hold his gaze and march right up. "Do you wanna get out of here?"

Wren's brows pinch together, an unreadable expression flickering across his face before he schools his features and wraps an arm around the woman's waist. "Actually, we were just about to leave."

A wave of nausea rolls through me as he looks at her with a charming smile, reaching up to brush a stray hair from her face. Bitterness paralyzes me. I don't know why it bothers me. I don't understand why it... *hurts* as my eyes bounce between them.

We're nothing to each other. I was foolish to think otherwise. Wren is attracted to the Doll. To my alter ego—not me.

My cheeks heat, chest tightening with humiliation for even putting myself out there. We've been playing this game for weeks, and I keep losing by showing him I want him. But I don't even want to play anymore.

I want to know him. To make a connection. But

even if Wren wants me too, he's made it clear he won't act on it, and he's never seemed interested in me personally.

Obsessions make us weak. My own words come back to me as I furiously blink back the tears that come for no reason other than the amount of tequila running through my bloodstream.

Regaining my composure, I ignore the way his face morphs into something like concern. "Right." I hate that I can hear the mortification in my tone. Backing away, I end my shitshow with a grand finale, my voice accidentally cracking as I let out a hoarse, "I'm sorry. That was stupid of me to ask. Have a good night, Wrenley."

His expression shifts like he's been punched in the gut. We both know I've never called him by his full name. I didn't even mean to. It just slipped out.

I inhale a shaky breath and turn, willing the tears not to fall as I walk away. Behind me, I hear Hunter growl, "What the fuck is wrong with you?" It's followed by a heavy thump—like he might have thrown something onto the pool table.

By the time I make it back to our spot, Bunny is staring at me with a sympathetic expression that makes my sinuses burn. "Oh, Love Dove. You wanna get out of—"

She cuts herself off, her eyes darting behind me

with sudden alarm. Spinning around, I see Hunter striding toward us like a man on a mission. He speaks to Bunny first, though his whiskey-colored eyes never leave mine.

"Bunny, I'm sorry for what I'm about to do." He doesn't stop walking, cradling my face in his palms as he bends low. "Dove, just fucking go with it."

Then his lips are on mine, and I'm too shocked to do anything but stand there frozen while the stupid man who's in love with my best friend kisses me right in front of her.

RED.

Scarlet, maraschino cherry, crimson—fucking candy apple shades cover everything in sight as Hunter grabs Dove's face and kisses her.

Apparently, my best friend wants to meet his maker early, and I'm all too happy to send him there with a one-way ticket.

Something roars inside me—a beast I didn't know existed, clawing to escape and murder my best friend before resurrecting him just to do it all over again.

Mine.

"Hey!" The woman—Cindy? Mindy? I don't remember her name—cries as I break free from her embrace and charge across the bar.

Bunny jumps down from her stool, pale as a ghost, and bolts. Dove finally—why the fuck did it take her so long?—shoves Hunter away, then yells after her best friend. "Bunny!"

Hunter glances over his shoulder, flinches, then spins quickly when he realizes how close I am. "I'm gonna go after her. You two, do us all a favor and get the fuck over yourselves."

"Hunter!" I growl, lunging for him, but he slips from my grasp and disappears into the crowd.

"What is *wrong* with you two?" Dove snatches her purse and follows after him, shouting over her shoulder, "Alex, I'll take care of our tab later." Without so much as a glance in my direction, she shoves past me and into the growing crowd.

The night air is cool as I step outside after her. Bunny and Hunter are nowhere to be seen, but Dove's dress shimmers under the streetlights as she storms toward her apartment—yes, I know where she lives— arms wrapped around herself.

"Dove!"

Her blonde curls bounce as she shakes her head, offering no response. I have to jog to catch up. For someone so short and wearing such ridiculous high heels, she's fast as fuck.

By the time I reach her, she's lighting a thin cigar. I balk, snatching it from her lips. "That shit will kill you."

Adorably, she stomps her foot, fists clenched at her

sides. "What. The hell. Is your problem tonight?" She motions back toward the bar. "Go back to your hook-up and leave me alone."

"Why? So you can meet up with Hunter?" I goad, knowing damn well she'd never do that to Bunny in a million years. Shoving my hands into my pockets, I follow her, trailing a few steps behind, keeping an eye out for creeps.

Sure, Wren. It has nothing to do with the fact that you're checking out her ass.

Okay, I'm the creep.

She glances over her shoulder, smirking. "He wasn't a bad kisser. I'd be into him if he and Bunny weren't up each other's asses."

I have a feeling she's verbally poking at me, but it sends a wave of jealousy through me all the same. "Knock it off, Dove."

"Ooh, burn," she says dryly. "Go back to your lady friend, Wren. I don't need you to walk me home."

"You drank enough tequila to kill a frat boy in his first year of college." I notice her shiver and pull off my jacket, striding forward to drape it over her shoulders. "Here, take this."

She stops, looking up at me as she clutches the fabric around her small frame. She looks endearing as hell in my clothes, and I'd be lying if I said I don't love it. It makes me imagine her in just my dress shirt—or nothing at all, my sweat and other bodily fluids marking her skin.

"Why are you here?" she asks, her voice weary.

I shove my hands back into my pockets in an attempt at discreetly repositioning my pants, trying to ignore my body's reaction. "Look, I'm sorry I didn't just say I wanted to go home with you, okay?"

Her brows draw together, and there's something slightly familiar about the motion I can't put my finger on. I'm sure I've seen her do it a million times before, but for some reason, it sparks a memory just out of reach—like déjà vu, but not.

"It's fine," she snaps, resuming her pace, sliding her arms through the sleeves of my jacket. "Really. Clearly, you don't need company."

"Someone sounds jealous."

She snorts. "Keep dreaming, Songbird."

It's strange how it no longer bothers me that she calls me by the same nickname my mother used. Well... it does. But less than hearing her say my full name. That, I hated. It felt like a slap, like she had taken all her hurt and weaponized it, aiming straight for my chest.

"I'm not letting you walk home drunk."

She doesn't argue, and we fall into silence, the city sounds filling the space between us. It's sort of... nice.

Almost like we're just a normal couple on a regular date.

"Why are you so obsessed with the Baby Doll Killer?" she asks quietly as we approach her street. "What is it about her that you're so attracted to?"

"Whoa. Attracted? That's a stretch," I lie with a nervous laugh. Memories of how easily I pulled the Doll into my lap the other night filter through my mind. How hard I was just from her presence. But how the hell did Dove conclude that I'm attracted to the killer? "I admire her. I wouldn't say I'm attracted to her."

"Your articles say otherwise. That's why we haven't published them. You know that, right? You put her on a pedestal and take away from the horrific things the men she kills have done." Dove throws her hands up. "You have an entire board of her in your office. You're obsessed!"

I walk faster until we're side by side. Her face is flushed from the cold, her chest heaving from how worked up she's getting. A smirk crawls across my face. "And you're cute when you're jealous."

She rolls her eyes but doesn't reply as she stops at her building's entrance. I happen to know Dove's unit was left to her by an aunt she visited often as a kid. The neighbors welcomed her when she was younger. With her bright and bubbly personality and the fact that most of them already knew and adored her, the other co-op members were all too welcoming when Dove moved to the city.

But I keep that to myself. Because why the fuck would I tell her I know any intimate details about her life?

She's right.

I am obsessed.

With her.

And I'm beginning to believe it might not be such a bad thing. I'm starting to see there's a lot more to Dove than the sparkly mask she shows the world. As much as I've tried to fight it, I want to know the real her. I want to crawl inside her head and settle in, the way she's made a home in mine. I want her to be just as infatuated with the idea of us as I am.

"Well, this is me." She won't meet my eyes, nervously digging the toe of her white platform into the concrete. I've never seen her nervous before. It gives me hope.

Of what, I'm not entirely sure. I still see my mother when I look at her, and that terrifies me. My past still has its deformed fingers hooked under my skin. Dove is like a bright new beginning I don't want to tarnish.

"Since you're already here, you might as well come up." She spins and heads inside without giving me a chance to say no. And I follow, because—newsflash—I've apparently become a simp.

Her place is bright and clean and so very pink. Cream and blush accents are everywhere, like something straight off a Pinterest board brought to life through decorative pillows, silk flowers, and even gilded crystal chandeliers. Dove's taste is like an old, rich grandma's—if that grandma had updated her appliances to match the century.

The rat greets us at the door. He looks like he's gearing up for a Skittles commercial, his sparse hair still bright and colorful. "What's up, little rat?"

"Don't call him a rat!" Dove chides, but Fang just jumps on my leg, tail wagging like we're old pals.

"He doesn't care. I think he likes me." I pick him up, tucking him into my arm like a baby. "Don't you, little dude?" Scratching his head, I follow her further inside.

She glances over her shoulder, glaring at Fang. "Traitor."

We reach her pristine, cream-colored kitchen with its custom blush refrigerator. "Do you want something to drink?"

She's still swimming in my jacket as she opens a cabinet, pushing up on her tiptoes, revealing more of her bare thighs. My pants tighten, and I wonder what she'd do if I picked her up and set her on the counter.

For some reason, though, I find myself asking, "What set off your panic attack when you saw Fang?"

Dove freezes, fingers wrapped around a blush-colored crystal goblet before she retrieves a water pitcher from the fridge and fills the glass. "What do you mean?"

"Come on, Dove. It set you off. There has to be a story there." I push the glass back toward her when she slides it across the counter. "You drink it. I had a few beers. I'm pretty sure you drank half a bottle of Patrón by yourself."

She fixes me with a sassy look. "I may be little, Songbird, but I can still drink you under the table."

"I don't doubt it." I smirk, holding her gaze as she lifts the glass and takes a sip. "So, what's the story?" I prod, setting Fang down and inwardly beaming when he begs for attention again.

Instead, I reach across the counter, refill her glass, and bring it over to the sofa. I place the cup on a coaster, patting the cushion beside me as I get comfortable. "You wanted to hang out, didn't you?"

Her lips twitch as she taps her nails on the gold speckled cream granite. "I don't think trauma dumping on a first date is exactly material for ensuring a second one," she states flatly.

"Is this a date, Dove? Or are we just two colleagues

hanging out?" I raise an eyebrow, patting the cushion again. "Come on."

Fang jumps up like I was calling him, curling into my lap and facing Dove like an endorsement. It seems to work. The corner of her lips lifts, a breathy laugh escaping as she shakes her head. "He likes men in general. Don't feel too special, Songbird."

"Tell me he doesn't like Ryan, at least? I don't think I can be friends with you if you liked that douche," I coo at the rat before realizing I just spoke to him in a baby voice.

Dove hides her smile in the cuff of my jacket, coming to join me on the sofa. She hugs a pillow to her stomach, resting her head against the back cushion. "Okay, I won't."

I drop a glare to Fang. He peers up at me innocently, tail wagging furiously, with big eyes half hidden by his long bangs. "You just lost two points in my book, rat." I turn back to Dove. "Story time. Fess up. What set you off?"

She exhales heavily. "Wren—"

"I'm trying to get to know you here, Dove. Give me something real. Deeper than what you show everyone else at work. Drop the sunshine act. You're in a safe space. A very pink, very safe space." I grin, gesturing around her living room.

"But am I in safe company?" she wonders aloud, melancholy creeping into her voice.

I meet her eyes, my earlier playfulness fading. "Yes. You're in safe company. Whatever you tell me stays locked in here." I tap my temple.

And in here. My heart chimes in.

Thanks, my dude, but I'm not ready to go spilling you at her feet just yet.

Dove inhales deeply, then exhales with puffed cheeks and pursed lips. "Okay. Well. Long story short, I got a teacher in trouble when I was younger, and the kids at school got upset. He was everyone's favorite, so they picked on me in retaliation. I grew up in a small town—one where everyone knew everyone. We lived in a tight-knit neighborhood, but people were angry about what happened. The kids took it out on my dog.

They paintballed my house, shot my dog, and covered him in paint. He died—both from the force of the paintballs causing internal bleeding and because the paint was toxic. He tried to clean himself, ingesting it in the process. By the time my mom and I got home, it was too late."

She ends her story with a nonchalant shrug. "It was stupid. I shouldn't have freaked out. I'm sorry."

"What's the long version?"

Her eyes snap up at my hardened tone. I listened the whole time, but my brain trips over the idea of her getting a teacher in trouble. A feeling crawls down my spine and spreads through my limbs, icy and bitter, leaving my skin pebbled with gooseflesh.

Something flickers through her pretty blue eyes. A hint of sadness. A heavy weight she's carried for years. A recognizable torment I hope to God I'm wrong about.

But like calls to like.

And right now, Dove is shining like a damn light-house in the middle of a dark, stormy sea.

"What?" she asks on a breath, long lashes fluttering as if my question confuses her.

"What happened with the teacher? How did you get him in trouble?"

I shift. Fang jumps from my lap and pads down the hall, likely sensing the unease creeping through me.

To my surprise, Dove answers. Her eyes fall to the cushion between us as she plays with a random curl, running her fingers over the flaxen strands. "My dad died when I was thirteen. He was away on a business trip. Just standing on the sidewalk, waiting for a seat at a restaurant, when a drunk driver lost control and hit him."

Tears fill her eyes, and my heart reaches for hers, aching to offer solace.

"We didn't really get along. He always made me feel like I was a burden. My mom took it hard, though.

She wouldn't get out of bed for days at a time. She didn't know how to do anything around the house. Dad paid the bills, managed their accounts, fixed things when they broke. She felt like her life was over. And while she was grieving... she sort of forgot about me."

I think about my own childhood. About how my mother *never* left me alone. I don't know which of us had it worse.

I want to pull her close, but Dove clings to the pillow in her lap like a lifeline, twirling her hair as she continues.

"That fall, I turned fourteen and started high school. Everyone was nice at first. Understanding. They let it slide when I didn't want to participate in class. Kids gave condolences in the halls. Teachers asked about my mom. But no one knew that I was taking care of myself. No one really cared to look that closely. Not until *him*."

Her voice cracks, and my hands clench. A lump forms in my throat because I already know the rest of the story without her having to say a word. But I let her continue anyway because I have a feeling she's never told her account to anyone who wanted to truly listen.

"He was everyone's favorite English teacher. Funny, smart, kind... handsome. All the girls had a crush on him. And I felt... *honored* when he started paying attention. At first, they were just little things. He'd ask how I was instead of my mom or if I needed anything for school. Then he told me he was impressed with my writing. Said I had talent. Asked if I'd ever considered pursuing it as a career, and offered to give me private tutoring lessons. Honestly, one of the only reasons I even became a writer was to spite him." Dove angrily wipes her tears from her cheeks and snorts a laugh. "When everything was said and done, he told me I'd amount to nothing, but look at me now, Mr. Patterson!"

I scoot closer and rest a hand on her knee, stroking gently in what I hope is a comforting manner.

"Anyway, I was elated. So, I said yes. It started with tutoring after school, then late-night sessions, then spending time at his house. By the time I realized how wrong it was, I was nearly seventeen." She sniffs. I make a mental note to find out everything I can about this guy.

If the Doll can do it, maybe I can too. Perhaps it's not about facing what happened to me but ensuring it doesn't happen to others. Maybe I can start that journey by rectifying Dove's stolen past.

"He knew I needed a father figure, so he stepped in and groomed me. For a year and a half, he walked that line between innocent and wrong. And once he crossed it," she exhales sharply, "he took most of my firsts. He ruined 'good girl' for me. I think I would've really liked that sexually, too." She pouts, forcing a joke because it's what she has to do to cope with the tragedy.

Dove meets my gaze, softening when she sees the unshed tears in my eyes. "Don't cry for me, Songbird. I'm not worth—"

I yank the pillow from her lap and pull her into mine, hugging her fiercely. "You're wrong, Dove. You are worth it."

She shudders against me, throwing her arms around my neck as she tightly returns my hug. We're nearly in the same position I was in with the Doll last weekend, but I know without a doubt I'd rather be here with Dove than with the stranger I admire.

When she pulls back, I smooth the tears from her face with my thumbs. Even sitting, I'm taller than her, and I can't help it when my dick grows hard beneath her, ready to say hello to the real thing instead of getting jerked off to the thought of her.

Her eyes drop to my lips. She licks her own.

Not the best time for our first kiss. I hate that Hunter's lips have been on hers tonight, and I hate that the same pink lips I've agonized over for weeks now just told me a tale that rivals my own.

It's not the time for intimacy.

Yet, as our breaths mingle, the space between us disappears. Gently, I cup her cheeks and guide her to me, tasting her for the first time. She tastes every bit as sweet as she looks, like candy and tequila, with a hint of citrus from the shots earlier. A reminder that she's had a lot to drink.

"Stop overthinking it, Songbird, and *kiss* me," she demands, winding her fingers through my hair.

She attacks my lips with a fervor that forces my eyes shut as I cling to her—to her scent and taste and the feel of her in my arms. So small and light and easy to escape from if I needed to.

So perfect.

She licks the seam of my lips, seeking entrance, and rocks against my erection. The tension shifts—from sexual to anxious. I pull back, hands firm on her shoulders.

She giggles. "What? Trying to make me work for it?"

I loosen my hold. Allowing her to nip at my lips as I say, "I... I don't like kissing... with tongue."

Dove blinks. "What? You afraid I'll try to bite it off?"

Running my hands down her sides and underneath my jacket, I rub the soft fabric of her dress with rough strokes. "It just grosses me out."

"Why?" Her question is genuine, and she stops

moving, hands steady on my chest while she waits for my answer.

"I don't know. They're... long." I realize how stupid I sound and try to distract her by kissing down her throat.

When I get to her collarbone, she drops her mouth to the base of my throat. "Of course they are. They're for licking." Her mouth traces a slow line upward. "And tasting." She presses an open-mouthed kiss on the pulse point below my ear before grabbing my chin and turning my face to her. "And kissing."

Kiss me now, Songbird! Just like I taught you!

Panic flares. Red-hot, all-consuming. A voice that isn't hers invades my head.

Danger.

We're in danger.

I can't see. Everything is a blur, but I'm vaguely aware of hands grasping at mine, even though all I see is red.

Danger.

We're in danger.

"...it's me," a soft gasp.

A sharp bark. Then another.

"Wren... it's me... it's Dove. It's just Dove." Hoarse and broken and begging.

"Wren!"

Another sharp bark.

I don't have a dog.

I don't have a dog.

I don't...

The world comes crashing back in a burst of cream and pink, and I release my grip as she stumbles off my lap, gasping for air and delicately clutching her throat.

"Holy shit. Dove, I'm so sorry." Shock and realization knock the air from my lungs. I push to my feet and reach for her, but she sticks a hand out to stop me.

"No. I'm sorry, Wren. I shouldn't have pushed you. Are you okay?" She doesn't look scared of me, but she should be by the looks of the red ring of fingerprints marring her skin. The sight makes my stomach roil as the beers I had earlier threaten to make an appearance.

I hurt her.

I hurt her, and she's asking if *I'm* okay. "Dove..."

"It's okay." She shakes her head as I approach her again. "Seriously, I'm good." Her voice is raspy and sounds so fucking painful, and it hurts *me* to know I'm the cause of it.

"Fuck!" What if I did permanent damage? What if I ruined her vocal cords, and I never get to hear her light-hearted, bubbly cadence again?

I reach out to her, but Fang puts himself between us, growling at me like he can actually stop me from getting to her.

"It's okay, baby. He didn't mean to," she coos.

I'm so sorry, baby. I didn't mean to. Another flash-back strobes across my vision.

I've never had something set me off to the point of violence before. "I'm so sorry."

Dove tells me she's okay again, but I don't hear it. I flee out of shame. Especially after what she told me.

Dove opened up, letting me in by sharing about the demon of her past.

I just let mine ruin our whole goddamn future.

"THIS IS A BAD IDEA," Bunny's concern bleeds through the speakerphone.

"Well, he won't answer my calls or texts. What else am I supposed to do? He won't talk to me. Maybe he'll talk to *her*," I grunt, struggling to zip up my catsuit. "I wish you were here to do this for me. You know I had nothing to do with Hunter kissing me. Why am I the one being punished?"

"Hunter can kiss whoever he wants. I don't care," she states flippantly. "And you're not being punished. I told you, I have plans tonight."

"You *do* care." I halt my mission, her last sentence finally resonating. Limbs contorted, I barely manage to pinch the zipper between my fingers. "What plans? You didn't tell me about any plans. Why wasn't I invited to the plans?"

"It's for work," she grumbles.

Something else filters through the speakers, but I can't make it out. "What was that?"

"Hunter specifically requested me for a job," she bites out.

I resume wrestling myself into this godforsaken clingwrap. "See? I don't appreciate him telling me to get my shit together when you two are way worse. I seriously don't understand why you don't just give in already."

"I have my reasons," she murmurs. "Anyway. Maybe Wren just needs space. Have you thought about that? You two went from hating each other to making out, and then he told you he doesn't like kissing with tongue, and you all but made fun of him."

Standing straight, I stomp my platform boot into the thick rug covering the hardwood. "I did not make fun of him! I thought he was making me work for it! You *know* how much I like a challenge." I try to keep my tone light, full of my usual energy, but my throat still aches, reducing my outburst to a whispery tantrum.

"All I'm saying is you should wait until Monday to see him at work." A page flips, followed by the crunch of Lucky Charms and the clink of a spoon against a bowl. "This isn't something to play around with,

Dove. If he finds out who you really are, it's gonna get messy. You know it will."

I secure my sleek black bob and check my reflection in the vanity mirror.

Most of my wigs are long and heavy, but tonight isn't about looking like her. It's about talking to Wren. Besides, I don't wear the catsuit to any of my killings. This wig won't draw as much suspicion, making it perfect for slipping through the streets unnoticed.

"I can't wait, Buns." I slip a few pairs of blackout contacts into the pocket of my ankle-length leather trench and strap my dagger sheath around my thigh.

"Damn, you got it bad. Jesus, maybe you should have married my husband instead. A man finally chokes you, and you want to put a ring on it," she jokes.

Like me, Bunny often uses humor to cope with her past.

"No one said anything about a ring," I reply flatly. "You weren't there. You didn't see his eyes. I think it hurt him more to see what he did than it hurt me."

"I mean, I saw your throat. He temporarily tattooed his fingerprints on you." I study the purple bruises in the mirror as she continues, "He's probably ashamed, embarrassed, and worried the cops will show up at his door any second now. And why *did* you let him get away with it? You could have gotten out of his grip."

I think back to two nights ago—to the glaze in Wren's eyes, the way he retreated into himself to deal with what I kept pushing him toward. I know that look well. And the words he whispered to the Doll still haunt me.

I'm already dead inside.

"Like I said," I murmur. "You didn't see his eyes."

NO GARLIC LINGERS in the air when I enter Wren's home. No errant clicking of fingers on a keyboard or the delicate scrape of utensils against a plate. Just my songbird, wrapped in the cold and dark, staring blankly at the TV from his place on the couch.

His eyes slide to me as I make my presence known. The dead, empty caverns burst to life, shining with the light of a thousand suns. "You came back."

"I didn't like how we left things last time." My modulator settings are unchanged, but the voice that escapes me sounds slightly *off*. Gently and as quietly as possible, I clear my throat as he shifts from his side to his feet.

Good god, those sweatpants should be illegal.

"I'm sorry about that." He sheepishly rakes a hand

through his hair, the silken strands feathering back, the front falling just enough to frame his forehead. "I'm glad you're here, though."

He flashes that damn smile and steps forward. But when I whip out my dagger and point it at him, he stops abruptly, hands raised.

He won't answer my calls or texts, making me look certifiably insane for how many times I've tried to reach him. But he's happy the Doll is here?

Can you be jealous of your alter ego?

"Why are you glad?" I sidestep. He mirrors my movement but keeps his distance.

Wren shoves his hands into the front pocket of his hoodie and fixes me with a look that is equal parts excitement and amusement. We step in tandem again, circling until my back is nearly to his couch. I creep around the edge of the coffee table and perch on the armrest farthest from him, keeping my weapon up in case he tries to rush me.

"Because I have questions." He's calm and cool and casual now. Entering his kitchen, he asks over his shoulder, "Would you like a drink?"

I shoot him a deadpan stare before remembering he can't see shit behind my mask. Sardonically, I point to the lips of my mask and ask, "Do you have a straw?"

"Didn't think about that." Wren laughs. He abandons any pretense of being a good host for his uninvited guest and pulls a kitchen chair halfway into the living room, flipping it around to sit backward.

"So, what are your questions?" I prop my forearm over my knee, letting the dagger dangle from my fingers, twirling it idly. Annoyance seeps from my pores at how friendly he's acting.

Do not lose your cool, Dove. You're a serial killer, for fuck's sake. That takes time and patience—both of which you need to exercise right now.

"How do you do it?" He crosses his arms over the back of the chair and leans forward, curiosity dripping from his lips, interest tucked into every chiseled curve of his facial structure.

"Do what?"

"*Kill.* I want—" Wren stops, his expression shifting. It almost seems like he's trying to rein in a sudden bout of anger. His fists clench, one leg beginning to bounce. "I *need* to learn." I can't stop the laugh that bubbles up, though the motion makes me wince—a painful reminder that the man across from me nearly crushed my throat two nights ago. "Who do you need to kill, So—" I cut myself off sharply, disguising the slip with a cough.

Fuck. I was just about to call him Songbird.

"Do you know Dove Carroway?" He squints, as if he can actually see behind my mask, searching for any hint of a lie. There's no evidence of him catching my slip-up. The question comes too quickly, catching me mid-fake cough—which, *again*, hurts like fucking hell.

If he'd had a straw and I'd taken the drink, I'm sure I would have choked on it. Pun intended. It takes every ounce of self-restraint not to react. Why would he be asking about Dove... err... me?

"No? I do love what she writes about me, though." My voice is light, flippant. "Why do you ask? Is she who you want to kill?" He says he needs to learn, and now he's asking if I know myself? Surely he's not stupid enough to try and kill little ol' *me*.

All over a bit of tongue action?

He doesn't answer my question. "No one else has the inside scoop on you like she does. And the first night you came here, you said a little birdie told you about my obsession."

"It's a saying. I wasn't being factual." I stand and stretch, letting out a fake yawn as though he's boring me. "I wouldn't mind meeting her, though. She does seem to *get* me."

Wren stands as well, approaching with heavy footsteps. "Dove writes about you for a reason," he stresses, making emphatic motions with his hands, as if they'll clue me in on whatever he's thinking.

Obviously, I know the reason for doing what I do. The fact that he's put it together so quickly is impressive and... adorable?

"I want to *murder* that reason." His words land like a hammer.

I nearly swoon.

Wren looks dead serious—a man on a mission.

My songbird doesn't want to kill *me*. He wants to kill *for* me.

Sadly, a quick internet search will tell him the man he wishes dead is already long gone.

Freddy Patterson was my first kill when I was twenty. After he was found not guilty and people in town started making threats, saying I'd lied for two years about what he'd done—what he'd *made* me do.

He'd been reinstated. Apologized to profusely. There had even been talk of a slander lawsuit, but my mother offered him hush money because she never believed me either.

Daddy issues.

Everyone said I just had daddy issues, and maybe I did—do.

But Freddy Patterson created the Baby Doll Killer. He liked dressing me up, buying me pretty things an adult woman would wear, and making me act younger than I was. He kept a room in his house just for me, filled with lace and frills and dolls—so many dolls that sometimes, at night, they scared me.

They would watch all the horrible things being done to me. Silent voyeurs to a nightmare where I was the beautiful, bright star—even when I no longer wanted to be.

Yet somehow, the dolls and the frills and the pretty pink persona stuck. A mask I'll never shed because they became a piece of me—a vital part of who Dove Carroway is. A reminder of why I do what I do and who I do it for.

"You're not a killer, Wrenley Campbell. You should leave that up to the professionals." Tears prick my eyes, making the blackout contacts slide and itch. I look away, focusing on the hall—my only means of escape—and the fact that he's standing in my way. All it would take is one contact slipping out, and he'd see my true identity staring him in the face.

Sniffing, I tuck my hair behind my ear. When I look back at him, he's frozen, a frown stretching across his painstakingly beautiful face. The dim lighting from the kitchen and TV casts shifting shadows over the living room, but he isn't looking at my mask.

He's staring at my neck.

Why would he be...

Oh, fuck!

<u>Wrenley</u>

It couldn't be.

"I need to get going. Consider your exclusive interview over." The Doll shakes her head, her hair falling back over her ear.

Call me crazy, but I could have sworn there was a bruise on her neck when she tucked her hair back—exactly where I grabbed Dove two nights ago.

"Wait!" I reach out but jerk back in alarm as she whips her dagger toward me, edging around before spinning and darting down the hall.

"Don't follow me!" she snaps.

But I couldn't even if I wanted to. I'm frozen in place, struggling to reconcile what I just saw. When she spun, her hair flew off her neck again, revealing the bruising once more. It wasn't a trick of the light.

Was it?

No. There's no way. She's taller than Dove. Her body felt...

Memories of that night crash to the forefront of my mind. The Doll and Dove have the same curves. The same dips and crevices in their thighs and waists, the same swell of their breasts pressing against my chest.

At least five minutes pass before I snap into action, grabbing my cell and dialing Hunter's number.

"Oh, are you speaking to me now?" he drawls, picking up after the second ring.

Annoyance floods my bloodstream. "No, and I'm going to rearrange your face the next time I see you.

You can't hide upstate at your parents' forever. But that's not why I'm calling."

"Is everything okay?" he asks, only marginally more concerned than two seconds ago.

"Uh... yeah." I can't tell him about what happened with Dove. It's got to be some sort of felony, and I don't need him put in the awkward position of asking if she wants to file a report. But I also don't want to share my suspicions about her just yet. "Can you email me the videos of the Doll?"

"Uh, no? You know that, Wren. What's going on?"

I hear shuffling and a voice in the background that sounds strangely like Bunny yelling about why she has to be "there."

Where is there? Last I knew, he wasn't in the city.

Shaking my head, I decide to ask about whatever is going on between him and his rabbit later. "Your boss knows I've seen some of them. Can't you send me those? I got the chance to publish, and I want to make sure I get the details right."

I hate lying to him, but honestly, I'm still too pissed to see him in person and not rearrange his perfect nose. Besides... it's not like it's the first time I've kept something from him.

Snapping open my laptop, I pull up a blank document and tap over the keys in unintentional strokes. As my fingers create a new language, Hunter sighs.

"They were leaked. Why can't you just watch them online?"

"Because the full versions weren't leaked. I won't tell anyone I have them, and I won't reference you in the article." I pause when I hear who *is* unmistakably Bunny, close enough now to make out her words.

"I have a date to get to, so if you can wrap up your...mrffgh!"

"Sending them over now. Gotta go, bye." The line goes dead.

"What the fuck?" I mutter, pulling my phone away from my ear to see my home screen staring back at me.

Why is he lying about where he is?

There isn't much time to ponder because less than a minute later, an email comes through containing exactly what I need. I spend hours watching and rewatching, looking for any sort of clue that wasn't caught before.

But there's nothing. The Doll is meticulous. The videos have been skewed in a way that would take a tech team weeks to unravel just to get some scope on her height.

Hunter calls back just as I'm rewatching the last video. "I had to come back for work. Mom and Dad say hi, by the way."

"Uh-huh. Did you release your rabbit into the wild for her date?" I take a pull from my beer and sit back, turning down the volume on the TV, where I've cast the videos from my laptop.

"Fuck her date," Hunter scoffs. "The dude was five-nine with a pedo-stache."

"And you know this *because?*" On the screen, the Doll saws through her victim's privates. My balls ache just watching it.

"Because I walked her to the bar where they were meeting. She's just trying to get back at me for kissing Dove."

"Hmm. Maybe she and I should team up. Swap a little spit in front of you two and see how you like it," I muse, getting up to grab a new bottle. The second the words leave my mouth, however, guilt punches me in the gut.

I've been ignoring Dove since I ran away like a coward the other night. She deserves better. She deserves more than a ring of bruises around her dainty neck and the pain I caused in her big blue eyes. No matter how panicked I was.

Even if she's the Doll. *Especially* if she's the Doll.

And fuck, if she is... was she right in front of me the whole time?

"Touch a hair on Bunny's head, and I'll charge you with sexual assault," Hunter grumbles. I know he won't.

"It's cute you keep threatening that, yet you had

the nerve to touch my..." My what? Dove isn't *my* anything. I ruined any chance of that.

Didn't I?

"Oh? Is she *yours* now?" Hunter sounds amused.

Movement on the screen pulls my attention back to the TV. The victim thrashes against his bindings, knocking the chair into the table holding the Doll's instruments. She backhands him with the pommel of her dagger. Her head falls back, shoulders rising and falling as if sighing, before she methodically readjusts the table to its original position.

I blanch, nearly dropping my beer.

Rushing back to my laptop, I rewind thirty seconds and hit play, vaguely aware of Hunter rambling about how he teased Bunny's date so bad the guy left before drinks were even ordered.

I watch closely as the scene replays, matching each second to how Dove reacted whenever I knocked something off-kilter in her office—how she'd pause before setting it back exactly as it was.

Holy. Fucking. Shit.

"Hey, Hunt? You never find any fingerprints at the crime scenes, do you?" I think about the way the Doll's fingers felt against my skin—smooth, with rough edges, like she'd taped something over the pads or coated them in glue.

"Nope." He pops his p. "The scenes are always wiped clean."

Sitting back, I drag a hand down my face, weighing whether to tell him. But at my core, I know he'd be obligated to investigate, and I can't stomach the idea of Dove sitting behind bars.

The Doll doesn't belong in prison. I don't care if she murders men. The disgusting bastards deserve it.

And it doesn't seem like Hunter is all that concerned with catching her.

"You guys don't seem too worried about catching the Doll or the Siren," I lead, hoping he bites.

He does. "This is off the record, obviously, Wren. But they kill the bad guys the world's better off without. Some of us aren't exactly *itching* to put them behind bars."

Long after we've hung up, after I've matched nearly every coincidence, I'm convinced.

Dove Carroway is the Baby Doll Killer.

THIS COULD HAVE BEEN *an email or a phone call. Why does it have to be a home visit?*

My inner voice sounds oddly like Bunny today.

I tug up my pale pink turtleneck—the only one I own because they look awful on me—until it sits just beneath my chin. The last thing I need is for Hunter to see the bruises his friend left and start asking questions.

This is the ultimate betrayal. I can hear Bunny screeching as if she's standing right beside me.

No, a betrayal would be actually fucking around with Hunter. This is harmless. It's Sunday, and this is a conversation I need to have in private.

I clutch a box of mini Merveilleux from Aux Merveilleux de Fred as I stroll down the street to Hunter's West Village brownstone. A good guest always brings a gift, and since Bunny talks about

Hunter more than she realizes, I happen to know these are some of his favorite treats.

His narrowed, whiskey-colored gaze greets me as he opens the door. "You know that kiss was just to force Wren to get his act together, right? I'm sorry, Dove, but I'm too obsessed with your friend to make room for you here." He clutches his chest, sarcasm dripping from his tone.

I roll my eyes and walk past him as he moves aside to let me in, shoving the box into his stomach. "Good afternoon to you too, Detective Remington."

"How'd you know I like these?" He wastes no time digging into the box, plucking out a coffee-flavored mini meringue. They really are good. I sampled two flavors while waiting in line and even placed an order to pick up on my way home.

Ignoring him, I take in his renovated space. It's cleaner than I expected—white and navy walls, gray-toned furniture, and light oak flooring giving it a crisp, balanced feel. "Nice digs."

"Thanks. So, tell me, Dove. What brings you here? You know if Bunny finds out, she'll skin us both, right?" He pauses and frowns, then nods for me to follow him into the kitchen. "*Does* she know you're here?"

"No," I sigh. "But I promise, I'm not here to

declare my undying love for you. Dark hair and jawlines that can cut glass just aren't my cup of tea."

He laughs. "I think that was a compliment, so thank you? Bet you prefer blonds, huh?" He winks before shoving another meringue in his mouth—the chocolate one this time. Around a mouthful, he asks, "Do you want a drink? It's too early for tequila... or is it?" He swallows, smirking. "I swear, sometimes I think you and Bunny run on the stuff. You guzzle it like it's fuel."

"Water is fine." I climb onto a tall stool at the far end of the white granite island, staring at the gray-marbled detailing. "Look, I know it seems weird that I called. I probably could have just asked over the phone, but..." I trail off, second-guessing myself. Wren is still ignoring me, and if he has any suspicions after I went to see him as the Doll last night, Hunter will be the first person he turns to.

But still... Hunter is also the only person who might have the answers I need. "I have some questions... about Wren."

He slides a glass of water and a small bowl of lemon wedges my way, then leans his elbows on the counter, fixing me with a wary look. "What type of questions?"

Averting my gaze, I squeeze two wedges into my water. "About Wren's past."

Hunter sighs softly, rounding the island to take the stool catty-corner from mine. "What happened?"

"Nothing in particular." I lie with a shrug. "There are just some things I've... noticed, and I wondered if you'd have some insight."

"Like?" I realize Hunter won't make this easy. If I want answers, I'll have to ask directly.

"Did something happen to Wren when he was younger?" *There. That wasn't so bad.*

Hunter's shoulders tense.

Or maybe it is.

He grabs the lemon bowl, spinning it idly on the granite. "Something like what?"

"Jesus Christ, Hunter." I push my water away, the liquid sloshing over the rim, dripping down the side to create a ring around the glass. "Stop avoiding my question. I'm not asking as a member of the press. I'm asking because I'm worried about him."

"I'll ask you again, Dove. What. Happened?" He won't look at me, but his tone has hardened, allowing me to believe my assumptions aren't unfounded.

"*Nothing,*" I stress. I almost say it takes one to know one. But I'm not close enough with Hunter to share my deep, dark secrets. I'm still annoyed I spilled them to Wren in an attempt to connect with him.

Silence stretches between us. When he finally

speaks, it's so quiet I barely hear him. "You look like his mother. The resemblance is uncanny."

My heart pounds, a slow, sickening thud against my ribs. An uncomfortable sensation rolls through me, like the first thawed drops of a frozen spring. "His mother?"

"Yeah. They always had a... close relationship." Hunter sighs, scrubbing a hand over his face. "His dad left when he was young. Said he wouldn't take part in raising a 'sissy boy' and complained that his mother babied him. Little did he know, Wren would have given anything for his father to take him away from her."

Tears prick my eyes, but I hold them back. If this is going where I think it is... why did Wren sit there and let me spill my past without sharing his own?

"Did... did she..."

"I don't know for sure," Hunter murmurs. "There were signs. It was a big accusation, and I didn't want to say anything to my parents without proof." He props his chin between his thumb and index finger, his leg bouncing. "When I confronted Wrenley, he denied it. I mean, vehemently denied it. I think he was embarrassed. And I tried–" He breaks off, exhaling sharply before continuing. "I tried to let him know I was there for him. That he didn't have to suffer through it anymore."

I take a shaky breath. How could Wren comfort me when he was carrying something just as heavy? Is that why he's so obsessed with the Doll?

Men aren't the only ones who abuse children.

I remember his words at the police department. A tear escapes, then another, clinging to my lashes.

"They were gone by the end of the week," Hunter concludes. "She packed them up and moved to California to live with her new boyfriend, according to Wren. We tried to keep in touch, but eventually stopped talking. Then we reconnected after college, and he seemed fine, so I never brought it up again."

"You think she sexually abused him?" The words taste bitter. What I went through was horrific, but if what Hunter is saying is true... what Wren went through is unimaginable.

And if I look like her... No wonder he hated me so much when we met.

I can't imagine kissing someone who looks like my abuser. It's no wonder he reacted the way he did when I tried to take things further.

Hunter shakes his head. "I don't know. Like I said, I have my suspicions. She clung to him harder than a koala to a eucalyptus branch and was overly—and I mean *overly*—affectionate. It was uncomfortable at times."

"Did he ever seem like she made *him* uncomfortable?" But I already know the answer. I did the same thing for years with Freddy. At first, because I felt special, and when I didn't anymore... Why would anyone believe a girl who let it happen for so long?

"He hid it well. Wren is nothing if not good at hiding his true feelings." Hunter steals a glance at me, his sharp features softening when he sees my tears. "You can't say anything to him, Dove."

"I won't." I rub under my eyes, careful not to smear my makeup. "Thank you for telling me."

"He likes you. He doesn't want to, but he does. Be patient with him."

Giving him a knowing look, I laugh. "Pot, meet kettle."

"Hey, if there's one thing I excel at, it's patience." He sighs. "Speaking of that—tell me one thing."

Sniffing, I reach for the roll of paper towels in the middle of the island and tear one off, dabbing my eyes. "What's that?"

"Am I wasting my time?" He fidgets nervously, rhythmically tapping his fingers to a tune only he can hear.

I don't need him to explain what he means or what he's talking about.

"Wasting your time? I suppose that depends. What exactly are you expecting from her?"

"Nothing," he breathes out with a shake of his

head. "I don't expect a damn thing from her other than to just let me in."

"She has let you in, Hunter. Believe it or not—aside from me—you're the closest thing she has to a real friend. You've been there for her for years. Don't give up on her now."

"I'm not giving up on her. But it's like every time I take a step forward, she takes two back. I just..." He pounds his fist on the island. Not in anger, but in frustration with his situation with Bunny. "I just want her to let me love her."

Bunny deserves that. She deserves a man who wants to take care of her and who will accept her just as she is. Especially after her husband tried to turn her into a Stepford housewife.

I know she wants that with Hunter more than anything. But I also know she's afraid, and I'm honestly not sure she'll be able to give him what he wants.

"My best advice is to take your *own* advice. Be patient. When her husband died, Bunny found out he had a pretty hefty life insurance policy." I nod my head along with my words, willing him to read between the lines.

He doesn't. He stares at me with notched brows like he doesn't know what that has to do with the conversation.

Sweet, sweet, Detective Dick—so pretty, but so simple.

"She's set for life, Hunter. She doesn't have to work if she doesn't want to. But she went back for a *reason.*" I don't flat-out tell him she went back because she missed him. Bunny hasn't even admitted that to me yet. I just know it's the truth.

Slipping from the stool, I press a hand to his shoulder and peer up at him with the most serious expression I can muster. "Bunny wants to be loved. She just doesn't know how because everyone she's ever loved has hurt her. Don't hurt her, Hunter. Or I'll have to kill you."

TWO DAYS. That's all it takes—two days of Dove calling out from work for personal reasons, and I turn into a stage-five clinger of epic proportions.

She's flipped the script on me now, refusing to answer my calls or texts. Well, except for a single, clipped *I'm okay*. I have to admit, that's more than I ever gave her, but it's nowhere near enough to quiet the gnawing need to talk to her—to see her.

I could go full stalker mode, show up at her house, and hypocritically demand to know why she's ignoring me. Instead, I rein it in—just a little—and settle for ambushing her best friend to see if she knows what's going on. Because, obviously, Bunny—whom I've been nothing but rude to and have said some not-so-nice things about—will have no problem spilling Dove's whereabouts to *me* of all people.

Imagine my fucking surprise when I walk into The Tipsy Taco, fully expecting to hunt down Bunny, only to find my girl perched on the edge of a pool table, talking animatedly with *Ryan*. Of all fucking people.

The feral beast that has taken up residence in my chest whenever Dove is near stirs awake. Curled horns and smoke and the inexplicable need to plant my fist into Ryan's modelesque face slither through me like a viper.

The bastard leans against the table, one hand gripping a pool cue, the other gesturing mid-story. Whatever he's saying makes Dove throw her head back in laughter, exposing the delicate line of her neck and the fading bruises that still mar her skin. His brows pull together, and he reaches out, fingers ghosting over them.

My anger surges as Dove inches away, waving him off, muttering what I assume is an excuse while she picks at invisible lint on her taffy-pink shorts. Sliding off the table, she tugs at the hem of her white shirt, adjusting the fabric that wraps around her back and forms a bow, while Ryan presses his questioning.

"How long are you going to stand there looking like a dumbass?" Bunny's dulcet tone interrupts my silent seething.

She's beside me now, dark-purple-polished fingers curved around a shot glass, which I assume holds tequila. Today, rainbow foil paw prints trail down her cheek, covering the scar beneath her eye at the highest point of her cheekbone. She watches the scene unfold with a wolfish grin stretched across her mauve-painted lips, and I *get* why Hunter is completely enamored with the dark-haired beauty.

Where Dove is bright, effervescent sunshine, Bunny is mystery and calculation wrapped in sensuality—like a wolf draped in a rabbit's hide. I swing my gaze back to Dove and Ryan, annoyed to find them locked in what looks like a full-blown argument. "Are they—"

"No. Absolutely not." Bunny crosses her arms, sipping her shot. "You should know by now that girl is wrapped around your finger, though she'd kill me for telling you that."

Then why the hell has she been ignoring me?

I study Dove as she speaks heatedly, trying to reconcile this version of her with the Doll and coming up short. I can't fathom it, and yet, I can. She's a paradox I need to unravel. I will her to look at me, sending every desperate wave of *choose me* energy across the bar. It tugs at her, invisible fingers tipping her chin in my direction. For a moment, she stares. Then, a warm smile tugs at the corner of her lips.

"God, you two are dense," Bunny sighs before sauntering off.

I nearly turn to tell her she and Hunter are no better, but just as Dove takes a step toward me, Ryan reaches out, grabs her belt loop, and pulls her back. It's not aggressive, but it makes her stumble in her chunky platforms, grabbing onto him to steady herself.

My feet carry me across the bar in six long strides—my intention to plant my fists directly into Ryan's face. I don't stop. I don't hesitate. I step into Ryan's personal space, chest to chest, forcing him to release Dove. "Get your fucking hands off her."

"Well, well, if it isn't Hunter's lapdog," Ryan clips, puffing his pecs like it'll somehow make up for the three inches I have on him. "This doesn't involve you."

"Wrenley, what are you doing?" Dove tries to push between us, her small palm splayed against my chest. If I wasn't already pissed that she was chumming it up with this asshole, I certainly am now—because she just used my *full name*.

"I told you to stay away from her," I seethe, fury radiating from every pore. If she knew the shit he's said about her, there's no way she'd even entertain a conversation with him. But we're drawing a crowd, and I refuse to embarrass her by airing his filth in public.

"Why would you say that?" she demands, still trying to wedge between us. "I can take care of myself, Wrenley."

I crack my neck, jaw tightening, but before I can

respond, Ryan cuts in. "You wanna know why I stopped talking to you suddenly?" He gestures at me. "Because this asshole threatened me."

My eyes snap back to his. "You wanna tell her *why*?" My voice is foreign to my own ears—raw, dripping with unfiltered rage. I've never felt such anger. Such unbridled need to destroy someone so thoroughly.

"It's okay. It doesn't matter." Dove curls her fingers into my jacket, stepping into me, pulling my focus back to her. "Let's get out of here. Take me home?"

A fraction of my anger ebbs at the urgency in her voice, in her eyes. My hand finds her waist, her warmth grounding me—reminding me that, once again, I've picked a fight with an off-duty cop.

"Nothing like a little hate fuck, I guess." Ryan smirks over Dove's head. "That's okay. Take her for a ride. She always comes back."

Dove gasps, affronted. She spins, hand flying. He catches her wrist mid-swing and shoves her back—not hard enough to hurt her, but enough that she stumbles.

I lunge, catching her while swinging for his face. He dodges, throwing his own punch. It lands, snapping my head to the side.

"Wren!" Dove twists in my arms, unharmed, but *fuck*, he could have seriously hurt her—and the look on his face says he knows it.

She presses a palm to the side of my mouth, glaring at him over her shoulder before shifting her worried gaze back to me. "Are you okay?"

"I've been hit harder." I spit, swiping the back of my hand across my bloodied lip.

Someone hands her napkins. A bouncer awkwardly arrives, escorting Ryan out. He glares at us as he's swallowed by the crowd and they part for him like he's got the plague. I'm not a cop-hater, but there are some who abuse their power, and Ryan is definitely one of them. The thought of him and Dove together —intimately—spikes a fresh rage.

"Come on." Dove tugs my arm, pressing an ice-filled bag to my lip. "Let's get you home."

"You didn't have to do that, you know," Dove murmurs, pressing a rose-shaped, raspberry-and-mint-infused ice cube—because that's all she has—to my lip. I wince slightly from the sting but refuse to show her any real weakness. I rushed in to be her knight in shining armor; I shouldn't be crying over a simple cut.

Ryan got me good, though, splitting my lower lip open so badly that Dove tried dragging me to the hospital for stitches. But I didn't want to sit in a stuffy waiting room full of sick people and overworked nurses too sleep-deprived to bother with a kind bedside manner.

I just wanted to go home. Apparently, that meant her place. I'm not mad about it.

Fang sets a paw in my lap, begging for attention, but before I can scoop the rat up, Dove gently shoos him away. "Your big, bad friend is hurting right now, baby boy. We have to nurse him back to health."

Suddenly, my brain is filled with images of Dove in a slutty little nurse costume, and a groan escapes my throat—which she mistakes for something else entirely.

"You really shouldn't have started shit with him," she repeats for the umpteenth time since we left the bar, letting me take the ice from her.

"Duly noted. Next time, I'll leave you to the two-hundred-pound beefcake whose sole mission is to let his dudebros gangbang you," I mutter, slowly massaging the cube around my lip.

Dove sits back on her knees, huffing air out of her nose like a tiny, angry dragon. I imagine sparkly pink smoke curling from her nostrils, infusing the air with glittering fury. "I still can't believe he said that. He totally had me fooled, and usually, I'm a pretty good judge of character."

Yes, I told her exactly why things went down the way they did. She also made no fewer than three calls to every police contact she had to report him for gross misconduct—even though, technically, I started it.

She pushes off the couch, arms crossed, one bare foot tapping against the floor as she stares at the wall. "I am a little proud of the Olympic blowjob reference, though. I *am* competitive in sports," she muses.

I can't help but laugh, wincing when the smile that threatens to split my lip all over again widens too far.

"Poor songbird." She sticks out her bottom lip mockingly. "That's what you get for being mean to me."

"*Mean* to you?" I repeat incredulously, tugging at my collar. Despite the ice against my skin, her apartment is stifling. I abandon the cube on a coaster and stand, shrugging off my jacket and tossing it over the arm of her couch before yanking my tie loose and unfastening the top three buttons of my shirt.

Dove hops onto a stool by the island, propping her chin in her hand, watching me unabashedly. Again, I try to envision her as the dark, unhinged Doll who goes around chopping off men's dicks.

For everything she went through when she was younger, she's so bright and happy.

Did I hit the bullseye when we first met and assumed she was being fake? That she was hiding something behind that cotton candy smile?

Do I even care?

At this point, Dove being the Doll would be the best thing to ever happen to me. I could selfishly have my cake and eat it, too. Black buttercream with a side of pink glitter sprinkles every fucking day for eternity.

"I told you my story, and you ghosted me, Wren," she says bluntly. "Even when I reached out repeatedly, you ignored me. See? Mean."

"I'm sorry. I didn't—" I trail off, realizing I never even considered it from her perspective. She let me in, and I slammed the door shut, as if her trauma was too much for me to handle.

I'm such a fucking idiot.

"Dove—" My phone rings, the shrill tone slicing through my apology.

Dove half-turns to peer at my phone where it lies next to hers on the counter. She blinks, murmuring, "It's your mother."

Leave it to *her* to ruin the moment.

"I'll let you get that." Dove is already disappearing down the hall before I can tell her I don't want to take the call. The bathroom door clicks shut behind her with one last, undecipherable look cast my way.

Thoroughly frustrated, I hit decline—only for Hunter's name to pop up a second later. I answer. "I'm assuming Bunny told you?"

"Yeah. How you feeling, buddy?" he asks in his best Deadpool impression.

"I'm fine, you sarcastic shit. What do you want? If Bunny told you what happened, surely you know I'm with Dove."

"Is the little hottie gonna nurse you back to health? Don't forget your sucker for being a good boy and taking your ass-beating like a champ. Or are you the one with the sucker for her?" He laughs.

"Goodbye, *Detective Dick*."

"Hi, Hunter," Dove calls behind me. I spin, still holding the phone, Hunter's laughter echoing in my ear.

"I gotta go," I mutter, hanging up as I stare, completely dumbstruck.

Dove apparently took me removing my jacket and tie as an invitation to get comfortable. Which, it's her place, and fuck, am I thankful for that.

She reappears in the living room wearing a tiny, bubblegum-pink satin camisole with cream lace trim and matching shorts that cut high on her thighs, hair piled messily on top of her head.

"What?" she asks. "It's time for pajamas. Get comfortable, Songbird. We're gonna watch a movie and talk. I'll make popcorn."

She pads past me into the kitchen, pulling out ingredients like this is an everyday occurrence for us. "Go!" she urges. "Wash the blood off your face and rinse with mouthwash."

"So bossy." I smirk, even though she can't see it. The playful banter does something to me, and I want it —fuck, I want it to be permanent so badly.

She mutters something that sounds suspiciously like, "Just wait till we move it to the bedroom, handsome."

Warmth blooms in my chest like a punctured water balloon. It makes me feel happy—almost *giddy.*

Dove and I have blown way past the usual awkwardness couples commonly experience in the first initial stages of courting. We've laughed, yelled, and pranked each other to the point that maybe we were always meant to skip straight to this.

But there are still so many secrets hanging over us.

Secrets I feel need to come to light if we're going to make a real go of it.

As I exit the bathroom, I feel like some of those secrets are hidden behind the ominous door on the left side of the hall. It looks just like every other door in her place, but this one *feels* different—almost like a cold, looming presence as I walk by.

Popcorn popping in the microwave tells me Dove is still in the kitchen. A strange tingle crawls up my spine as I reach for the gilded doorknob and turn it slowly, ensuring I don't alert Fang.

Locked.

"What are you doing, Wrenley?"

SHIT!

Her question startles me, and I nearly launch myself back against the wall.

"Jesus, you scared me." Breathing deeply, I clutch my chest, letting a light chuckle escape as I step toward her.

"What were you doing?" she asks again, caution tightening her features. I don't like that look directed at me.

Playing it cool, I shrug. "You caught me snooping. I was curious."

One light brow arches. "Curiosity killed the cat, Songbird."

"But answers brought it back, and knowledge kept it alive."

My attempt at redirecting her works. "It's too late for philosophy, Wrenley."

Why *does she keep calling me that?*

"Don't call me that," I snap, rougher than I intended. I'm sick of her using my full name. She changed the way I see my stupid nickname, and now she wants to call me by my full name like I'm in trouble?

No.

"Call you what?" Dove asks, full of sass, planting her fists on her hips as she cranes her neck to look up at me. "Your name?"

Slowly, I step forward, forcing her to retreat a step. "You never use my full name."

Another step. "What am I allowed to call you then? You don't like Songbird. You weren't partial to Wren. If I can't use your full name, then what else do I call you?"

This game of cat and mouse has me hard, my dick tapping against my zipper. Her eyes flick down, tongue shiny as she licks her lips.

Nervous, baby?

"Yours. You infuriating fucking woman." In a flurry of limbs, I lift her onto the stool, and she jumps at the same time, ready for me to catch her.

Our mouths meet roughly, and I battle the pain, soldiering through the ache to claim the little piece of heaven she's offering. It only lasts a mere moment, though, before I taste blood on her lips.

"Are you okay?" she asks with a light laugh, palms warm on my cheeks. She rests her forehead on mine, licking the crimson from her skin like a vampire.

"Yeah. I'm fine." I smooth a few of her fallen strands back. The gesture feels natural, like I've been doing it for years.

Grasping her hip, I pull her close until our bodies meld together. Dove belongs in my arms, against my body, living rent-fucking-free in my head. If I could go back a month and a half and do it all over again, I'd get on my knees for her that very first day and pledge my fucking life.

"Did you really mean it?" She grips my shirt, the force of her clenched fists tearing two buttons open to reveal half my chest. Her gaze dips, locking onto my heart. "Do you really want to be mine, Songbird?"

"Yes." I nuzzle her nose, kissing her softly with the uninjured side of my mouth. Goosebumps break out along her flesh as my hands slip beneath her camisole. "A thousand fucking times, yes."

"Do you want me to make you feel better, baby?" Her voice drops to a husky rasp, hands sliding inside my shirt to explore.

"I would never make you do something you didn't want to do," I murmur as she leans forward, pressing a kiss to the spot she'd been staring at, claiming the organ beneath as her prize for conquering me so thoroughly.

Dove pulls back, looking a little sad, a little sheepish. She refuses to meet my eyes. "I would never make you do something you didn't want to, either, Wren. I'm sorry I pushed you the other night."

Guiding her chin up, I caress her lips, telling her it's okay with my mouth. I place her hands on the rest of the buttons, silently encouraging her to remove my clothes.

"Are you sure?" she whispers against me, reaching for my zipper next.

"Yes," I moan, breath heavy.

Free from the confines of my pants, my cock throbs in my boxer briefs as she runs her palm along it.

This has been *his* dream since day one. We never imagined we'd be such lucky bastards.

Stepping out of my pants, I hook her legs around my waist and carry her to her bedroom. Her soft giggles against my neck spur me on as she laves at my skin. "Am I allowed to use my tongue as long as it's not to kiss you with?"

I don't know why she keeps checking in on me. Yes, I had a breakdown last time. But she doesn't know why. A little voice in the back of my head says we should talk about it before going further—

Then her teeth scrape across my nipple, and I nearly come before I've even seen her naked.

"I'm not glass, Dove. I'm not going to fall apart on you like last time." I try to lay her down, but she instantly rolls us over, guiding me to the head of the bed, where decorative pillows in cream, soft gold, and blush are piled high.

"Oh, I *plan* on making you fall apart, Songbird." She peels the last of my clothing from my body, the soft glow of the vanity lights casting her in an ethereal halo as she peers down at my cock in awe. "Lucky me," she hums appreciatively, running a finger over the veins lining my length. "Ribbed for my pleasure."

"Fuck," the word rides a long moan as she drags her tongue over my skin, settling on her stomach between my legs. My cock taps against my abs, begging for her attention when she abandons it to smile sweetly up at me.

"Put another pillow under your head so you can watch me, baby." She rests her weight on one arm, grabbing me between her thumb and middle finger to idly stroke while waiting for me to obey.

I've never seen anything as fucking hot as Dove ready to make my cock her bitch.

Her glistening tongue darts out to lick my crown, swirling around the tip sensually before pulling back to blow cool air over the slit. I'm already weeping, precum leaking to mix with her saliva as she takes me into her throat with precision.

It feels like all my nerves are on fire, electric pulses igniting with every pass she makes. Each stroke goes deeper, her fist working the part of me she can't fit in her mouth.

Oh, but she fucking tries.

I can't take my eyes off her as she picks up the pace, spit frothing at the corners of her lips as she sucks every last inch of me, savoring it with her eyes locked on mine.

Do not fucking come yet. Do not fucking come yet.

Her lips curve around me as a whimper fills the air.

Damn, is that me?

Dove pops off my cock, a string of saliva still connecting us as she lazily strokes me. "I think that's the most erotic thing I've ever heard. Sing louder for me, Songbird."

She drops back down with renewed vigor, reaching for my hand, which is fisted in her plush comforter, and threads my fingers into her messy bun. With her silent permission, I lift my hips into her face, pushing her down gently as I unleash exactly what she wants to hear from my throat.

Her contented sigh around my length has my eyes rolling back. I'm so fucking close to dumping months' worth of pent-up tension down her throat.

It's never been like this with anyone. Dove has all the control, yet somehow, she makes me feel like I'm the one who wields it.

We move together, pleasured moans and sighs mingling with the slick, wet suction of her mouth.

"Fuck, Dove." I'm so close, but I never want it to end. I could fuck her sassy mouth for hours and never tire of watching her choke on my cock. "You're so pretty when you're making me yours."

"Mmhmm," she moans around me, the vibrations shooting straight up my spine.

My balls tense, both hands clutching her hair like a lifeline. Her free hand strokes unintelligible symbols on my hip, a soft, maddening contrast to the way her mouth consumes me. I try to focus on them, desperate to stave off my impending orgasm.

M

"I'm close," I warn, my voice ragged.

I

She nods, never slowing, her determination clear. She's on a mission—to unravel me as she sucks my soul from my body.

N

From this moment on, I'll do anything she wants. If she's the Doll, I'll be her accomplice. I'll help her bury the bodies. Whatever she asks—so long as I get to have this. Have *her*.

E

Her name spills from my lips like a prayer as I release down her throat in hot, thick bursts. My entire body jerks, a shuddering wreck beneath her, and still, she keeps sucking, determined to strip me down to nothing. Like she's trying to get to the center of a Tootsie Pop.

"Fuck. Fuck. *Fuck*." My hips chase her mouth, a tear slipping from my eye as she works me through every last aftershock, until I'm soft against her tongue.

When she crawls up my chest, I'm convinced I've died and gone to heaven. And she's the angel waiting for me at the pearly gates.

Her soft giggles vibrate against my skin. "Well, I'm sorry to report there are no pearly gates, but there were definitely pearls of cum involved."

"Did I say that out loud?" I ask in a daze, feeling utterly boneless. I'd ask for my soul back, but I want her to keep it.

It belongs to her now, anyway.

I massage her scalp where I gripped her hair, pressing a kiss to her forehead, then the tip of her nose, then finally her mouth, savoring the way I taste on her lips. "You're fucking incredible."

Dove doesn't reply. She simply smiles, lacing her fingers over my chest and propping her chin on them. "Do you want some clothes to sleep in?"

"Turtle Dove, in what world do you think your clothes will fit me?" A lazy grin tugs at my lips as warmth spreads through my chest. Her cheeks are flushed and sticky, and the slick heat between her thighs seeps against my skin.

I want to flip her over and mark her as mine—just as thoroughly, just as devastatingly, as she's made me hers.

"You just called me Turtle Dove." She beams, lighting up the whole damn room. "I think you like me just a little bit."

"After what you just did, I like you a lot-a-bit." How could I have ever hated her? The thought of our stupid rivalry—and let's be honest, it's not much of a rivalry because Dove always gets her way—seems so pointless now.

As if she can read my mind, she rolls onto her side and props her head on her hand. "What made you change your mind, Songbird? You hated me so much before. Now you want to be with me?"

I mirror her position, uncaring that my thoroughly spent dick flops onto her bed—grower *and* shower, folks. "Honestly?"

At her nod, I trace her lips with my thumb, memorizing each and every perfect feature of her beautiful face—from her long, thick lashes to her button nose.

I've never been more at peace with anyone than I am at this moment.

When I look at her, I'm not immediately reminded of the horrible childhood I had. Slowly, the past ebbs away, and the future I thought I fucked up begins to look a whole lot brighter—*pinker*.

"You feel like home."

TRYING to keep the tears at bay burns my sinuses.

Wren sleeps curled against my side, peacefully unaware of my turmoil. Gently, I press a kiss to his head before resuming my slow, soothing strokes through his silken strands.

You feel like home.

Does he mean like his mother?

Or does he mean it for real?

"No one will ever hurt you again, Songbird. Not while I'm around," I whisper to his resting form.

His mother is alive. Alive and still in contact with him.

Do they speak?

Does he forgive her?

Is this why he's so obsessed with the Doll?

Everything makes so much more sense now.

A strange calm settled over me when I caught him trying to open the door to the room where I keep everything for my alter ego.

He knows.

He must have seen the bruises the night I returned to his place. My clever songbird pieced it all together and still sought me out. Still let me devour him while at my mercy. Still begged me to make him mine.

Do you know what it means to be mine, Wren?

Do you understand that once you're mine, I'll never let you go?

White flashes at the edge of my vision. Fang lifts his head from the edge of his bed, eyes locked on my nightstand as the glow pulses in the darkness. Once again, my mother is calling, though I haven't picked up in months.

Seems like we both have mommy issues.

I do not forgive my mother.

I have no desire or reason to speak to the woman who sided with the boogeyman.

But now, I do harbor an intense need to rid Wren of the monster lurking under his bed.

He stirs, as if my errant thoughts have bled into his dreams. Dark blond brows pinch together as he clutches me tighter. "No..." he murmurs.

"No what, baby?" I tilt my head to see his face better.

A deep shudder racks his body. His fingers dig painfully into my hip where he grasps me. "No, don't!"

"Wren," I whisper, shaking him gently. "Baby, wake up. You're having a nightmare."

As tightly as he holds me, the force is even greater when he tries to push me away, shooting upright. "Don't touch me!"

"Baby, it's me. It's Dove," I soothe, quickly turning on my bedside lamp before scrambling across the duvet to cup his cheeks. "It's Dove."

Unfocused eyes lock onto mine for a few seconds before clarity sets in. "Dove?"

"Yeah, baby." I push against the prick of threatening tears. "It's me."

Wren is burning up as he pulls me against him, plastering our bodies together like I'm the only thing keeping him afloat in an endless sea.

"You're okay." I rake my fingers through his hair until his breath evens out against my neck.

"I'm sorry. Did I... did I hurt you again?" he asks fearfully.

"No, Songbird. You didn't hurt me. Here, lie back down." I know I'd feel vulnerable naked while my partner remained clothed, so I retrieve his boxer briefs and wait for him to slip them on before settling into his side. "Bad dream?"

"Just the same fucking nightmare." He sighs, running a hand through his hair. The strands fall messily over his forehead, and I take a moment to simply admire him.

Wren is beautiful. A tragic kind of beauty—the kind that's been weaponized against him, the kind that hides an undercurrent of sadness only visible if you know where to *look*.

"What?" he murmurs, shifting to meet my gaze. His fingers trail warm paths along my skin, shoulder to elbow and back again.

"Nothing." It physically hurts to break our gaze, but I nuzzle against his chest, clinging to him harder than the redhead did to Vince Vaughn in *Wedding Crashers*. "Do you want to talk about it?"

A resigned sigh escapes him. I know his answer before he even speaks. "Not tonight."

I don't push. Instead, I trace idle patterns on his skin with my nails. His hand slides around my knee, hiking my leg higher until I'm half draped over him. "Tonight, I'd rather do other things."

Every pass of his lips against mine causes him to wince, so I abandon them in favor of nipping my way down his throat. His hands roam, exploring—leaving no part of me untouched.

He shifts me beneath him. "I want to taste you,"

he murmurs, dragging his nose over my nipple before grazing it lightly through my camisole with his teeth.

"Songbird." I stop him before he can go further south. "Your lip can't handle it." His erection is unmistakable, straining against his underwear like a neon sign flashing *ready to go*. "Why don't you let me take care of you again? After all, I'm supposed to be the nurse."

The look he gives me is unamused. Before I can register the glint of mischief in his eyes, he flips back over and pulls me onto his lap, leaning back against my mountain of pillows.

"Aren't good nurses supposed to care for all their patient's needs?" he moans huskily into my ear. Every nerve in my body ignites as his fingers ghost down my arms, lifting my wrists behind his head. "I *need* to feel you, Dove."

"Oh, fuck." A guttural moan escapes me as he shoves a hand into my shorts, two fingers sliding through my slick heat.

"So wet for me." He nuzzles into my neck, his free hand pulling my top down to palm my breast, pinching and rolling the peak between his fingers. "Were you this turned on the day we met?" A soft laugh bubbles in my throat, cut off by a sharp gasp as he plunges two fingers inside me, his thumb gathering my arousal and smearing it over my clit with devastating precision. "Oh god, Wren. That feels so good."

"Yeah?" he moans, as if my pleasure fuels his own. "Answer me, Dove. Are you always dripping when we're in the same room?" He groans, low and long, as I arch my back, grinding against his erection.

I'm breathless as he picks up his pace, heat surging through me like wildfire. "Yes!" I cry out. "I've wanted this since I propositioned you."

His chuckle is throaty as he nips at my ear. "I would have gladly fingered you right there in front of everyone and claimed you as mine."

"Why didn't you?" I whine, rolling my hips until I'm dry humping him just as well as he's finger fucking me.

"Is that what you want, you dirty, dirty girl? A very *public* declaration?" I feel powerless in the best way as Wren winds me higher and higher, his fingers relentless. "Fuck, Turtle Dove, you're gripping me so tight." His fingers rub my G-spot, and I nearly see stars. "Spread your legs. Let me see you."

He withdraws only to shove my shorts down, spreading my thighs apart before sliding back inside. We both watch as he enters me again. His fingers sliding through the sticky mess he's created to finish what he started.

"I've never seen anything as perfect as this" he whispers, forehead resting against my temple.

"You haven't watched my pussy swallow your cock yet," I tease breathlessly.

His lips ghost over mine.

Wren abandons my nipple and curves his arm up to cradle my jaw. I've always known there was a sizable height difference between us, but it's not until this very moment that I realize how tall he is compared to me.

"I meant this. *Us.* Come apart for me." He kisses me gently with the uninjured corner of his mouth. "I can feel your walls fluttering against my fingers. Let go, Turtle Dove."

A silent moan catches in my throat, then melts against his mouth as the dam inside me shatters— waves of liquid fire surging through me, spilling over his hand.

"That's it. So good." He skirts around the phrase I told him I didn't like, and it works. I still feel the praise —the euphoric reward—without my body locking up. It makes me want to reward him in return.

I writhe against him, digging in harder, working for all the little moans that slip from his lips. His cock wedges between my ass cheeks, the friction relentless, and he thrusts until he erupts with a ragged roar.

We lie there for what feels like hours, sweaty and spent and tangled in each other without pushing for more. Even as we shimmy out of our sticky clothes. Even when I retrieve a warm washcloth to clean up. Even when he admits that he's never spent the night with a woman before.

"Will you stay, though?"

Wren pulls my naked body flush against his, back to chest, and tugs the duvet up over us both. "You're never getting rid of me."

I trace my fingers over the back of his hand where it rests against my stomach. "I don't want to get rid of you, Songbird. I've decided I quite like having you around."

TAPPING MY FOOT IMPATIENTLY, I check my watch again. Only a few minutes have passed since the last time. With a sigh, I reload the browser, hoping—irrationally—for a new message in my inbox. It refreshes in real time; I know it's empty. Still, I check.

The office buzzes with chaos, as it always does when the site is under construction. You'd think by now Joe would stop publishing on the four days a month maintenance partially downs the system.

Finally, the browser loads.

Nothing. Again.

A flicker of irritation sparks somewhere between my chest and stomach, unsure whether it wants to rise to my throat or sink into my gut. Dove still hasn't returned from her absurdly long lunch break, and she refused to tell me where she was going or why she needed the extra hour away.

Today was *supposed* to be the day she vouched for me to Joe. Not because I made her come three times last night—fingers and toys only, since she still won't let me go down on her until my lip fully heals and neither of us has broached the subject of full-on sex yet —but because the article I wrote on the side of my regular workload had moved her to tears.

Instead of putting the Doll on a pedestal, as Dove once so eloquently put it, I wrote about how hurt people *hurt* people, exploring the possibility that perhaps the Doll was once abused herself—thus the reason for doing what she does.

A low blow, maybe, using Dove's experience. But I used my own, too, wrapping our pain in pretty words that gave nothing away to indicate I was writing about us. I watched her carefully, searching for any hint that might confirm my growing suspicion—that it's been *her* all along.

She remained silent after she finished reading, polishing off the rest of our bee pollen pancakes before leaving me in the middle of Tanner Smith's to pay the bill while she freshened up. When she returned, she said she'd talk to Joe.

So far, though, it's been radio silence.

Tiny footsteps approach hastily from down the

hall, curving my lips into a smile that only faintly stings now. Fang bounds into the room, wiggling excitedly as he darts around my desk and leaps into my lap, licking my face in a flurry of kisses.

"Hey, little dude."

The rat has grown on me.

When Dove mentioned she might visit her mother in a few weeks, I even volunteered to babysit.

You would have thought I single-handedly brought on the apocalypse with the way Bunny went off on me, calling me an interloper and insisting I was just a passing fancy. No way in hell would she let me watch her dogson—and if you don't know what that is, it's godson in dog mom language.

"Where's your mom?" I scratch behind Fang's ear, where the faded colors of his wiry fur resemble pastel dragon's beard candy.

"He sure was excited to see you, and it's been less than twenty-four hours. I'm starting to wonder if I should be jealous, Songbird." Dove's voice fills my office, flooding my veins with an instant dose of happy.

And sappy.

Fuck, I've got it bad.

The smartass quip on the tip of my tongue dies the moment I look up.

"What did you do to your hair?" I ask, equal parts horrified and stunned.

Dove's beautiful blonde hair is a few inches shorter. Where it once hung to nearly the middle of her back, it now curls around the tops of her breasts. Streaks of pastel pink run through the strands from mid to tip in sporadic bursts.

I've never had a real girlfriend before—is she even my girlfriend?—so I have no idea how to navigate this situation. I don't think you're supposed to tell a woman you don't like what she's done with her hair, though.

I hate it. I hate everything about it because it doesn't look like her.

She twirls, holding out her hands. "Do you like it?"

"Shouldn't we have talked about it first?" I ask weakly.

Her hands drop to her sides, her expression flattening. "I don't need your permission, Songbird. Besides," she perks back up, "I thought it was time for a change."

She rounds my desk to scoop up Fang. Her fingers brush against my cock—intentional, no doubt —but both he and I are too stunned for him to high-five her. "You told me to be honest about my feelings."

Dove releases a short, breathy laugh and nods. "I did."

"Okay." I scrub a hand down my face, taking a deep breath. "This makes me extremely worried for the safety of my own gorgeous locks because I assure you, they will never be pink again."

"Goodness, Songbird. Lighten up. No one asked you to color your hair again."

"*I* didn't color it in the first place!"

"Mmhmm. Well, you still have no proof it was me." She lilts the words, cocking her head before spinning in her four-inch pumps, the ruffled skirt of her dress sailing high enough to expose the curve of her cheeks and a pair of white lacy bikini-cut underwear.

"Why'd you do it?" I unglue my eyes from her ass when she turns back around.

A somber smile replaces her playful grin, not quite reaching her eyes. "I think you see someone else when you look at me sometimes, and I don't want to remind you of someone who brings up bad memories." I stare at her, trying to decode her meaning. I haven't spoken about my past with her...

Maybe she knows you're onto her as the Doll.

Do her words have a double meaning? She knows I'm not afraid of the Doll.

"Anyway, I need to get back to work. See you in a few hours." She blows me a kiss.

I catch it, making a show of slapping it against my cheek. It's our thing now, and we're corny as fuck. I don't know how we went from hating each other to being the poster couple for Hallmark, but they can start cutting us checks any day now.

"What about my article, Dove?" I call out to her retreating form.

She spins, flashing me a devilish grin with a wink. "Not quite there yet, Songbird."

My smile drops, my heart sinking into my stomach.

Infuriating woman!

<u>Dove</u>

"It's fine. I was going to go upstate with Hunter to visit his parents anyway," Wren says when I tell him I'm busy this weekend and can't hang out.

He chews his cashew chicken thoughtfully, his grip tightening around the spoon as he clearly winds up to ask a question. I've been waiting all night for him to ask why his article didn't make it into this week's edition.

"You have every Saturday on your calendar marked out for C.W. What is that?" he asks, his tone careful, guarded.

I swallow my bite of broccoli, dragging tofu and peppers onto my fork, pulling them between my lips to buy time to think of an adequate answer. The little Chinese-American restaurant where Wren eats three times a week has a fondness for spice, giving me a few extra seconds as I chase the heat down with lemon water.

C.W. stands for culling weekend—whether that means recon or stripping evil men of their privates before brutally murdering them—but it's not like I can tell him that. I'm nearly one hundred percent sure he's onto me. Wren has always watched me with fierce attentiveness, but now it's heightened, like he's waiting for me to slip, to catch the tiniest thread he can trace back to the Doll.

There's only one other thing I can think of for C.W.

My mother.

"I have a standing date with my mother on Saturdays. She drives in from Rochester and stays the night. C.W. are her initials—Charlotte Woodsbury. She got remarried a few years ago."

I don't tell Wren that my mother and I don't speak. That she tried paying off my abuser. That she never believed me. So he should be none the wiser about my little white lie.

Wren pauses mid-chew, eyes narrowing slightly. He doesn't look up, doesn't meet my gaze. "Hmm."

Silence stretches between us for the next few minutes. He's lost in thought while I focus on the fact that I need to get my shit together for this weekend. Wren and I have been spending so much time together that I haven't put in the effort it takes to ensure things go off without a hitch.

It's more than luring a bad man to a random place and eviscerating him. I have to learn his likes and dislikes, memorize his habits, know details like his drink of choice so it's easier to drug him. I have to select the right wig, the right nightie, ensure I have enough supplies to scrub my DNA from everything.

It takes time. Planning.

And lately, I've been far more interested in getting very acquainted with my songbird's gorgeous cock than ridding the world of immoral men and their nasty, tiny, shriveled peckers.

"Why didn't you publish my article, Dove?" Wren's question cuts through my thoughts, his voice low, tired.

I feel bad.

I really do.

But it's *my* thing. I abandon my fork, pushing my plate back. Fang lifts his head from his bed by the sofa, tail wagging in hopes of a bite. As he stretches his tiny body, I hold up a hand. "No, baby boy. It's too spicy for you."

Wren's eyes never leave mine. "Honestly, Songbird,

you're not going to like what I have to say, but I'm not going to sugarcoat it. The Doll is my thing. I picked *Metro Media* up from the ashes and I've been writing about her ever since. I'm sorry, I know it's territorial, but how would you feel if I showed up at your last job and started writing about your shtick?"

A muscle ticks in his freshly shaved jawline. "I'm writing good pieces—"

"You write beautifully, Wren. No one's saying you don't. But I'm not going to roll over and let you take my job just because I let you roll me around in the sheets now." I try hard to mask my irritation, but it bubbles just beneath my skin as I try to get him to see reason. "You write about other things. I don't. If you want to write about a serial killer, write about the Shadow Siren."

"I don't want to fucking write about the Siren, Dove. I want to write about the Doll." His anger vanishes in an instant, replaced by a smug, boyish grin. "I have an in."

I nearly laugh at his conviction.

"She approached me."

Remembering to act surprised, I cock my head, eyes narrowing. "Why would she approach *you*?"

He throws his hands out, still grinning. "What can I say? I guess a little birdie told her I was obsessed." He flings my own words back at me.

I know what he's doing. He's testing me, trying to catch me in a lie, playing on my jealousy, thinking I might slip.

So I step it up. If it's a show he wants, I'll give him one.

"So you let a serial killer near you?" I sneer, dripping with false jealousy as I lean forward. "Are you so obsessed with her that you just... oh, I don't know, forgot she kills men? Tell me, Wren, did she let you get close? Did you confess your love and devotion to her? Are you a two-timer, Songbird?"

"What? No!" Wren looks genuinely confused.

"So what?" I scoff. "You think just because she visited you, I should roll over and let you take my job?" I know I'm being selfish. Petty. But I'm not budging on this. Wren needs to stay in his lane and stop trying to crash into mine.

"You told me you'd put in a good word with Joe!" he snaps. Guilt tugs at me. "Why even say that if you had no intention of following through?"

I brighten, bouncing back to a chipper tone with a careless shrug. "I don't know. You looked so hopeful, and I didn't want to crush your dreams over pancakes."

Wren stands abruptly, grabbing his suit jacket from the stool and sliding it on. "I don't know what I'm doing there if you won't even try to work with me. You're being callous and treating me like shit."

"No one's treating you like shit, Wren!" I laugh, incredulous. "You're being sensitive."

"And you're being insensitive."

"Holy fuck, Songbird. I thought *I* was the woman in this relationship." It's a mean thing to say. I know it is. But I need him to go. I need space.

Because this is getting too real, too fast.

This argument makes me want to throw up my tofu veggie stir-fry. I hate the thought of Wren being upset with me. I hate that he feels like I'm silencing him.

But I won't give myself up just to make him happy.

"Nice, Dove. Keep being a bitch."

"Only to you, Songbird." I flutter my lashes, flashing him a sardonic smile.

Wren stares at me for a long moment. So long that the tears threatening to surface nearly prick my lashes. He's searching my face for a white flag.

All he'll find is an enforced wall and a fuck ton of bombs.

I don't know why I thought we could have a relationship. There are too many secrets between us. Too much horror and pain.

And I don't want to emasculate Wren, but I'm not sure he can handle the truth.

I do what I do for a reason.

The Doll has a purpose.

I can't let anything change that.

Not even the man I might be falling in love with.

I DON'T KNOW what I'm doing anymore.

The days blur together, bleeding into the weekend without so much as a flicker of acknowledgment from the woman I'm dangerously close to falling for. Things return to how they were—work rivals at each other's throats—except now, I'm also getting the silent treatment.

On Wednesday, I wait outside her office for her to finish a call. It drags on longer than it should, and I have to abandon my attempt at a white flag or risk standing up a source for a piece I'm working on. Thursday, I take her last yogurt in full view of our coworkers, waiting for her to storm over and berate me for stealing her snacks. But she never does. Today, she ignores me completely when I step into her office and ask if we can have dinner.

No ghost of a smile. No smartass quip about me caving first. Just silence. Dove stares at her computer screen, her pink sparkly nails catching the light as her fingers tap steadily on her keyboard as if I'm not even there.

I let my gaze drift across the space, moving toward where she keeps her things. She's focused enough not to notice when I lean against the ledge where her small purse sits, slipping a tracking device onto the back of a pink Zippo she hasn't used since we became serious—because she knows how I feel about her smoking.

The point of writing about the Doll was to get close to her. I wanted her attention, her time. I crossed the country in hopes that my public praise would get her to notice me.

I wanted a relationship with her—to get an exclusive look into her beautifully fucked-up mind and convince her to bare her soul to a lowly man who could only hope to hold her interest beyond one lucky evening.

To my absolute, utter luck, I got more than that. At least, I'm ninety-nine point nine percent sure I did.

And I really don't want to fuck that up.

"Are you seriously not going to speak to me?" I turn back around, but her attention remains fixed, her posture indifferent.

I *did* call her a bitch. I suppose I deserve this.

I'll get on my knees and beg for forgiveness if she lets me.

"Dove," I sigh, moving to stand beside her. "I'm sorry."

The clicking of the keys falters. Encouraged, I push forward. "You were right. I shouldn't have barged in and expected anything to be handed to me. Hell, I shouldn't have even assumed I'd get the opportunity to write about the Doll. It was presumptuous. Sexist. And I'm sorry. I understand where you're coming from, and I don't want to fight with you."

"We aren't fighting, Songbird." She resumes typing, her voice light, airy—completely devoid of anger or concession. "We just aren't fucking."

I don't point out that we haven't actually fucked yet.

We've done a lot of things. But anytime we get close to the actual act, Dove pulls away like a not-so-virginal virgin convinced God will smite her if she puts a P in her V before marriage.

Reaching out, I twirl a lock of bubblegum-and-vanilla hair around my finger. "What do I have to do to make it up to you?"

From my angle, I see her eyes flicker away from the screen. But instead of relaxing into my touch, she stiffens, edging away. "I'm trying to work, Wren."

Still pissed.

Point taken.

Or maybe she's pushing you away because you hurt her.

But Dove said some things that weren't exactly kind, either. Calling me an emotional woman when I was just trying to explain the unfairness of her making me think I had a chance at publishing a Doll article? Yeah. Not my favorite moment.

Still. I get it. She's clawed her way to success in a male-dominated field.

"Okay." I lean down, pressing a kiss to the crown of her head, inhaling the sugary scent of her shampoo. "I'm here. When you're ready to talk."

She hums noncommittally, and it spears through my chest like the tip of her dagger—if she *is* the Doll.

Back in my office, I pull up the tracker app to confirm it's working and pray to God she doesn't smoke before Monday. I need to know if she's telling the truth about her mother. Or if there's a more nefarious reason she's lying.

One that involves babydoll nighties and a mask that haunts my dreams.

WELL. She's definitely lying about her mom.

Saturday evening, I follow Dove to an isolated area

between Poughkeepsie and Hyde Park. I spend the long drive convincing myself that maybe she's meeting her mother somewhere outside the city. Or that she's working over the weekend, hunting a lead.

But when her rented black sedan parks outside the seediest motel I've ever seen—the kind with metal keys instead of keycards—I know she's not here for a family visit.

A slow, crawling anticipation settles over me as I watch her haul a sizable black duffel into a room, surveying her surroundings like she's mapping easy exit strategies should things take a turn and she needs to flee quickly.

With every passing second that brings me closer to the truth, I become more certain.

I'm watching the girl of my dreams set up for a murder.

Inky black darkness settles over the sky, the stars winking to life one by one, like glittering diamonds as the night grows longer. Parked in the vacant lot of a run-down store next to the hotel, I watch through binoculars.

I nearly text her and ask how things are going with her mom, but she's not talking to me anyway, so I know it won't matter even if I do. My phone sits abandoned in the cup holder, the screen lighting up now and then with messages from Hunter checking in.

He's staking out Bunny's newest date and apparently, this one actually has him worried. I feel slightly bad I'm not there. But he thinks I'm chasing a lead upstate.

Which... technically, I am.

Technically, this is a type of lead. It didn't seem like there was much in Dove's bag, though. Is her costume in there? Her weapons? Whatever it is she paints on her skin to avoid leaving DNA all over the place?

At this point, I know she doesn't film every encounter, and there's no way professional film equipment would fit in the bag with everything else. So, unless she's recording on her phone, I don't think tonight is the type of confrontation she documents.

My thoughts shift to my ever-present question of why she sends videos to the police. Yes, they have the victim's personal information, but what is the point of the show? So they can see that she catches more pedophiles than they could ever hope to? Or does she just enjoy the song and dance—pun intended.

An older-model silver Tacoma with a black bed cap pulls up beside Dove's sedan, interrupting my rambling thoughts as I try to deconstruct her purpose for doing things the way she does.

The beast inside me roars to life when I see a man step out, dressed in black, with a baseball cap pulled low. Even through the binoculars, I have to squint to see his face.

Is that...?

No.

"No. She wouldn't do that to me," I say out loud, trying to convince myself that what I'm looking at is a trick of the light and not cruel reality staring me in the face.

Fucking Ryan.

Hunter said Ryan was suspended after what he pulled at the bar. Even if I deserved a punch, shoving Dove sealed his fate. That's what ultimately landed him in the most trouble.

So why the hell is she meeting him in secret all the way out here?

My stomach drops, acid rising in my throat. I told her everything he'd said. How could she? *Why* would she?

It feels like my heart has cannonballed into my stomach, splashing bile back up into my esophagus.

Ryan pulls his hat down, further obscuring his face as he knocks on the door, glancing over his shoulder as he waits.

If they were meeting like this on purpose, wouldn't she expect him to just walk in?

The door opens. A sliver of peachy light appears on the dirty, cracked concrete walkway outside the room. I shift, trying to see Dove with what little room

Ryan leaves as the hulking dickwad takes up most of the doorway.

She's... surprised?

Dove's light brown brows shoot into her hairline as she stares up at him, frozen with one hand on the door and the other on the frame. My knuckles whiten as I grip the binoculars tighter when I see she's wearing a pink and red babydoll, her hair pulled up in pigtails.

Just like the Doll sometimes does.

But the look on her face isn't one of a stone-cold killer. No, she looks scared. And that pisses me off.

Ryan surges forward. One second, he's standing still. The next, his hands are around her throat, shoving her backward, kicking the door shut behind him.

What the fuck?

I'm out of my car before I realize I've moved, charging toward the room—until a sick thought claws its way into my brain.

What if it's all a scene?

What if she needs this?

I slow, doubt creeping in like poison.

She's dressed like an adult version of a little kid. She was abused as a child. What if this is her way of coping with it? What if that's why they were even—are even?—a thing. He's an asshole, but maybe he gives her what she needs to deal with her past.

I know it's a rational, and even potentially therapeutic, way to deal with trauma. Sometimes, it takes returning to the bad place to face it head-on.

But I can't even face my own trauma. I stayed in the same state as my abuser for years because I don't know how to confront her or heal from what she's done. She's like a sticky substance I can't scrub from my skin—the shadows deep in the recesses of my mind I can never escape.

How the fuck can I be that for Dove if I can't even help myself?

I hear no sounds coming from the building.

No struggles. No cries for help.

What if that's why she's been avoiding me? She basically called me weak when we fought, and I am. I really fucking am.

I don't know if I'm equipped to help her with her trauma if this is how she deals with it. I know it's unfair—I haven't been honest with her about my past.

What if she needs this and I can't give it to her?

Lowering to a squat, I thread my fingers over my head as turmoil creeps through my body like a thick, noxious gas.

I thought I was coming to confirm her alter ego as the Doll.

Dove looked scared, though. Genuinely surprised to see Ryan.

"Arrghh!" I growl, pushing forward.

If they're fucking, I'll quit. I'll go back to California and pretend none of this ever happened. If she's been playing me—using me—this whole time, even if it's a way for her to cope, I'll never be able to forgive her.

But there's still a tiny part of me that wonders if she's truly in trouble.

"They're probably laughing about how pathetic and stupid you are," I mumble as I approach the dilapidated building, letting my intrusive thoughts tear her to pieces as my mind gears up to protect me from what I'm about to see.

But what if...

What if I'm wrong?

Ryan being on the other side of the door instead of Thomas Hardy was not on my bingo card for tonight. Then again—Tom Hardy—fuck, I should have known better.

This was supposed to be an *easy kill*.

There's easy: when they look just like any other murder. Medium: when it seems like an average break-in homicide. And then there's hard: when I dress to the nines, record myself, and release my feminine rage in the form of a deranged psychopath for the night.

Thomas Hardy was supposed to be simple—a quick way to quell my frustration, restock Fang's jerky supply, and call it a night.

Never in a million fucking years would I have done this without the copious amounts of research I usually do. But my stupid, stupid songbird just had to go and make things difficult, didn't he? He had to go and distract me with hurt feelings and his gorgeous dick that I miss entirely too much for only having had it for a few days. And now I have to kill a cop—an asshole cop, but one with a nice penis and a talented tongue. A shame, really, for the future women who would have taken him for a ride.

Some women are into assholes. We listen, and we don't judge.

Ryan's eyes widen, mirroring the shock in mine. "Dove?"

Fuck. Fuck. Fuck. I drop the strand of hair I'd been twirling around my finger, scrambling for something to say. But before I can, his face twists into pure malice. Surprise steals the breath from my lungs as his hands wrap around my throat, shoving me into the room, kicking the door shut behind him.

"What the fuck are you doing here?" He shakes me like a ragdoll. Terror seeps into my bones as I claw at his hands. My poor neck can't take much more choking. It's too delicate to be handled so roughly.

Ryan shoves me onto the bed, finally releasing my throat to jab a meaty, gloved finger in my direction. "Start talking, Carroway. What the hell is going on?"

"What are *you* doing here?" I stall, buying time. Maybe I can spin a story about baiting a creep. After all, this wasn't my usual meticulous setup. It was rushed and reckless. I should have dug deeper into the fake persona Ryan used on the website where I typically meet my easy kills.

"What's it *look* like?" He laughs bitterly. "I got suspended without pay because of you. But when I return with the Baby Doll Killer, I'll be welcomed back with open arms." He eyes my outfit, scoffing. "How fucking stupid is Hunter? You were right under his nose the whole time."

I was under yours too, dickwad. Trust me, I've thought long and hard about that more than once.

"I don't know what you're talking about." I flash him an airy laugh, rising to my feet. "What makes you think I'm the killer?"

Ryan whips out a pistol—one eerily similar to his government-issued sidearm—and aims it at me. "Don't fucking move."

I raise my hands in surrender, giving him a broad, toothy smile and shrug. "Maybe I just have a thing for role-play, okay?"

"Stop lying, you bitch." His grip tightens on the gun as he pulls a set of handcuffs from his belt. "I fucked you on and off for two years. I think I would have figured that out." He stalks toward me, taking slow, measured steps. "You know, I've been after you for months now. Trying to catch the Doll before

Hunter." A laugh bubbles from his lips, tinged with disbelief. "Never would've guessed it was you."

With a detached sigh, I flop back onto the bed, the mattress bouncing beneath me. "See, that's the thing about people like me, Ryan. We hide our kinks well."

He's so preoccupied with thinking he's caught the Doll that he never notices the dagger strapped high on my thigh. Just a few more steps, and he's mine. His eyes flick between my gaze and where my fists clench onto the rough fabric of the old comforter. His breaths come in shaky exhales, likely from the rush of believing he's finally caught a serial killer.

There's a reason why Ryan never passes the evaluation for a promotion to detective. He likes to play alone.

Rule number one when hunting a killer: you never go after them alone.

I reach up, causing him to flinch, his finger twitching on the trigger. "Relax, Ryan. I'm just taking these ridiculous pigtails out. Man, imagine how stupid you're going to look when you haul me in, and I tell them I just like being railed by older men who have a thing for adult women who look like little girls." I huff a laugh while removing the first hair tie, letting the right side cascade over my shoulder. Ryan's grip slackens, his gun dipping a fraction. "It's embarrassing for me, sure. But you're already in trouble for manhandling me, and now you're following me to hotels and roughing me up? You're just begging to get fired. Talk about stalker status." I pull out the second tie, hand drifting near my thigh as I discreetly hike my nightie up.

Ryan lowers his gun even further. "I'm not roughing you—"

In less than three seconds, I palm my dagger and lunge, driving the shiny silver blade deep into his chest, right over his heart. Before he can register what's happening, I knock the gun from his grasp and drag the blade downward with every ounce of strength I have. His eyes bulge, his gaze flicking from the weapon embedded in him to my face.

Usually, I wait until I've had the chance to drug my victims with a drink, then take my time to roll out a tarp to make cleanup easier.

What's a girl to do, though?

"You know, I thought you were such a nice guy at first," I whisper, maneuvering him back toward the bed. Our height difference makes it a little tricky, but I cradle his neck and guide him down so we're more at eye level. A choked cough splatters blood onto his chin in flecks of crimson. Luckily, none of it gets on me.

"You were sweet, and so kind to Fang. And really, that's the most upsetting part of all this." I yank the dagger free, flipping the handle to drive it just below his ribs. "My dog really liked you. And now I have to feed him your penis."

"Dove?"

I freeze as an all-too-familiar voice sounds to my left, calling my name with a singular, horrified syllable.

Ryan's blood escapes the wound in small rivulets, seeping into his shirt. I let go to avoid getting it on me. He gurgles out a wet cry for help as I slowly turn toward my songbird, who's standing in the open doorway, his wide, unbelieving eyes flicking between Ryan and me.

How did I not hear the door open?

Worst serial killer ever.

Something dark stirs in my belly. Slowly, it slithers around my organs, constricting some while causing others to work overtime to process this fucking nightmare of a situation I find myself in.

"Close the door, Songbird," I murmur, pulse thundering in my ears. "I don't need any more interruptions."

I should have known he'd find a way to follow me. I knew he was suspicious. I should have cleaned up my killer cave and shown him the room to ease his doubt.

Now what the fuck am I supposed to do?

I don't want to kill Wren.

"Fucking... monster," Ryan spits out.

Rolling my eyes, I press my palm to his forehead

and shove him backward. "Monsters are survivors, Ryan. You're the one who got yourself into this mess. I'm just a survivor of this unfortunate situation."

Wren continues to stand frozen in the open doorway, dumbfounded. "Wren!"

He snaps out of it, stepping into the room and shutting the door behind him with an audible slam.

I like this hotel because even though it's cheap, the walls aren't paper-thin, and they never ask questions when I book three rooms next to each other. Sound still travels, so when I use their fine establishment, I take the utmost precautions.

"Don't look so surprised, Songbird. You've known for a while, haven't you?"

Ryan uses the last moments of his life to beg Wren for help, but all he does is stare while I roll my former lover into a life-sized sushi roll with the comforter. It may be old as fuck and scratchy as hell, but it's thick enough to keep the blood from seeping through to the sheets.

Humming *Ten in the Bed*, I push Ryan until he topples off the side, landing with a hard thump. "And one fell out!" I finish with a flourish, spinning to face the other man in the room with a vulpine grin.

My man.

Well, he's not screaming or running for his life. That's a good sign.

But why would he?

He loves the Doll, and now he knows she's been near him the whole time.

Still, my muscles ache from how tightly I tense, waiting for him to speak.

Wren blinks from Ryan to me. When he finally admits softly, "I've had my suspicions for a while now, yes." I'm genuinely surprised.

He regards me as I take slow, measured steps toward him, each one in sync with my heartbeat. I can only imagine what's going through his mind. Is he recalling the times I showed up as the Doll? Is he disappointed to know we're one and the same?

Wren nailed it when he wrote his last piece about the Doll killing the men she does because she was abused as a child. Did he write it to coax me out of my shell like a scared turtle? Is he really obsessed with her, or has he been trying to uncover her identity all this time for a life-changing exposé?

Thought after thought races through my mind as I approach him. "What now, Songbird?"

Wren reaches for me. I go rigid as his hands settle on my waist, his brows furrowed. The air grows thick with tension, the *unknown* stretching between us as he asks, "What do you mean?"

His fingers are soft and warm through the thin material of my babydoll—no roughness, no intent to subdue me. His thumbs rub soothing circles along the dip of my waist as he steps into me and—is that?

Looking down, I see he's *hard.*

Like, really hard. Straining against his pants, dick-trying-to-fist-bump-me hard.

Arching a brow, I glance back at his face just as a slow smile stretches across his handsome features. "Does watching me incite violence turn you on, Songbird?"

Wren digs his fingers into my waist and lifts me abruptly. My legs lock around him, arms winding around his neck as he murmurs against my lips, "Every fucking little thing about you turns me on, Dove."

Dove. Not Doll.

Me.

"Besides, I never liked him anyway," he whispers before crushing our lips together and walking us to the bed.

The fingers that caused death just minutes ago tangle in his hair as a desperate moan escapes from my throat. Wren gently runs his tongue along the seam of my lips, asking for entrance for the first time.

Greedily, I part for him, keeping my tongue glued to the bottom of my mouth so he can explore without feeling overwhelmed. I want to cry at the tenderness with which he lays me on the bed, lowering himself between my legs as they dangle off the side.

"You're so fucking perfect," he whispers against my skin, trailing kisses between my breasts.

"Perfect doesn't exist, Songbird," I murmur to the ceiling, raking my nails against his scalp as he shoves up my nightie and presses his warm mouth exactly where I want to feel it the most.

"Yes, it does." He sucks softly before moving my underwear to the side to run his tongue through my aching center. "I'm tasting it right now."

The bundle of death on the floor twitches—a chemical reaction that should concern Wren and shove him back into the reality that there's a dead body on the floor next to us while we get our freak on.

Meanwhile, my nerves feel like they're melting in euphoric bliss as Wren eats me out like his life depends on it.

Maybe he thinks it does.

Pushing up on my elbows, we lock eyes as he continues licking and sucking with alternating tenderness and wild abandon. "I need to feel you, Wren."

I don't have to ask twice. He's on his feet, his belt and zipper undone in seconds. Wrenley is eight inches of velvet skin, rock-solid pleasure, and enough veins that it looks like his dick is a bodybuilder on steroids. I've dreamed of having him inside me since I first saw it outlined in his gym shorts.

Yet, there are still moments when he flinches at my

touch. Moments when I pause, ensuring he knows it's *me* there with him, not *her*. So whenever we come close to consummating our relationship, I pull away, pretending I'm not ready.

But he's ready now.

And I'm so ready, I feel like I'll burst into a million vaporized particles if he doesn't fuck me this second.

"Are you sure?" he asks, fingers grazing my jaw reverently as I stroke him. "I don't have a condom."

"I don't care." I nearly climb him, pushing to my knees as he removes his pants and kneels on the bed, letting me lay him down so I can get on top.

Our limbs tangle in a frenzy, his hands thrusting into my hair while he kisses me. He has to let me go, our height difference making it impossible while I line his cock up with my entrance and lower myself slowly. Wren's moan cuts through the air as his fingers dig into my skin—that musical, high-pitched, purely sensual sound I love so much.

"Fuck, Turtle Dove, you feel so good." He helps me ride him, our skin breaking out in a glistening sheen as we rock together slowly but with so much purpose.

I wanted our first time to be monumental— memorable. I suppose having a rapidly cooling body stuffed like a sausage in a prickly, coarse casing next to us fits the bill.

"Yeah?" I ask, pinning him with a heated stare. Using one hand on his chest to anchor myself, I arch my body back as I grind myself on him. We're a tight fit, and I can feel each and every corded vein as it drags against my walls. "How does it feel to fuck your obsession, Songbird?"

"Like heaven." He looks me dead in the eyes. "Use me, Dove. Use me in whatever way you want. Every breath in my body and every fragment of my soul... it's all yours. I belong to you irrevocably."

He flexes inside me with his beautiful words, eyes screwing shut as he tries to stave off his impending climax. I blink away the tears that try to form, knowing what it costs him to give up control to me.

"Look at me, Wren," I command softly. He does as I say, and I slow my hips, rolling them with longer, deeper passes. "You don't have to belong to me. We're both broken. We can heal together."

A tear slips from my eye as the dam in my lower body breaks, unleashing a tidal wave of warmth that sends electricity down into my toes.

My mouth opens in a silent cry as Wren comes undone, moaning, "Fuck, I'm coming. Fuck. Fuck. *Fuck*."

I can feel him pulsing inside me, every ripple spearing me with his release, claiming me as his own. He says he belongs to me, but I belong to him just as much. I'm convinced our souls were meant to find each other in this life. Everything happens for a reason, and this is ours... our way of helping each other heal.

We move together until we're both spent. I lay my head against his chest, listening as his heart beats in time with mine.

I don't know how much time passes, but we're both still shimmering with sweat when he asks, "Do you... need help? With him?"

I flinch.

Way to make it awkward, Songbird.

"I'm sorry." He immediately reads my body language, grasping my shoulders to try and stop me as I push myself up and get off the bed. "I didn't mean to—"

"It's okay." Holding a hand up to stop him, I wait until he's got his pants on. "I got this. The less you're involved, the better. And your DNA is all over the place now. It'll take longer if I have to tell you what to do. You're better off just heading back to the city."

"Okay," he says quietly.

"You can't say a word to Hunter, Wren." I give him my back, hating how he couldn't just allow a little time for us to be *us*.

I'm not mad, just... disappointed with the situation.

"I wouldn't do that, Dove." Irritation laces his

tone, and his warm hand wraps around my bicep, forcing me to look at him. "I'm serious. Your secret is safe with me. But we *do* need to talk about it."

It's a pivotal moment for our relationship. Wren sees and accepts me for who I am, but where do we go from here? Hunter is his best friend. *Can* I trust him to keep my secret?

"Okay." I nod curtly. "Good. I'll see you later then."

He scoffs a little at the dismissal, flashing me an incredulous look before he lets me go and turns to leave. He doesn't even make it two steps before he spins back around. "What did you mean? When you said we're both broken?" He chews on his lower lip, unable to meet my eyes. When I don't answer—because I don't want any more secrets between us—he asks, "You know. Don't you?"

Remaining quiet, I bite the inside of my cheek to keep the tears at bay. Wren nods, taking my silence as confirmation. Sorrow pools through my veins as he turns to leave.

"Wren?" I call out as his hand touches the door-knob. He pauses but doesn't turn.

I don't take the opportunity to tell him how sorry I am. People who have been through the things we've experienced don't want pity, even if we share the same sense of loss.

I also opt out of saying that I love him. And I do. I never thought I could love someone as much as I love the man standing across from me. But now isn't the time. Wren has a lot to process on his drive home. He doesn't need me throwing that at him as well.

"Drive safe. Will you let me know when you make it back?" I'm proud of how solid my tone is even though I feel myself breaking inside.

With a nod, he leaves, reminding me to lock the door behind him. When he's gone, I heave a sigh and grab my phone to call Bunny as I cross the room and twist both locks.

As soon as her sleepy greeting echoes through the speaker, I know she's gonna be pissed I'm pulling her out of bed. "I need a cleanup on aisle three," I inform her, back to my jovial mood so she doesn't spend the night pestering me with questions I don't yet have answers to.

"Cleanup?" Her exhaustion snaps into alertness. "Easys aren't supposed to be messy, Love Dove. What happened?"

I glance at the floor, where blood finally begins to seep through the blanket. "It's more than messy," I sigh, nudging the tuna roll to keep his wounds topside. "It's Ryan, and we're gonna need the suits and saws."

SMACK!

Dove's skin flushes beneath my palm. A new patch of raspberry blooms to melt into her already reddened ass as her breathy cries echo throughout my bedroom. "Oh fuck!"

"It should be harder," I whisper, digging my fingers back into her hip. The wet sound of my cock slamming into her pussy over and over urges me to go faster, harder, even as the headboard bangs against the wall with every thrust. "Did you enjoy playing me, Dove? Did it get you off watching me agonize over your identity?"

Roughly, I pull out, scooping the mess between her legs with three fingers and yanking her head back with the hair that's twisted around my other hand.

"Taste yourself when you're being a greedy little slut for my cock."

Dove moans as she sucks her arousal off me, wiggling her hips back in search of the part of me she loves the most while one hand slips between her legs.

Smack!

"No, no, no, Turtle Dove." I thrust into her once more, palming her chin with my fingers still in her mouth to gently, but firmly, pull her back onto me. Once my pelvis meets her ass, I curve over her, twisting her locks further around my fist until I have her body bowed inward. "Remember what I told you? You don't get to come until I say so," I whisper against her cheek.

She whimpers and tries to move her hips, looking for any sort of friction after I've edged her back from the brink of an orgasm twice. A tear slips from the corner of her eye while she laves at my fingers and begs around them. "Please. Please let me come. Fuck, Wren. I need to come."

My entire body feels like it's going to erupt. I relish her squeal when I remove my fingers and slap her clit. "You should have thought about that before you lied."

"I didn't lie. I just didn't tell you," she argues, and I slap her core again for her sass. This time twice in quick succession as I remain unmoving inside her. My cock throbs, swelling in her tight, warm heat. It's a miracle I've managed to stave off my own orgasm. Dove likes to be the one in control. But tonight, that honor is mine.

And holy fucking shit, is she spectacular when she submits.

"Wren! Please! Please, please, please," she cries out, so pretty as she writhes against me.

She's a fucking vision.

The locks that aren't wrapped around my fist stick to her face in sweaty strands. Her eye makeup is smudged from sweat and frustrated tears. But my favorite part is the smear of lipstick over her mouth. When I pull out slightly, I can still see the remnants of it around the base of my cock from when she choked on it earlier.

I slam into her, plastering myself to her back even though my legs are beginning to cramp from the angle. Our size difference makes things difficult—only a handful of positions work to our advantage, and most of them require her to be in control.

A familiar wave begins to crest, so I pick up my speed. "No more secrets, Dove."

"No more! I promise!" she cries, clutching the sheets like a lifeline as I return my fingers to her clit. I rub her in rhythm with the quick snap of my hips, pounding into her at a punishing pace that cuts her moan into short, jagged sounds.

"Fuck, Turtle Dove, I'm gonna come." I clench my teeth, trying to hold it at bay for a little longer. She feels so good I never want to leave. If I could live out the rest of my days in bed with her, I'd die the happiest man ever.

"Wren! I'm coming! Fuck, baby, I'm coming. Thank you. Thank you," she wails as she clenches around me, her pussy holding my cock in a vice grip as she milks it. Both our climaxes go on and on to the point where I think I might start spilling out of her by the bucket load if it doesn't stop.

I've never come so hard and so much in my fucking life. The more sex we have, the more I realize it will be this intense every time. And at this rate, I'll have to learn how to administer banana bags at home.

Dove sinks to the bed, breathing heavily as she releases a chuckle. "Oh my fucking god, Songbird. You can take control more often. I give it up. From now on, you're the master in the bedroom."

She shivers as I spread her cheeks, watching as my cum spills from between her perfectly pink pussy lips when I pull out. With a reverent moan, I push it back in, massaging the hot liquid against her walls. She jolts in surprise before squirming against my hand. "Wren—"

"Don't worry, Turtle Dove. I'm nowhere near finished with you," I promise. "But we're going to have a little chat before you sit on my face."

She rubs her legs together as I release her, hiding her face in my comforter. "I don't wanna," she pouts.

"Tough shit." I make my way to the bathroom to retrieve a warm washcloth and return to find her kicking the plush blanket off my bed as she wraps herself in my top sheet. "Come here."

She squeals with surprised glee as I grab her ankle and drag her back to the edge of the bed. Shoving the sheet to her hips, I take my time and tease her as I remove our combined release from her thighs.

"Can we stay like this forever, Songbird?" Her question makes me pause, a lance pricking my chest to let in a warm flood of elation at her words.

"For me, forever started the second I saw you." I kiss her inner thigh, watching her through the hair that's fallen over my eyes, as she graces me with a lazy smile. "I just didn't know it yet." I quickly wipe myself off before joining her in bed. Dove hikes her leg over my stomach, suctioning to my side as she threads a hand in my hair and kisses me like she needs to steal my very breath to survive.

Kissing her is like going to Disney World for the first time, every time. It's magical. Somehow, all my fears evaporate when her lips touch mine. Using my tongue doesn't even bother me anymore. It's second nature now. I can't imagine kissing her and not feeling like we're fusing our souls when our lips lock and mouths part for each other.

It's as easy as breathing.

"You're not going to get out of talking about it," I murmur against what's left of her watermelon-scented lipstick.

She laughs on a sigh, flopping to her back dramatically. I follow suit, holding my weight on one elbow and cradling her face with the other hand. "Dove..."

"What do you want from me, Songbird? When would have been the best time to say something? When I was dry-humping you in your living room?" I arch a brow at her damn sassy mouth, already imagining stuffing it full of my cock again as a form of punishment.

Although, does it really count as punishment if she enjoys it so much?

Flashing me a daring look, she rolls her eyes when I shake my head slowly. "It's not a casual topic, Wren. It's not like I could have brought it up over dinner." She waves one hand in the air while doing her best impression of me. "Hi, honey. How was your day?" She moves to her other hand as she switches to her bubblegum persona. "Mine was great, thanks for asking. I took Fang to the groomers, finished my article, and, oh! I sawed a man into pieces after hacking off his little smokie. How was your day, sweetie?" She drops both with a thud and gives me a pointed look.

"Turtle Dove, you know how I feel about her."

"You know, for a second there, I thought maybe you just wanted to reveal her identity so you could write an exposé I couldn't turn down. One that would skyrocket your career and fuck me over."

Now, it's my turn to fix her with a pointed stare.

"What?" She edges away, head bobbing with attitude. "Oh, and technically, I consider what you did cheating. You didn't know we were two different people."

Infuriating woman!

"We weren't together, Dove. I didn't cheat." I shift to nuzzle her neck as I pull the sheet from her body.

Her fingers dig into my shoulders as she tilts her head to allow me better access. "Don't try to distract me now, Songbird. You wanted to talk."

"Are you going to keep doing it?" My cock hardens at the sound of her throaty gasp when I graze my lips along her collarbone and continue south.

Her nipples pucker, the rosy buds rising to meet me. I pinch one while rolling the other between my teeth and tongue. "The less you know, the better. And no, this does not mean you get to write about me."

I pinch hard, twisting her stiffened peak and biting

down on the other before sucking it with enough force to make her cry out. Popping off with an audible smack, I grin up at her, moving further down her body. She widens her legs to make room for me between them.

"I got everything I wanted, you know," I tell her, each word leaving my lips as I trail soft caresses along her skin. "Except a published article."

"Don't even think about blackmailing me, Wren." Her legs clamp around my head as I dip my mouth toward her center. "After Ryan, I got a taste for the blood of men who can't keep their noses out of other people's business."

I see red at the mention of another man's name while I'm mere centimeters from her pussy. Unapologetically, I clamp my teeth over her clit and pull.

"Fuck!" She sucks in a breath, digging her nails into my scalp before slapping against the top of my head. "The term eating is *just* a term, Songbird! It's not for actual consumption!"

I laugh and release her so I can lick it better—only to freeze moments later as something about her words register uncomfortably in my gut.

Lifting my head, I will away the bile threatening to rise as I rapidly piece my thoughts together. "Dove?"

"What's wrong?" She laughs. "I was only kidding.

Well, not about the consumption part, you know I like it a little rough, baby, but—"

"Dove!" I clamber off the bed as I gaze down at her in horror. Even though it was weeks ago and has long since left my body, everything I've eaten in the last two days threatens to reappear. "What kind of jerky do you feed Fang?"

Dove's lips curl in, and her shoulders begin to shake. She slaps a hand over her mouth to muffle her laughter as she scrambles up with the sheet. "Baby, listen. That's on *you*."

Covering my mouth, I run to the bathroom as my stomach cramps. I barely make it as the chunks of the rice and yellow curry I ate for dinner splash into the white porcelain in a spray of bright canary flecked with orange.

"Oh, baby," Dove coos sympathetically as she enters the bathroom, her cotton candy rasp reverberating off the tile.

I almost tell her to go away, but she's literally played with human entrails. I'm sure she can handle a little puke.

"Sweet, sweet, Songbird." The bubbly tone that once grated my nerves reappears. Her nails scrape against my scalp in a soothingly way before venturing down to rub along my shoulders. "It's okay. I've eaten dick before. Hell, I went to town on yours earlier. It's not that bad."

"Sucking it and eating it is not the same! *It's not for actual consumption!*" I reprimand to the best of my ability, parroting her earlier words.

"Touché, Songbird. Touché."

NIGHT DESCENDS SWIFTLY as Dove prepares her duffel. Gilded rays slash through the forbidden room of her apartment, glinting off the blades in her dagger collection, desperate to soak into the costumes and wigs before fading with the sun.

My angel of death checks the screen of her pink iMac again, humming the *Legally Blonde* theme as she reviews her target's *requests* for tonight. She returns to her clothing rack, selecting a light pink-colored babydoll.

A slow simmer heats my blood. The thought of another man seeing her in lingerie, *touching* her, drives me bat-shit crazy.

The feeling worsens as she glances over her shoulder, offering me a soft, knowing smile. "I'm sorry,

Songbird, but the answer is still no. You can't come with me. I don't need the distraction."

A low growl rumbles in my chest. Fang, who's curled in my lap, immediately pushes to his feet, turns in a half-circle, and plants his front paws on my chest. He stretches lazily before offering a single, placating lick to my nose. Then, satisfied, he circles once more and resumes his nap.

Dove giggles, dragging my gaze from the rat back to her. "You're cute when you pout."

"It's not cute," I mutter. "I don't like you going alone." The thought terrifies me. How the fuck has she lasted this long without getting seriously hurt?

"Wren, I've been doing this for a while. I've had no problems." She scrolls through her computer again before crossing the room, selecting the wig she wore the first night she came to me as the Doll.

"Things are different now, though. You don't have to do this alone." The realization hits as I say it—I mean it. The delusion of becoming romantically involved with her is now reality, and I'd willingly be her accomplice.

Just months ago, we hated each other. Now, I can't imagine my life without her. Without her, the world is dull. Dim. A monochrome wasteland.

I need her—her sweet, sugary scent, her saccharine smile, her bubblegum persona. She makes me want to live my life in color... in *her* color. In spun shades of cotton candy, even when the darkness threatens to take over.

Dove must know I need her like I need air. I want to be her sanctuary in the chaos she surrounds herself with. "I know it's hard to adjust to having someone you can rely on, Dove. But I need you to know—I'm here for you."

She carefully places the wig in a hairnet before tucking it into a pink satin bag. Fang senses the shift in her energy before I do. He stands, jumps from my lap, shakes his stringy mane, then trots out of the room without a backward glance.

When I look back at Dove, she's leaning against her white dresser, arms crossed, appraising me with those big blue eyes. She bites her bottom lip, barely suppressing a smile painted in strawberry lip gloss.

"What?" I rise to my feet, closing the distance, relishing the way lust darkens her gaze as it meets mine.

The tiny cut-off shorts she's wearing barely conceal the curve of her ass. I palm it, effortlessly lifting her onto the glossy surface. I'm hard within seconds as she wraps her legs around my waist, rolling her hips into mine.

"I love how easily you've accepted this." She slides her palms up my chest, nails digging into my neck as she pulls me down. "It's hot to think of you by my side while I seek justice."

One by one, she slowly undoes my buttons, pressing kisses down my chest as she goes. "But you'd be a distraction, Wren—one I can't afford."

"You know, I do realize that you use sex to distract *me* every time I bring this up." I thread a hand through her hair, smirking as she presses a kiss to my abs, finishing the last button. My dick is granite, and all I want is to watch it disappear between her teasing lips. But before she can start on my pants, I grip her chin, tilting her head back.

A surprised squeal morphs into a giggle as I push her down, her legs tightening around my waist. "What are you doing?" she laughs, squirming as her ass barely balances on the dresser's edge.

I make quick work of her shorts and lace panties, peeling them off one leg at a time. Her pussy is the most perfect thing I've ever seen. Pink and glistening with evidence of how turned on she is. Warm and wet and just waiting for me to sink my tongue into it.

"You're so fucking beautiful, Dove," I whisper, kissing my way up her thigh as I sling one leg over my shoulder.

"Who's distracting whom now?" she teases, but her words dissolve into a guttural moan as I lift her other leg and bury my face between them.

Her hands fly overhead, fingers stretching against the wall as she writhes, her shoulders the only thing still touching the surface. I rip the thin strap of her tank top down, exposing her heaving breasts.

"Wren!" she gasps, searching for anything to grasp onto. Her head falls back as I thrust my tongue deep into her heat, stroking before sliding up to tease her swollen clit. "Baby, that feels so good," she whimpers, voice broken by desperate moans.

I love how easily she submits to me now. How fucking beautiful she is when she surrenders. It makes me feel powerful, the emotion so intense it's like getting drunk. She's intoxicating, and I'm an addict fiending for her all the fucking time. I never thought I'd find a woman who makes me feel the way Dove does. She's awakened a power in me I didn't even know existed.

Her hands find mine as I palm her breast, her hips bucking against my face. She tenses when I hit that sweet spot. "There! Right there! Just like that. Don't stop, baby. Please don't stop," she begs.

I stop.

"Wren!" she cries, nails digging into my wrist. "No! Why?"

"Bring me with you." I smirk against her pussy, smearing her arousal over my lips as I gently kiss her everywhere but her clit. Soft, closed-mouth kisses. And she can't reach my head to pull me closer.

"I swear to God, if you don't keep going, I *will* murder you in your sleep, Songbird." Her tone is utterly non-threatening, making me grin wider.

I press another soft, chaste kiss to her swollen flesh. "How badly do you want it, Turtle Dove?"

God, I love having her at my mercy—bent nearly in half, upside down, her pussy on full display, ready for me to devour however I want.

Dove moves with intent, trying to escape my hold, but I can't have her getting away just yet. I tighten my grip around her thighs and bite lightly around the spot she craves most.

"Ah!" Her back arches and a whine parts her lips on a moan. "Suck, Songbird, or your dick is becoming Fang's next jerky batch!"

My chuckle ghosts over her wet, swollen flesh before I give in—not because she threatened me, I know she loves my cock too much to ever remove it from my body, but because I'm close.

Too close.

And fuck—I come.

Hard.

My dick jerks in its confines as Dove's thighs clamp around my neck tightly when she comes. I'm sure she intends to suffocate me as a form of punishment.

Little does she know, I'll gladly die from asphyxiation with her release on my tongue and her flesh in my mouth.

No, wait. That makes me sound like a cannibal.

Dove's giggle pulls me from my spiraling thoughts as they return to the day I ate Fang's jerky. "Fuck, Songbird, you're really getting better at *tongue-vincing* me to do things."

A flicker of hope ignites in my chest as I lower her, helping her down until her feet touch the ground. She hums appreciatively, licking her lips before curling the bottom one between her teeth as she trails a teasing finger over the wet spot on my shorts.

"Why is it so hot that you came while fully clothed?"

"So I can come with you?" I divert, my voice filled with so much hope and desperation it makes me sound like a naive juvenile.

She smirks. "No, Songbird." She guides me back to the chair I occupied earlier, settling herself with a knee on either side of my waist as she straddles me, raking her nails through my hair. Neither of us cares that it makes an even bigger mess of my shorts. "When will you learn that you can't make me do what you want just because you know how to play my pussy as well as you play pool?"

"I *am* a pool shark," I murmur against her lips.

She giggles, kissing me, taking her time as she tastes herself on me before seeking entrance with her tongue. I like kissing her this way, but she's still respectful every time, always ensuring I'm comfortable.

We still haven't discussed my mother—or what Dove thinks she knows. I suspect she's waiting for me to bring it up, and I will, eventually, be ready to tell her everything.

Like how I'm finally seeing the light at the end of the dark tunnel I've been trapped in for years. Just months ago, I wouldn't have even entertained the idea of confronting my mother, let alone seeking the closure I so desperately need.

But seeing Dove's strength up close—watching her shape her past into something that saves others—it's empowering. My girl is inspiring.

When we part, she graces me with a vulpine smile. "Will you wait for me? *Naked*. In my bed."

"Why don't you break into my place instead? Take advantage of me while wearing your mask. Make all my fantasies of your alter ego come true."

I grin as her face falls comically.

"Only you could make me jealous of my serial killer self, Songbird," she deadpans.

"It's not cheating, Turtle Dove." I nuzzle her with my nose, grasping her wrists and holding them behind her back when she tries to get up. "You're the same person."

"Yeah, okay, *Ross*," she pitches her voice higher and mocks, "We were on a break!"

"I don't... know what that means?" I release her as I stupidly try to recall where I've heard that before.

She giggles, the sound ringing through the room as she heads toward the bathroom. "Guess we have a new show to watch, Songbird." She winks over her shoulder before disappearing down the hall. "Another *first* I get to give you."

At her possessive tone, warmth spreads through my chest. I release a lovesick sigh, tracking her backside with a dreamy gaze until she vanishes from view. "Sounds good to me, Turtle Dove."

I WATCH as the tiny dot representing Dove continues traveling northwest. At least I know she hasn't been smoking those disgusting little cigars, because she still hasn't found the tracker I stuck to her Zippo.

While both those facts comfort me, my nerves are fraying as she gets further and further from the city. She can't have left more than thirty minutes ago, and with each passing second, my resolve to stay put weakens.

Hunter slides another beer in front of me before dropping onto the stool beside mine, snorting. "Can you believe this guy?" He gestures with the neck of his bottle toward where Bunny sits across the bar, deep in conversation with her date. "What, did Dove dress him?"

I huff a laugh, setting my phone screen down and taking a pull from my drink. The guy in question is wearing a salmon-colored button-up, his long, sandy-colored hair tied up in a bun secured with what looks like a pastel pink scrunchie.

He doesn't seem like Bunny's type, yet I think this is the happiest I've ever seen her. They talk animatedly, completely absorbed in each other, while Hunter continues his futile attempt to incinerate the guy with sheer force of will.

Bunny greeted me earlier, but she didn't ask about Dove, which I find odd. After seeing me here alone, why wouldn't she ask where my girlfriend, her best friend, is?

It's a little weird.

Does she know who Dove really is?

I've always wondered how those videos make it to the police station. Dove doesn't seem like the type to edit footage into the eerie, cinematic style they always appear in. She hates it when marketing asks about layouts or design choices, always huffing about how she can't figure it out to save her life.

Is Bunny in on it?

"The Shadow Siren struck again. We haven't released details yet. Want an exclusive?" Hunter asks, tearing his gaze away from Bunny's table.

"Yeah, that sounds good. Dove sure as hell isn't letting me write about the Doll anytime soon, so I should probably give that one up for now."

"How are things with you two?" Hunter asks, and for once, he sounds like he genuinely cares—even though his knee bounces restlessly, his fingers flex around his beer, and his eyes keep flicking sideways, trying to catch glimpses of Bunny in his peripheral vision.

"Things are good." My foot taps against the stool's lower bar. Whether it's Hunter's anxiety bleeding into my space or my own unease about Dove's where-abouts, I don't know. "They're great, actually. Life-changing, once I got out of my own way."

He claps me on the back. "I'm happy for you both, truly. You seem a lot better. I don't think I've ever seen you so happy with a girlfriend before."

I pick up my phone, giving him an opening to let his gaze drift where he wants. "Why don't you man up and make a move?"

"You think I haven't tried?" he asks bitterly.

"I hate to say it, Hunt. But maybe you should let her go then. Or force her hand. She doesn't like seeing you with other women. She went ballistic about you kissing Dove—which I still haven't forgiven you for—so give her a taste of her own medicine. She clearly cares. Maybe if you act like you *don't*, she'll finally face her feelings."

He scoffs. "I *can't*. She's got me so wrapped around her finger I'd sit and watch while she let him fuck her if she asked me to."

My head whips toward him, an incredulous look on my face as I try not to choke on my drink. "I'm sorry... *what*?"

He snorts. "I'd kill him afterward, of course. But that goddamn woman has me under her spell, and I'm at my fucking wit's end. I know she has feelings for me. I just can't push her. She puts up this strong front, but that's all it is—a facade of indifference because her husband hurt her so badly I don't know if she'll ever trust another man like that again."

I don't know the full extent of Bunny's story. Dove keeps telling me I can ask, but it's not hers to share. I think she encourages Bunny and me to spend time together because she doesn't want her friend to feel left out now that she's in a relationship.

But honestly? I just want Bunny and Hunter to get their shit together so we can all be happy.

Hunter exhales sharply. "A man's pride can only take so much."

"Ever wonder why she keeps dating?"

"What do you mean?"

"Have you ever just offered her a one-night stand? A chance to fuck yourselves out of each other's systems?" I think back to that night—Dove, sitting a few stools away, making the same proposition.

The memory of how she felt beneath my fingertips. The warmth of her skin and the heated look in her eyes. The moment I realized she felt the same way I did.

The moment everything changed.

Hunter's gaze shifts, now studying Bunny with something new simmering in his amber depths. "I want more from her than that. I'd rather have nothing than a taste of happiness just to have her rip it away."

"Maybe she needs a taste first." I shrug. "Then she'll be hooked. And you can go on to have annoying little babies that look exactly like you, just like you've always dreamed."

Hunter has always wanted a big family. As an only child, he never had siblings and only had a few friends besides me. He always used to say he wanted enough kids to make a baseball team. I don't know Bunny well, only hearing one-sided bits and pieces of their history from Hunter, but I think his need to settle down scares the shit out of her.

"Tone down the long-term intensity, Hunt. I know you love her, I still have no idea how, or why, but I know you do. But maybe what Bunny needs is a good fucking, and that's it. I hate to be crude about it, but I think Dove would agree if she were here."

Hunter mulls over the information as he continues watching the object of his obsession with renewed curiosity. "Where *is* Dove tonight?" he murmurs, uninterested.

I check my phone discreetly. Her dot is still moving. In one swift moment, my resolve snaps.

"Working late. I'm gonna meet up with her."

I follow his unwavering gaze to see Bunny heading to the bathroom. Hunter is off his stool and walking away without so much as a goodbye, giving me the perfect opportunity to slip away unnoticed.

Go get her, man. I'm going after my girl, too.

RICH PEOPLE CAN BE SO FUCKING dumb sometimes.

Aside from his proclivity for fucking women who look younger than they are while scouting his next victim, Marcus Westfield doesn't ask for a shred of proof about who I am. No collateral, no NDA, no precaution ensuring I'll keep his identity a secret.

Nothing.

Most men of his caliber—scummy, high-ranking Wall Street types—have protocols. NDAs, security measures, exit strategies. Not Marcus. He thinks his remote farmhouse on the New York–Pennsylvania border, miles from the nearest neighbor, is enough to ensure discretion.

It's where he takes his victims. It's fitting that it's where he'll meet his bloody end.

Marcus is a medium kill, but I have a lot of pent-up rage to burn.

Winding down the long gravel driveway, the crunch beneath the tires of my rented white sedan is swallowed by the storm rolling in. It's an older-model Chevy with no GPS, but I still slapped on a fake license plate and prayed to whoever was listening that I wouldn't get pulled over.

Wren was right to be worried. Generally, I wouldn't agree to meet somewhere so isolated. But this is precisely why I work alone. Even Bunny and I don't usually do jobs together. Sure, we help clean up the mess, but it's too much trouble to worry about another body in the mix. People are unpredictable.

And my songbird is too sweet to get tangled in this chaos.

The farmhouse's distant glow grows closer, blurred by the rain that now pours in heavy sheets. The windshield wipers struggle to keep up as I reach for my purse, fishing out my pack of Black and Milds and the Zippo I keep next to them. My thumb glides over a raised smooth surface on the lighter, and my heart stops. I slow the car as I hit the map light to inspect it.

Motherfuc— I abruptly cut off my internal curse, vowing never to use that word again. But goddammit, Wren. This must be how he's tracking me. That smart-ass knew I wouldn't find it because I promised him I'd quit smoking. And I have—mostly. A frustrated sound escapes my throat as I toss the pack and lighter back into my bag.

A heavy sense of dread settles in my lungs. What if he doesn't listen? What if he follows me again?

This is a bad idea, Turtle Dove. His voice rings through my head, clear as if he were beside me.

I inhale sharply and press my foot to the gas. Another day that Marcus gets to live is another child at risk of becoming his next victim.

The farmhouse looks perfectly normal—cream-colored with a gray shingle roof, a detached three-car garage, and carefully manicured landscaping, the kind that suggests he hires someone to maintain it when he's not here.

It's bigger than what a single bachelor needs, but my research shows he likes to throw parties for his finance bros.

This house has seen some shit.

Tonight, that shit will look tame compared to what I'm about to do to him.

Pushing thoughts of Wren from my mind, I collect my duffel, open the umbrella I always keep in my purse, and make the short walk to the door. Marcus greets me with a glass of red wine and a charming smile.

He has the kind of face that inspires trust at first

glance—freshly shaven, sharp features, a wolf in finance shark clothing. In his tailored suits, he's the man who can double your investment while making himself even richer. Dressed down in joggers and a white tee, he looks like he could be the hot basketball coach at a local high school.

Which is probably exactly how he hooks the teenage girls he likes to fuck.

"Wow. You are beautiful." His eyes roam my body, lingering. He shuts the door behind me and motions to an umbrella stand in the corner.

Even though I have a costume to change into, I took my time selecting the perfect summer dress to highlight my curves. My makeup is carefully done to make me look younger. The whole package is designed to put him at ease, to make him think I'm just a tiny slip of a woman, unable to defend myself when his instincts kick in and he starts playing out his rape fantasy. He's smart to hire sex workers between his victims so he doesn't draw too much attention to himself. Unfortunately for them, no one cares if they go missing.

Unfortunately for him, he's caught the attention of the wrong woman.

"Thank you," I reply, keeping my tone light and breathy to sell the innocent act. It's what he requested, after all. And I'm nothing if not a professional.

"Listen," he says, handing me the wine with an apologetic smile, "I'm sorry to have to do this, but I have to take a quick Zoom call for work. Shouldn't be more than half an hour. Make yourself comfortable. There's charcuterie if you're hungry. Help yourself to anything."

Charming *and* considerate. He's trying to put me at ease, too. Having researched him, I know not to drink the wine. The food is probably safe, but the alcohol? Almost certainly drugged.

"It's okay. I can wait. Would you... would you like me to get ready?" I peer up at him with big doe eyes, willing a blush to rise to my cheeks as I bite my lower lip demurely.

Marcus doesn't bother hiding his erection as it springs to life behind the charcoal joggers. "Sure. Third room down the hall on the right." He steps into my space, blue eyes tracing my features. I force myself not to flinch as he cups my chin. "Forget the wig. Dress in the lingerie and wait for me on the sofa in the living room where I can see you." He pulls on my lip with his thumb. Every nerve in my body screams in revulsion. I mask it with a shy smile and fluttering lashes as he whispers, "Fuck, you're perfect."

"Thank you." I lower my gaze, glancing timidly at the bulge in his pants that threatens to brush against my stomach if he comes any closer. It makes me want to retch. Guilt lances through me for being so intimately close to a man who isn't Wren.

Turn it off, Dove. This is what you do. It's who you are. Wren doesn't change that.

"How old are you?" Marcus asks.

"Fifteen," I lie, providing the age he requested I play.

His smile is downright diabolical. The contents of my stomach curdle as he says, "Good girl."

A shiver runs through me. He mistakes it for desire and chuckles. "Go get ready for daddy."

Gag.

Bile rises in my throat, but I swallow it with a thin smile and turn to do as he says.

The hall is devoid of personal touches. No photos, no shelves with knickknacks. The off-white walls are blank. But stepping into the room he directed me to is like walking into a nightmare. A ledge borders the top of the space, and every inch of it is occupied by dolls—porcelain collectibles, the same kind Freddy used to keep in my room at his house.

What the fuck is it with psychopaths and dolls?

A shudder racks my body. I toss my bag onto the pristine ivory comforter of the queen-sized bed before setting the wine on the large white vanity.

I retrieve an alcohol test strip and dip my finger in

the red liquid, dropping some onto the strip. I let out an unladylike snort when it turns blue instantly.

Amateur.

I check the time and pull out my lingerie, inwardly cringing as Wren sneaks back into my thoughts. If he saw what Marcus is about to see tonight, he'd lose his goddamn mind.

I know I have to reevaluate everything. Every painstaking detail I put into my kills washed away because my boyfriend discovered my identity.

Wren makes me sloppy. Distracted.

But I refuse to give him up.

Or the Doll.

I have to change *something* to make this work. And I want it to work so badly. I've never wanted anything like I want Wren. He makes me feel alive. Being with him awakens a protectiveness in me I never knew I possessed.

It's not like a mother's instinct—the kind that drives a woman to do whatever it takes to protect her offspring.

No, it's something far more primal. A feral need to protect my mate.

I need to be willing to do whatever it takes.

Marcus is talking shop when I return to the main living area, laughing with whoever is on the other end of the screen as he lounges at the dining room table.

The open-concept layout makes it easy for him to see me, and I allow another shy smile to grace my lips as his approving gaze drags down my scantily clad body.

Lazily, I peruse the room. As he continues working, I do things to catch his attention—bending slightly to read the titles of books on the inlaid shelving so he gets a perfect view of my ass beneath the babydoll nightie, or slowly pushing my hair over my shoulder before running my fingers over my breast.

By the time he finishes his call, he looks ready to chase me through the house and fuck me senseless.

I've never been drier.

"Did you not like the wine?" he asks, joining me where I sit with my legs curled beneath me on the sofa.

"It tastes a little funny." I scrunch my nose and move to my knees, reaching over to take his glass as he sets it on the coaster. Holding his gaze, I take a drink. "Yours tastes normal. Maybe mine still has soap residue from the dishwasher?"

The most common date-rape drugs are tasteless. Marcus likely knows this. He frowns and cocks his head. "Huh. That's strange. I'm sorry. I can get you a new glass."

"Maybe I'm just being silly. I'm not usually a big wine drinker. Here, try it." I grab my drink and lift it to his lips.

"What do you drink? I can get you something

else." He jolts off the couch, giving me his back as he strides into the kitchen.

Quickly, I pour half of my wine into his glass, then set them both back on their coasters, my drugged, now half-empty drink where his was. "That's okay! I'll just drink it." Marcus turns as I pretend to take a sip. "It's really not that bad. I was just trying to play into the fantasy."

Nice save, Dove.

He huffs a laugh and strolls back, picking up his glass and taking a large gulp. "Well, you're certainly worth the money, aren't you?"

I flash him a saccharine smile and rise to my feet. A flicker of light flashes through the large front windows, catching my attention for a split second before it vanishes into the dark. My brows knit together as I glance back at Marcus, but he doesn't notice my momentary lapse in attention.

Is he expecting someone?

My hackles rise. A gut feeling tightens in my stomach—a whisper of warning that I may have gotten in over my head this time.

"I'm going to use the bathroom before we get started. I'll be right back." I take my glass with me, returning to the room with my things to text Bunny—only to realize I left my purse, and my phone, in the car.

"Shit." Sighing, I dump the wine into the toilet and flush, letting the sink run for a few moments before retrieving my mask.

For whatever reason, the mask is what always puts the fear of death in their eyes. Maybe it's because they finally realize who I am. Maybe it's just downright terrifying. To me, it's just a mask. Without the blackout contacts, it's not even that creepy.

Men are so weak.

I give it a few more minutes. The light wasn't far away—if Marcus is expecting someone, they'd be here by now. Once I'm certain it was just a trick of the house's reflection against the glass, I return to the living room.

Marcus' head swings toward me, slow and sluggish, a sloppy smile curving his lips. He doesn't even notice the mask as he pushes to his feet, swaying. "Did you tell your parents you were at a sleepover?"

I swallow the disgust threatening to crawl up my throat. "I did, *Daddy*. Now, why don't you sit back down so I can sit in your lap, and you can sing me a lullaby?"

His features melt from confusion into stark realization as I slip the mask over my head. "You... You're—"

"So eloquent, Marcus." I take a step toward him, giggling as he stumbles back. He's a big guy, and it's only been a few minutes—the drugs will take a few more to really kick in. "Wanna play your game now?"

In his requests, he mentioned playing hide and seek. But now that the tables have turned, he looks more ready to piss himself than chase me through the house before raping me.

Sweat beads on his forehead as he takes a step back for every one I take forward. He skirts the massive kitchen island, leaving the large knife he used to cut cheese up for grabs. "Please don't kill me," he sobs.

"Does the name Sophia Madden ring a bell, Marcus?" It's my voice that echoes through the room, not the modulator, as I ask the question.

He shakes his head, tears beginning to flow from his face, when I ask another. "How about Brianna Turmond? Chloe Singleton? Sarah Weaver?"

Each step backs him closer to the French doors. The less mess I make inside, the better. By the time anyone finds Marcus, he'll be a pile of mush—if the rain keeps up.

With a trembling hand held out like it will stop me, he sobs, "I thought they were of age, I swear!" His other hand scrambles at the latch as his back meets the glass.

"Funny how you suddenly know exactly what I'm talking about." I cock my head and grin, though he can't see it behind the mask. "Do you know they're all in therapy now because of what you did? Did you think picking girls from different places would keep you from getting caught?"

A flash of lightly tanned skin darts into the backyard. From the corner of my eye, I catch Wren slipping into the bushes. He's wearing dark clothes, but he's not even trying to be stealthy.

Fucking hell.

With a sigh, I mumble, "He's never gonna learn."

Marcus tilts his head in confusion and looks behind him. When he swings his unfocused gaze back to me, he cries, "I promise! I'll learn! I swear I will!"

He finally fumbles the latch open, and the door swings outward abruptly, catching in the wind as he stumbles into the storm. The drugs are reaching their final stage, making his limbs clumsy. He falls, grasping at mud, and I follow.

Lighting flashes in the sky, the fat clouds above backlit by a grayish blue before a roar of thunder claps therapeutically. The chaos soothes me, helping to ground my psyche as I catch up with the blubbering mess who army-crawls away.

With a quick downward thrust, I plunge the dagger into the meat between his spine and shoulder. His cry is lost to mother nature as she throws a tantrum and takes it out on the mortals who keep fucking up her zen.

I honestly don't blame her.

Marcus flips over and tries to crabwalk away, his injured arm now useless every time he puts weight on that side. He sounds sleepy as he continues to beg for his life. "Please. I have money. I'll give you whatever you want."

I heave a deep sigh, removing my mask and tossing it to the ground before tipping my head back toward the sky to let the rain wash over my face.

I hate the ones who think money will change anything. They've been taught their whole lives that money can get them out of any bad situation—even at the expense of someone else's life.

"They wanted it! I didn't force them! They were old enough to know better!"

Freddy's voice echoes in my ears. *You were old enough to know better.*

Fury rips from my throat in a warrior's cry as I drop to my knees, straddling him. The dagger plunges deep into his stomach. Blood spurts from the wound, splashing onto my face. I grimace and reach for my mask and slip it back over my head, shielding myself from the revolting spray of blood and spittle as they leave his body in shuddering bursts.

I want to play my games and torture the man within an inch of his life. I want to wait for the drugs to wear off so he feels everything when I finally end him.

But, of course, my songbird had to go and fuck up everything. So a quick death it shall be.

Marcus swings his arms weakly, a lazy, pathetic attempt to fight me off. His screams gurgle through the blood flooding his throat. My goodbye lullaby joins his cries from behind my mask.

"Ring around the rosie."

Pierce.

"Pocket full of posies."

Slash.

"Ashes. Ashes."

Stab.

"We all fall down."

Okay, so I get a little carried away. His stomach is a shredded, meaty ruin, bubbling with blood and slick intestines spilling onto the grass. My final blow lands with a sickening squelch, and I watch the light fade from his eyes.

And I won't lie—knowing that Wren watched the whole thing without making a sound? Kind of turns me on.

Laughter bubbles up from my lips, dark and breathless. I remember when Wren told the Doll that he wanted to kill for me. Now, he's watched me take a life.

Twice.

I told him not to follow, and yet here he is, even after seeing me murder Ryan.

If that's not love, I don't know what is.

My laughter dies as I turn toward the bushes. "Come out, Songbird. I know you're there."

Wren steps from the shrubbery, dressed in black, eyes dark with something I've grown to covet.

Hunger.

Need.

Heat curls low in my stomach. My breath quickens. I'm acutely aware of how little my nightgown covers, the rain making the thin fabric cling to every curve. Wren doesn't try to hide his appreciation as his gaze sweeps over me.

The rain eases. He says my name in a low, rasping growl. "Dove."

Dropping the knife, I tear my mask off and break out in a run toward him. There's no fear in his gaze, nothing but lust and admiration and relief to see that I'm okay shining in the depths of his deep brown eyes.

Wren bends, arms wide, waiting. I leap, crashing into him, locking my mouth to his. The impact knocks us backward, sending him sprawling onto the wet earth with me in his lap.

But it doesn't stop us.

We're a flurry of lips and tongue and teeth—

desperate, insatiable. My fingers fly to unbutton his pants, freeing him. His hands tangle in my rain-soaked hair, pulling me impossibly closer, until there's no space left between us. I shove my panties to the side to sink down onto his hard length with a shuddering gasp.

He groans. I whimper. We move as one, frenzied and raw, our bodies as wild as the storm raging around us. Wren grips the grass behind him, anchoring us as I grind against him, chasing the edge of my climax.

"Fuck, you feel so fucking good," he moans with his head thrown back in bliss.

I tip mine toward the sky, eyes slipping shut as the heat coils tight, the rain mixing with sweat, with blood, with the heady rush of power and lust. It crests, bursting inside me, a violent, shuddering release.

White explodes behind my eyes. "Wren! I'm coming! Baby, I'm coming!"

"Me too. Fuck, Turtle Dove. Me too."

His grip tightens at the back of my neck, pressing our foreheads together as his hips stutter against mine, his moan melting into my lips. We breathe each other in, the storm still crackling around us, the world reduced to nothing but this.

Wren kisses me softly, then shifts, pulling my legs more firmly around his waist.

"I was so fucking worried about you," he murmurs.

I laugh lightly, nipping at his bottom lip.

"I told you—I can take care of myself." Then, with a wicked grin, say, "I think my violence does turn you on, though. You have a thing for necrophilia."

Wren makes a face, pulling back slightly. "Gross, Dove. That's when someone has sex *with* dead bodies. Not next to them."

I giggle. "Okay, so you have a thing for fucking *next* to dead bodies."

"Only fucking you." He grins, pressing a slow, teasing kiss to the tip of my nose before flexing his still semi-hard cock inside me. "Because you're right. Watching you incite violence *does* turn me on."

A DEEP HUM reverberates in Wren's chest as I squirm in his arms. "If you keep pressing your ass against my cock like that, Turtle Dove, I'm going to fuck you again."

My giggle bounces off the bathroom walls, wrapping around us as I wiggle my butt against him once more. The bathwater sloshes, sending pink-tinged bubbles spilling over the porcelain to drip onto the tile. "Don't threaten me with a good time, Songbird."

Even though I'd be more than happy to go another round, I relax against his chest, settling into the warmth. Wren nuzzles my neck before pressing his cheek to my temple. "From now on, I want to go with you."

Since leaving the farmhouse, he hasn't stopped touching me—except for when we had to drive back in separate vehicles. It's like he thinks if he lets go, I'll vanish.

His hands slide under my arms, cupping my breasts as his thumbs gently stroke over my hardened nipples. It's not meant to be sexual, just grounding—a quiet moment of comfort for us both in the warm, strawberry-scented water.

"How about I put a pin in it, and we figure it out together?" I hope he understands what this means to me. What it means to invite him into this part of my life, to consider and include his feelings in my plans.

"Would you really do that?" he asks, shifting to look at me.

I nod. "Yeah. I will."

I hope that by sharing something so deeply personal, he'll finally open the door to the part of his life he's kept hidden from me. "Can I ask you a question?"

"Of course, Turtle Dove. Anything." He pulls me back against his chest, resuming the slow, soothing strokes over my skin.

"What tipped you off? About me being the Doll?"

Wren laughs. "In one of the videos your victim knocked your tool tray askew. You paused just to fix it. I notice you do that whenever I move something in your office."

I snort. "Fucking Freddy. The asshole instilled that

in me. Everything always had to be clean and perfect or he'd—" A shiver has Wren wrapping his arms tighter around me. "Let's just say the punishments were less than savory."

"I'm sorry, Dove," he murmurs, nuzzling the back of my neck.

"Can I ask another?" I don't ignore his sympathy, I just don't want to waste more time on a man who doesn't deserve any more of my thoughts.

"Sure." Wren skims his fingers down my stomach before trailing back to my breasts.

"Do you... do you still see her when you look at me?" I hate how timid my voice sounds, hate the vulnerability that seeps into my words. I need to be strong for him, need to be ready to carry the weight of what I've just unearthed.

Wrenley's fingers never falter as he exhales softly. "No. Not anymore."

At first, I think that's all he'll give me. But then he holds me tighter, shifting me higher on his body so he can rest his chin on my shoulder. "My dad left when I was little. He hated how my mother coddled me. Said he didn't want to raise a sissy boy for a son, and didn't care enough to really look past her obsession."

My breath hitches. I was prepared for Wren to give me a few snippets, but it seems like my songbird is finally ready to tell me his tale. I only wish he'd let me look him in the eye while he does.

But I understand the need to hide when revisiting our demons.

"My mother... she was... overly attentive." A shudder rolls through his body, sending ripples through the water. "When I was young, I didn't think much of it. A tight hug here. A kiss on the lips there. Other moms did the same with their sons, so I never questioned it. But as I got older, it got worse. She'd come into the bathroom while I was showering and open the curtain like it was nothing. The hugs became caresses. The kisses turned..." His voice trails off, barely a whisper.

I exhale slowly, pressing my tongue against my teeth in an attempt to hold back the tears burning my eyes. "Wren, it's okay. You don't have to—"

"No. No, I *need* to. I've never told anyone. I... I need to get this off my chest." The desperation in his voice echoes my own when I first spoke up about what happened to me. My heart clenches, aching for him.

"Okay, baby. Take your time."

He waits a few beats before continuing. "In high school, Hunter started noticing. By then, she'd come into my room at night. Three, four times a week." His voice quickens, turning slightly frantic. "She said it was my job as the man of the house to make her feel good.

That in return, she'd make me feel good. And I knew it was wrong. By then, I knew. But I didn't stop it. I could have, but I didn't."

"Baby, it's not your fault." My stomach roils, and the tears spill freely down my cheeks. Wren presses his forehead to my back, his own tears hot against my skin. When I try to turn, he shakes his head.

"One night, she let Hunter stay over. She never let anyone stay before, and I was never allowed to go anywhere overnight either. I thought maybe I'd be safe from her that night. Figured since Hunter was there, she wouldn't try anything. But after we fell asleep, I woke up to her standing over me, holding a finger to her lips. She motioned for me to follow her. I didn't want to, but it was clear she wasn't going to leave until I did. I didn't know Hunter was awake. He followed us and made a show of going to the bathroom just to let her know he wasn't asleep." Wren catches his breath, squeezing me like a life raft. "He asked if something was going on. I told him no. I was too ashamed. Too embarrassed. A few days later, she put the house on the market and pulled me out of school. We moved to California to live with some guy she'd met online. Hunter and I lost touch."

We remain silent for a long while, until our tears have dried, and he finally lets me turn and pull him into my arms. "Hunter told me I look just like her."

"You do." He draws back to meet my gaze. "If I didn't know better, I'd swear we were related. But I do know better. And we aren't, thank god."

"A lot of things make sense now," I murmur, dropping my gaze to the bubbles in the space between us. "Now I know why you hated me so much at first."

"I just... It was hard. She was always the picture-perfect mother to everyone else. But behind closed doors..." Wren lifts my chin. "I thought that maybe you were the same way. It wasn't fair. And I'm sorry."

"But I am... sorta, anyway. The pink and the glitter and the happy-go-lucky *are* me, but then there's the Doll."

"And you're perfect. Either way. So goddamn perfect, and I'm an idiot for almost letting you slip through my fingers."

Emotion swells in my chest as he presses his lips to mine. "I can't help but wonder if you'll always think of her when you look at me. You say you don't, but... have you... Would you consider sex therapy?"

Now it's Wren's turn to frown. "I think our sex is pretty fantastic, Turtle Dove."

"Yeah, but... I don't know." I push away, needing a little distance. "Maybe it would be therapeutic for us both?"

Wren gives me a contemplative look before grabbing my ankle under the water and pulling me back into his lap. "If that's what you want, we'll do it."

"I mean, should I change my hair? I don't think I can pull off being a brunette, but I'll try if you think it will help—"

"Dove, stop." Wren grasps my cheeks as I start to spiral. "I don't want you to change a damn thing. I lo —" he catches himself as my heart skips a beat. His eyes dart between mine, brows notched together in perplexity as he breathes a gentle laugh. "I fucking love you, Turtle Dove. Just the way you are."

An overwhelming wave of emotion crashes through me as tears prick my lash line and I smile. "I love you, too, Songbird."

Our lips meet in a slow, tempered sweep of passion, laughter spilling between us—part disbelief, part wonder, that just months ago, we were ready to tear each other apart.

Later, rinsed clean and tangled in bed after two rounds of what I can only describe as the most sensual experience of my life, Wren asks, "How did you get so comfortable with sex?"

"Reading," I admit truthfully. "Believe it or not, it's therapeutic. It let me experience things while still having the power to close the book—stop the trauma, so to speak."

I'll never forget the first time I picked up a book at

the store and skimmed through it. Some dark romance had been misplaced, buried among historical novels featuring women in dresses that weighed more than they did and pirates who took pleasure in plundering what lay beneath.

A giggle rumbles from my lips at the memory. "At first, I was like, what the hell did I just buy? But four hours later, I was hooked. When Bunny and I met, we realized we liked the same kinds of books, so we started our book club. Even though we see each other all the time, Sundays are sacred—we always get together to talk about whatever we're reading."

I leave out the part where we also discuss our targets. I can't tell him she's a fellow serial killer without her approval first. And something tells me Wren will have to work really hard to get on Bunny's good side after implying he'd be a better choice to watch Fang than her—and after calling the Shadow Siren basic in her form and not as interesting as my alter ego. A tidbit I let slip to Bunny one night while complaining about him when we were still rivals.

"Can I be in the book club?" Wren asks, and he sounds genuinely interested. I giggle against his chest, already imagining my friend's face when I tell her everything.

"I'll have to ask Bunny."

"She hates me," he muses, then pauses thoughtfully. "Although, who knows? After tonight, she might be more fond of me."

I prop my chin on his chest, raising a brow, waiting for him to elaborate.

He smirks. "I may have sent Hunter into the bathroom after her to fuck her brains out while she was on a date. He's always going on about being her Mr. Right. I told him to say fuck it and just be her Mr. Right Now."

My jaw drops, and I let out a shocked squeal. "Did he?"

Wren shrugs. "Guess we'll find out tomorrow at book club."

Northern California doesn't feel like coming home.

Home has always been New York, even when I wasn't living there.

It's the chaos of the city, the inescapable air of superiority on one block while the next is full of laid-back artistic types. It's grabbing a slice at any time of the day, walking down the sidewalk and spotting a random movie star filming on any given night of the week.

Home is hues of pink and glitter and the ever-present scent of cookies and vanilla. It's curling up in Dove's bed, a bowl of popcorn in her lap and Fang in mine.

Even though I spent over ten years of my life in this godforsaken state, arriving back in California feels more like turning myself in for a crime I didn't commit than returning to a place full of happy memories.

"I see you're just staying the one night. Passing through?" The front desk attendant at the hotel asks. Her tone is suggestive, and if the smile she's flashing me is anything to go by, she's about to offer to show me around the shit small town my mother dragged me to during my senior year of high school.

I answer with a noncommittal hum, hitching my overnight bag higher on my shoulder as my phone dings.

The woman flutters her lashes as I pull it from my pocket. "Well, the hot tub closes at eight, but—" she leans forward and winks, "if you want to use it after hours, I won't say anything. Sometimes, I like to relax after I get off work."

I give her my best *what the fuck is wrong with you* stare before dropping my gaze to my phone.

TURTLE DOVE

> How's Hunter's parents? I miss you.
> 😢 I know, I know. So sappy.

I can't help the grin that curves my lips. I like it when she's sappy because I might as well be a sugar maple when it comes to her. How I managed to withstand her allure for so long, I'll never know. All I know is that I never want to be without Dove again.

Seizing the keycard from the woman—whose cheeks flush in embarrassment as she avoids my eyes due to my glaringly obvious dismissal—I head out of the main office without another word. The air is thick with petrichor from the afternoon rain, the parking lot nearly full as the hotel's patrons settle in for the evening.

I wait until I'm in my room before replying. Another ripple of guilt courses through me as I carry on my fabricated lie.

> I love the sap, and I miss you more.
> It's fine. They have chickens.

Dropping my bag onto the bed, I send her a picture of Hunter and his mother, who's holding a black chicken with a crazy hairdo and wearing a diaper. He sent it earlier as evidence, but also because I hadn't believed Carla now spends her days tending to a diaper-clad chicken.

Dove came clean about C.W. not really standing for her mother's initials. She admitted the trip she claimed she was taking was an excuse to leave for the weekend to target another douchebag. So I had to come up with a reason of my own for my absence.

Hunter was all too willing to provide an alibi,

which worked perfectly since he was already heading to his parents' anyway. He's been in a great mood since his little rendezvous with Bunny in the bathroom at The Tipsy Taco. I have a feeling they fucked like her namesake—even she's been friendlier since.

TURTLE DOVE

Eeee! So cute!

A picture comes through of her and Fang. Dove blows a kiss at the screen while the rat looks at her like she's crazy. A smile curves my lips again as I collapse into a chair and scrub the day's travel from my face.

Fuck, I miss them already.

TURTLE DOVE

We're headed to Bunny's for book club. I swear I'm going to make her tell me what happened in that bathroom.

Hunter won't tell me. If Bunny tells you, I think it's safe to say she wants him just as much as he wants her.

Dove's reply is almost immediate.

TURTLE DOVE

> Duh! I could have told you that!
> They love each other. She's just
> worried about getting hurt again.

> Anyway. Bunny's house has shitty
> service, so if you call later and I
> don't answer, that's why. Talk
> tomorrow?

I need a long, hot shower to ease my tense muscles. More than anything, I wish I'd just been truthful with Dove and told her what I was really doing.

> Talk tomorrow. And when I get
> home, I plan on having a very long,
> very serious conversation with your
> pussy while you discuss future
> living arrangements with my cock.

Just typing the words has me hard. If I hadn't lied, I'd FaceTime her so we could mutually masturbate to relieve the frustration of being apart for the first time in weeks.

TURTLE DOVE

Guilt eats away at me for lying to her. She's given me the strength I need to face my demons, but I refuse to drag her into my mess. I know she'd be by my side in a heartbeat if I asked her to come with me.

But now I finally understand why she doesn't want me there when she becomes the Doll.

My mother is unpredictable. And I won't put Dove in any situation that might put her in danger.

I can take care of myself, Songbird. I can hear her as though she's beside me—hands on her hips, a pretty scowl on her face, amusement dancing in her big blue eyes.

Turtle Dove

Even though I know she can take care of herself, I need to do this alone. I have to face this to live the life I want with Dove. Otherwise, there will always be a tiny speck of splattered ink on every page of our story, an ever-present blemish in the margins.

Steam rolls out of the small bathroom as I turn the shower as hot as it will go. The water scalds my skin, but I barely feel it. The pain is nothing compared to the terrors that occurred in the house I'll be visiting tomorrow.

For years, I suffered. Unable to walk away. Unwilling to face the proverbial monster under the bed. When I was old enough to know better, I should have stopped it. I could have left. Yet I did nothing.

What kind of sick fuck does that make me?

A traumatized one, Songbird. This is why we need to go to therapy.

Dove's words from a few days ago echo in my mind as I wipe the fog from the mirror. Since interviewing Ginny Tailor about the new family center she's opening, I researched their accommodations. Therapy happens to be one of them, and the branch near the Upper East Side has people who specialize in sexual trauma.

Dove is interested in various support groups, but I need something more solitary. I'm not ready to talk about what happened to me with a bunch of strangers.

My phone rings, startling me so abruptly I nearly stab the back of my throat with my toothbrush. I expect it to be Dove again, even though we already said goodnight, or maybe Hunter checking in. But when my mother's name flashes across the screen, all the tension that melted in the shower returns tenfold.

Each shrill ring tightens my chest. The feeling of a thousand insects skitter across my limbs.

It's like an out-of-body experience as I answer her call for the first time in months.

"Oh! I finally got you, my little songbird!"

Songbird.

Vomit rises in my throat, bitter against the minty foam of the toothpaste, when she uses the nickname I only want to hear from Dove's lips. I screw my eyes shut as memories flood the graveyard in my mind where I've buried them for so long.

A warm wetness where it shouldn't be. "It's okay, my little songbird. Mommy's going to make you feel good."

Frantic cries of embarrassment as she coos, "It's okay, Songbird. It's a perfectly normal thing for your body to do."

"Kiss me now, Songbird! Just like I taught you!"

"Wrenley?"

The room snaps back into focus. Panic surges through me. I clear my throat and press the mute button. Acrid bile mixes with sharp spearmint, and I vomit as she squeals, "Mommy misses you, sweetie. How are you? How's New York?"

It takes a moment to compose myself after spilling my stomach into the sink. I hate that my body reacts so violently to just the sound of her voice, how a single word drags up everything I've tried to lock away. A name that once made my skin crawl—until Dove turned it into something sacred.

After a deep breath, I unmute the phone. "I'm back in California. I'll be stopping by tomorrow."

Another squeal. I press my palm into my temple, trying to block out the throbbing that begins at her cries of joy. "Oh, baby boy! You have no idea how happy that makes me! Why aren't you here yet? Where are you? You're alone, right?"

The familiar warning edge sharpens her last question. I was never allowed to date, never permitted to show interest in a girl without my mother making thinly veiled threats about telling everyone what a disgusting little boy I was. She always said no one would believe me if she said *I* forced myself on *her*.

She always said men aren't victims, that women will always be believed over them.

I wasn't willing to take that chance in high school. Even in college, I was careful never to tell her my whereabouts.

"Yeah. It's just me." I keep my answers short. "I'm staying nearby. I'll be there tomorrow in the late afternoon."

There's a pause so thick with suspicion I can feel it through the phone. "Why didn't you come home, Wrenley?"

"Late-night work call," I lie, staring at my reflection in the mirror. "Hunter says hello, by the way."

It's a warning.

An indirect way of saying someone knows where I am. Someone expects me back in New York.

Her voice hardens. I can picture her gritting her teeth, her fake smile faltering as she speaks through them. "Well, tell him I say hello, too. I'll see you tomorrow then, my little songbird. I'm so happy you've come home."

She hangs up without waiting for a goodbye. And for some reason, her parting words feel final—like I've come to stay.

Or like she doesn't plan to let me go again.

I toss and turn all night, debating whether to call Dove regardless of the late hour, just to hear her voice.

In the end, I decide against it, and I don't sleep worth a damn.

Nothing has changed since I left.

The old two-bedroom house still needs a paint job, but the multitude of flower pots and various-colored blooms in the garden beds out front manage to make the chipped cream exterior look warm and cozy.

My mother's Camry sits in front of the ostentatious red garage. The color always made me feel like the house was a target—a giant bullseye. A complete contradiction to the rest of the aesthetic.

A predator lives here. Stay away.

And people did. Despite my mother's friendly demeanor and penchant for joining every social club that would have her, no one ever visited. She always went out, always needing to control how others saw her. Out there, they didn't see past her mask. They only saw a good mother and a son in desperate need of a father figure.

A fly on any random wall in this house could have told them tales that would churn their stomachs.

The freshly trimmed grass catches my attention. Who's taking care of it? Did she finally get a boyfriend? Or should I worry about her attentions turning to one of the neighborhood boys who mow lawns for easy cash?

My foot barely hits the first step before the door swings inward. My mother appears in the entryway, wearing a flowing sky-blue dress and a bright smile. Her long blonde hair is pulled back in a ponytail. She's the picture-perfect image of warmth and welcome, even if she towers over most of the women in town at five foot eleven.

"My sweet songbird has finally returned to me," she greets with wide arms.

I stop on the top step, neither returning her smile nor stepping into her hug. "Mother."

The side of her mouth twitches. For a moment, we're frozen. Just a boy and his mom. The person who should love and protect him from the world. I hate that the little boy inside me still wants his mother's love.

Just not the way she wants to give it.

A gentle breeze lifts strands of her hair, sending them drifting over her face. Her dress sways. She drops her arms with exaggerated disappointment. "Well, geez, Wrenley. You look like you've lost your best friend. What's wrong with you?"

"I'm not here to visit, Mother. We need to talk." My gut clenches. The steel nerve I've built up begins to liquefy into something cold and anxious.

She turns her back to me, leaving the door open as she storms inside. "What do we need to talk about, Wrenley? How you're coming back home?"

Following her is like wading into the ocean. You know you're at risk of the waves becoming tempestuous at a moment's notice, yet the water can be calm and warm before the storm.

Robyn Campbell *is* beautiful. It's part of why I hated Dove so much when we first met. Because no matter how deranged and fucked up my mother's actions are, I still think she's pretty.

Call it a coping mechanism. The woman is ugly as sin on the inside, and that's the difference between her and Dove. My girlfriend is beautiful, inside and out—even when she's stabbing men to death, covered in their blood.

"I'm not coming home. I'm staying in New York. Permanently." I set my keys and phone on the small kitchen table and sit as she flits around, gathering items to make tea. I have to admit the smell is nostalgic as she opens the bag of loose leaves while the kettle heats. It infuses the air with a warm, fruity fragrance with a subtle undercurrent of rose.

My mom is unresponsive as she begins to hum to herself, as though she didn't hear what I said. A second later, she chirps, "We should go to the store for lasagna ingredients. It's been so long since I made it for you."

She disappears down the hall without waiting for a reply. A few seconds later, my phone lights up with a message from Dove.

TURTLE DOVE

A smile touches my lips just before the air stirs beside my face. I jump, looking over my shoulder to see my mother standing over me, staring at my phone with a disapproving grimace. I didn't even hear her return.

Goosebumps break out along my skin. A shiver racks my body at her proximity. My muscles remember what my mind tries to forget.

"Is *she* why you're staying?"

I swallow. "It isn't only her."

She straightens and returns to the counter to prepare our tea.

I push my tongue against my cheek, fighting for the strength to say what I need to with the same eloquence Dove delivers her monologues.

"She's a pretty little thing."

I stare at the photo on my lock screen showing Dove and me cuddled up in bed. Her head is resting on my chest, my arm curling around her bare shoulder while the other is extended holding the phone. Fang is in it too, lying on his back in my armpit, squished against my side.

This is why I'm here. They say you can't choose your family.

But I did.

"You can't hurt me anymore." The words slip from my mouth before I can stop them. They aren't wrapped in an articulate bow, but as my mother freezes, I know they land exactly as intended. "What you did to me was wrong. You know it was."

Like sour milk, she curdles. Her shoulders hunch, her head dipping between them before she rolls it side to side, a grotesque mimicry of nonchalance. "Whatever do you mean, Songbird?"

"Don't call me that!" I snap, slamming my fist onto the table. My keys rattle, and the vibration makes my phone light up again. Dove's face stares back at me from the screen. I take a breath, steadying myself.

"You no longer have the privilege of calling me that." My voice is steel. "You need to stop calling me. I want you to leave me alone. As of this moment, you are no longer my mother, and I am no longer your son. And if I ever hear that you've hurt another child the way you hurt me, I will make sure you suffer."

Each word is slow, deliberate, thick with such disdain that it makes me want to gag. My leg bounces, restless, and when she slides a cup of pink, strawberry-scented tea toward me, I drink, hoping to soothe the tight dryness in my throat.

A heavy darkness coils inside me like smoke as the warm liquid courses through my body. I cling to it, let it fortify me like armor. "You are a disgusting, vile woman. You should be in jail. But we both know there's no point in reporting you. There's no evidence. And, just like you once told me, no one would believe me now." I lift my gaze from my phone to her. Her cornflower-blue eyes narrow in something like pity, as if I'm telling her about someone else's suffering.

"So this is me, getting the closure I need. After this, I never want to see your face again. You can't hurt me anymore, Mom."

The familiar pressure of tears builds, flooding my sinuses, burning beneath my eyes and into my jaw. I clench my teeth to keep them from falling. The darkness I wielded as a shield suddenly turns inward, its fangs bared at me, an unfamiliar panic rising at an alarming speed.

My gaze drops to the tea as my limbs grow heavy, my voice alien in my own ears as I rasp, "What did you do?"

She smiles. And just like that, the liquid in my stomach sours.

I think of Dove as the edges of my vision blur, then darken. I think of all the things we planned, the places we said we'd visit. The promises we made to each other over the last few weeks.

I'm sorry I wasn't strong enough, Turtle Dove.

The gleaming lemon-colored linoleum rushes toward me as I try to stand, but my legs buckle, sending me crashing to the floor. My head lolls, my brain sloshing like soup in a pot. I try to shake the haze away, but it only worsens, dragging me deeper.

Hands clamp around my biceps, and I jolt, clawing at the floor, desperate to escape the monster who has so easily reclaimed me.

"Shh. It's okay, my little songbird. Mommy's got you now." I want to retch as she smooths my hair back and presses a kiss to my forehead.

Please don't touch me. The little boy inside me sobs.

"Don't worry, sweetheart." Her voice is syrupy, sickly sweet. "When you wake up, Mommy will have your lasagna ready, and we can talk about you moving back home. With me. Where you belong."

Dove...

The last thing I see is a pair of big blue eyes.

Then, everything goes dark.

CALIFORNIA SUCKS.

Well, at least the northern part does.

It's so isolated I have to take an extra flight from a bigger airport just to reach the town where Wren's mother whisked him away in high school. And I'm not a snob about accommodations, but there's only one hotel with vacancies.

ONE.

Who is visiting this place?

It shouldn't be you, that's for sure.

As I drive through a town that looks abandoned—neglected stores and vacant streets—I release a long sigh and tap my heart-themed nails on the steering wheel.

I shouldn't be here.

But they say revenge is a dish best served cold.

And I am cold. Or... I was because Wren decided to fuck off with Hunter for the weekend, leaving me to sleep alone.

Technically, the saying means you're supposed to *think* about extracting revenge for it to be carried out in the best way. Plan. Prepare.

Not hop on a plane the second your boyfriend is out of town to murder his disgusting pedo mother.

A knot tightens in my gut as I recall everything Wren confided in me. He's still harboring so much animosity. Is it fair to take away his opportunity for closure? Should I have discussed this with him first?

I took my revenge when I was ready. But I needed the chaos, the violence—an outlet for all my pent-up rage.

I love my sweet songbird, but what *he* needs is four walls and someone licensed to help him start his healing journey.

Is that really your call to make, Turtle Dove?

I have a love-hate relationship with the fact that I can hear him at any given moment, as though he were really right beside me. It's become constant when he's not near. Sometimes it's comforting. Other times it drowns out my intrusive thoughts, and I need those to carry out my justice-seeking duties.

At a red light, I check my phone. Wren hasn't replied since I messaged him the second I got off the plane. It's late afternoon there, and all he's sent today is a simple *I love you.*

That's... not like him.

If necessary, I'll fly all night, even if it takes four layovers, to make it back to New York before he gets home in the morning.

The town Wren grew up in isn't the typical place you think of when you hear California. The roads are dusty, cracked, and riddled with potholes. The houses are sturdy but rundown, desperate for a good power wash. I do like that they're not stacked on top of each other, though.

It took some digging, but I found a floor plan for the home Wren's mother, Robyn, rents. There's a basement below ground, and the house sits on a corner lot, meaning there's extra space on both sides.

No one will hear her scream.

See? I did plan a little.

And it seems my luck just keeps rolling in.

My rental creeps toward the gaudy red garage with two vehicles parked outside. I plan to drive by a few times, then stop and ask for directions like I'm lost. But half a block away, one of the cars pulls out. I'm too far away to see the driver, but I pick up speed, trailing the light blue Camry as it heads toward the main street.

A little more time to study my target won't hurt. My research didn't indicate Robyn is seeing anyone.

You should've grabbed the license plate on the second car.

I can worry about that later, though. I follow the Camry to the local grocer, parking a few spots down on the opposite side of the row. I have to choose a place with a few empty spaces so I can back in. As a New Yorker, backing up and parallel parking are not my strong suits, so I need a spot with some breathing room.

I watch as Wren's mother steps out. Seeing her in person is surreal, after scouring the internet for the handful of photos that exist. Robyn Campbell is beautiful, though I loathe to admit it. I understand why Wren thinks we look alike—same wheaty blonde hair, similar blue eyes.

Though in height, I'm the equivalent of Bilbo Baggins, and she's Gandalf.

Don't do Gandalf dirty like that, Dove.

It must be where Wren gets his size from unless his good-for-nothing father is also as tall as a giraffe.

I stay a few steps behind as she grabs a cart and sets her beige crossbody in the baby seat. Robyn looks like every other middle-aged woman. Shopping for groceries, smiling at everyone who passes, and stopping to chat with people who greet her by name.

An upstanding citizen, fooling everyone with her

charm and good looks. No one would ever guess a monster lurks beneath her painted face.

Wren's initial reaction to me makes so much more sense now. He knew a monster when he saw one.

To stay inconspicuous, I steer my cart down an aisle, nerves fraying each second Robyn is out of sight. A relieved breath exits my lungs as I round the corner to see she's now coming down the same aisle the opposite way.

I grab a random can of pasta sauce and throw it in my cart along with—I check the bright orange box—chickpea pasta.

Huh. Sounds gross.

Robyn pays no attention to me as I sneak up beside her humming a tune I don't recognize, a dreamy look in her eyes as she browses canned tomatoes. Her purse sits open, her phone peeking out—easy pickings for any pickpocket worth their salt. I slow my cart beside hers.

"Excuse me?" I lace my voice with sugar. "Could you grab me a few cans of diced tomatoes with basil, please? The brand with the yellow label?"

Robyn perks up, snapping from her daydream. "Of course, honey. How many?"

"Oh, four would be lovely. Thank you."

As she busies herself with that, I scan the aisle to

ensure no one's watching. I slip her phone from her bag, flick it to silent, and shove it in my purse.

She turns, arms full of cans. The moment her gaze lands on me, she falters, nearly dropping them. I snatch two before they hit the ground. "Thank you so much. They make it hard for us short people sometimes."

Robyn stares, eyes wide, brows dipping like she's trying to place where she knows me from.

She doesn't. She can't. Wren and I aren't social media official, so if she's keeping tabs on him that way, she'd never make the connection.

"I'm so sorry." She laughs, shaking her head. "You just look so much like me. Wow! It's uncanny."

Duh, Dove. That's why she was staring at you like she saw a ghost.

"We do look similar, don't we?" I chuckle and shrug my shoulders. "They say if you've seen one blonde-haired, blue-eyed woman, you've seen 'em all."

Robyn lets out another loud laugh. "Too right. I'm sorry. I wasn't trying to be awkward."

"Oh, gosh, you're fine." I wave her off. "Thanks again. Have a nice day!"

Before she can respond, I beeline for the checkout with the items that I don't—and will never—need. Is chickpea pasta even a thing in New York? Or is it a California thing?

Wait… it's a gluten thing, isn't it?

Ugh. If I'm eating pasta, I want the real deal. Isn't there a grain-free flour that makes better noods?

Dialing Bunny, I slide into my car. "Did you know chickpea pasta exists? Please tell me you find that as gross as I do."

Her answer is a tummy grumble that I can hear clear through the phone before she releases the most disgusting belch I've ever heard from her. "Chickpea pasta fucks up my stomach. It's not that bad, though," she says weakly once she's exorcised her inner gaseous demons.

"What was that?" I snort a laugh as I drive away, intent on finding the elusive In-N-Out that Wren has on a pedestal. He claims they have the best burgers ever.

He's wrong. When it comes to chains, Shake Shack does, and no one can change my mind about that.

But… when in Rome…

"I think that pizza we ate yesterday was bad. I've been sick in bed all day."

I feel fine. Maybe she caught a stomach bug.

"Oh, poor baby. Why don't you ask Hunter to bring you some soup when he gets home tomorrow? Maybe he can kiss it and make it better," I coo in a baby voice.

Bunny stays quiet for a beat before an irritated sigh fills the speaker. "I did," she laments softly.

"Wow. You must really feel bad. DoorDash would have had it there way faster than Hunter. Duh."

The bright yellow arrow I'm looking for catches my attention, and I turn on my blinker.

Found it! Now, what did Wren say? I need to try it animal style?

"He said, and I quote, 'Sorry you aren't feeling well. I'm not in town, but even if I were, I don't want to get sick.'" She blows a raspberry.

"Whoa. What'd you do to piss off Detective Dick?" I cover the speaker as I place my order.

"Are you getting In-N-Out? Oh my god, fries and a shake sound so good," she groans.

"I thought you felt sick? And yes, I needed to see what Wren is always going on about. And don't deflect. What's going on with Hunter?"

Bunny's been tight-lipped about her and Hunter's night in the bathroom. She won't tell me what happened, no matter how hard I try to pry it out of her. I think it's safe to assume they had sex, and now she's terrified he's going to hurt her.

If I didn't know any better, I'd think Hunter's response was just him being a typical guy. Now that he got what he wanted, he's not interested anymore. But I *do* know better, and I know Hunter isn't like that.

Maybe he really just doesn't want to get sick.

"I think I'm going to throw up again. Call me when you're back and tell me everythi—" The line goes dead just as the sound of yesterday's regurgitated pizza cuts off her words.

I pop a French fry into my mouth and sip my strawberry milkshake as I head back to Robyn's, mindful to park on the street a few houses down, but still within sight of the driveway.

I don't have to wait long before her blue Camry pulls up, giving me just enough time to finish my food. Wren is crazy. The burger is nowhere near as good as Shake Shack.

Robyn carries in her groceries, and I let a few minutes pass, sipping on my shake while I pull her phone from my purse and switch it off silent mode. Once she's closed her front door, I slip my dagger up the sleeve of my jean jacket and tuck my bag beneath the seat.

Hopefully, she hasn't realized her phone is missing yet. Wren once told me she doesn't use it often because she'd rather talk to people in person. I'm banking on that one snippet of information.

As I approach the house, the neighborhood feels eerily quiet. No hum of lawnmowers, no kids playing in the street. Strange for a weekend afternoon, but it works to my advantage.

My heart hammers as I step onto the driveway. There's still time to turn back. I keep thinking that if I'm not meant to do this, Wren will call or text—some sign that the universe is intervening.

But my songbird is unusually quiet today. I know Hunter's parents wanted help around the house, but even he managed to text Bunny back.

A gentle breeze sways the hanging flower pots, sending a thick floral scent wafting over me. I don't have to knock because the second my foot hits the top step, the door swings open, and Robyn stands there, wide-eyed in confusion.

"Hi! I'm so sorry. I know this is probably weird!" I hold her phone out. Her eyes dip to it before narrowing with thinly veiled suspicion. "You dropped this at the store. I tried waving you down when you were leaving the parking lot, but you didn't see me. I hope it wasn't weird that I followed you home."

I'm a walking red flag.

Anyone with an ounce of stranger danger would know that, no matter how old or trusting they are.

Robyn just blinks, and a second later, the monstrous visage twisting her features melts into fake gratitude. "Oh, goodness! Thank you! I can't believe I didn't realize it was missing."

She takes the phone and widens the door as she steps aside. "Would you like to come in for a cup of tea?" She releases a breathy laugh, patting her ponytail. "I know, it's probably weird to invite a stranger in, but my son moved away, and I could use some help bringing some things up from the basement." She tosses up her hands and snort-laughs, rolling her eyes. "Yeesh, Robyn. You couldn't sound more like a murderer if you tried."

No wonder people like her. She oozes the same friendly assurance Freddy did, even making a lurid joke sound harmless.

I let out a giggle, smiling at her. She's making this too damn easy.

But it reminds me a little too much of myself—how I lull my victims into a false sense of security before I strike. This woman has over a foot on me and can probably toss me over her shoulder like a sack of potatoes.

She's not weak like a man. I'm not a vice for her. From what I know, she sexually abused Wren but wasn't otherwise physically violent. My guard is up because I know what she is, but I'm not getting any *"I'm going to lock you in the basement"* vibes.

"I'd love to help. I know I'd want someone to do the same for my parents if I moved away." I step inside and take in my surroundings.

The living room is small, with a single loveseat and an old recliner that's seen better days. Brightly colored crochet animals lay in a pile on a small table next to an unfinished project. Photos of her and Wren clutter the walls, a montage of their life together.

Robyn leads me down a long hall, past the kitchen. I notice there are two cups on the table. "So, where did your son move to?"

"New York. He's only been gone a few months but can't wait to come home. Says it's just awful there," she lies, her voice thick with syrupy sympathy. "Have you ever been? I don't think I've seen you around. We don't get many visitors in our little town."

"Oh, I love New York. It's such a shame he doesn't like it. I'm just passing through on my way to San Diego," I say as we reach a wooden door at the end of the hall.

As she opens it, a thud sounds from beyond the kitchen area. My breath catches. Per the floor plan, I know the bedrooms are where the sound came from, and a sense of dread creeps along my bones.

Wren was sure she never touched anyone else. But what if he was wrong? What if, now that she doesn't have him in her grasp any longer, she set her sights on someone else?

"Oh, that's the dog. When I saw you coming up the driveway, I put him away. He's not real friendly to strangers." She ushers me through the doorway and down the rickety stairs.

All my senses are on high alert as we descend into a dimly lit room that smells muggy and fresh all at the same time. When I reach the bottom of the stairs, I spot a washer and dryer against the far wall, the source of the clean scent.

Another thud sounds from upstairs—closer this time. My grip tightens as I slide my dagger into my palm, eyes snapping to the open doorway.

It's that moment in a thriller when the music builds, and you know the jump scare is coming—but that knowledge doesn't make it any less terrifying. Something about this entire situation sends my serial killer Spidey senses into overdrive.

"Dove!" Wren's sluggish cry from upstairs sends my heart plummeting to my stomach.

What are you doing here, Songbird?

Blue flashes in my peripheral.

I jerk back just in time, slashing my dagger across Robyn's body as she lunges at me. The blade skims her stomach, slicing fabric and flesh. She shrieks, clutching the wound as blood pools between her fingers. It's shallow, nowhere near fatal, but enough to drop the giantess onto her ass.

"What did you do to him?" I seethe, straddling her in an instant.

She thrashes beneath me, one arm pushing at my

shoulder while the other presses to her bleeding stomach. "If I can't have him, no one will!"

"Dove!" Wren cries again. A crash follows, and my head whips toward the stairs just in time to see him stumbling down like a newborn foal, unsteady and disoriented.

"Baby, what did she do to you?" I growl, slamming the pommel of my dagger into Robyn's cheek before shoving off her and rushing to Wren's side.

He greets me with open arms, sighing in relief the moment his eyes meet mine. "Thank God. I thought she hurt you," he breathes against my hair.

"Get away from her, Wrenley!" Robyn snarls. "She's poisoned your mind against me!"

The aggression rips from my throat before I can stop it. I tear from Wren's grasp, blade poised to sink deep. "You disgusting, despicable—"

Wren's arm locks around my waist, yanking me back, but not before my weapon finds purchase, biting into the meat of her calf as she scrambles away.

"Dove, no." His harsh command mingles with her pained scream.

"Go back upstairs, Songbird. You don't have to watch me do this." I twist in his arms, clutching his shirt as I stare up at him, vision blurred with unshed tears. "Let me avenge you."

"You have no right to call him that!" Robyn sobs,

her voice raw and shaking. "He's mine! My little songbird!"

"Baby, please." My forehead presses to his chest, my tears soaking his shirt. "She can't live after what she's done to you. I know I should've asked first, but I—"

"Stop, Turtle Dove." Wren's fingers slip under my chin, tilting my face up. He kisses me softly. Once. Twice. The third time, his tongue sweeps against my lips, and I let him in, letting him ravage me.

Behind us, Robyn sniffs. "Wrenley, how could you?"

"I love you so fucking much for wanting to do this for me," he murmurs, pulling back just enough for me to see the hazy devotion in his eyes. He sways slightly on his feet.

His fingers smooth my hair back as his deep brown gaze shifts—first to me, then over my head to his mother. I glare at her over my shoulder as he continues, voice steadier than before. "But this is something *I* need to do."

"Baby, I already told you—you're not a killer." I reach up, cupping his cheek.

Wren smiles. It's full of so much love and reverence that my heart aches from the force of it.

"Now that I have my angel of death at my side," he murmurs, "I'm feeling pretty invincible, Turtle Dove."

WRENLEY

"Did you really come to avenge me, Turtle Dove?" I ask before downing the last of my bottled water.

Whatever my mother drugged me with has my head pounding, and my body still feels weird, like I'm wearing someone else's skin. I vaguely remember her dragging me into my old bedroom, lifting me onto my bed. I fought the effects as hard as I could but ultimately lost the battle.

Until I heard Dove's voice.

Like a shimmering light in the haze, her bubbly tone gave me the strength to push against the murky waters trying to keep me under.

I've never felt the type of panic I did when I realized Dove was really here, in California—in my mother's house, talking to her.

"Of course I did, Songbi—"

Mother's low growl cuts her off. Dove's hand flies out, backhanding her across the face before she resumes shackling her in the chains we found next to an old toolbox. "Hey! What did I tell you? Shut it."

Dove stands, dusting off her hands, surveying her work before turning to the other things we found. "I'm a thousand percent sure this house belonged to a serial killer before you lived here. Or she's picked up some new, untoward tendencies because this looks like a serial killer starter kit."

Besides the chains—which have locks—and the toolbox, there's a tarp, rope, and a crowbar. Either Dove is right, or my mother had a hobby I never knew about. A surge of anger splinters through my chest at the thought.

"Did you hurt anyone else?" The question is for my mother, though I step to where Dove stands and pick up the crowbar.

Like I told her earlier, having Dove with me makes me feel invincible. Alone, I panicked, drowning in the past. But this woman flew across the country to confront my demons for me, and that gives me a renewed sense of purpose.

I *can* do this.

"You don't have to do this, Wren," Dove whispers. "You can say what you need to say and walk away and never look back. You can let me handle it. Or, if you want her to live—and I won't judge if that's what you want—we can leave together."

"Listen to her, Wrenley, baby. You don't have to do this." Mother's syrupy lilt makes my skin crawl.

Dove turns, ready to shut her up again, but my body moves first. With a roar, I pivot and stride forward, bringing the crowbar down on one of her restrained hands. She shrieks as her skin splits, blood spilling down her fingers, splattering as I strike again. This time, I hear the crunch of knuckles beneath the steel.

"Did you hurt anyone else?" I yell into her tear-streaked face, shaking with rage.

"Wren! Baby, stop!" Dove grabs my elbow, tugging on it before I can strike again. "You're going to give yourself a head rush! And I haven't put down a tarp yet! Do you know how hard blood is to get out of concrete?" She steps on my foot to try and gain lever-age, trying to pry my arm down.

"I didn't touch anyone else, I swear! You're my only special boy!"

Her words make me impossibly furious.

After all those years of feeling so hopeless, I finally hold the power.

Dove is wrong.

I am a killer.

Shaking her off, I bash my mother's other hand

where it's chained to the arm of the chair. "You were supposed to protect me!"

Bits of bone and splattered blood fly through the air.

Dove barely registers above Mother's screams. "Oh, this is going to be a fucking mess to clean, but go on, Songbird. Have at it."

A sickening squelch fills the basement as I reduce her hands to bloody, meaty stumps. "You should have kept me safe! You should have loved me like a mother is supposed to!"

"Peroxide. Maybe she has some peroxide," Dove mutters, heading upstairs.

"Why did you do it?" My voice cracks. Vulnerable. Tears flood my eyes. "Why did you hurt me?"

"I didn't mean to hurt you, my sweet boy." Her voice is weak, her ashen skin glistening with sweat. "Mommy just loves you so much. I wanted you all to myself. I thought if I made you feel good, you'd stay with me forever."

She sounds so earnest, like she genuinely still believes what she did was okay.

Dove reappears as my tears fall. Her soothing hand slides up my back, then down again, trying her best to comfort me. "He would have been yours forever if you'd just acted like a sane mother." Her voice is thick with emotion, and I don't have to look at her to know she's crying. I can hear the pain in her voice as she speaks. "Adults who prey on children are the worst kind of predators. You deserve what you're about to get, Robyn."

Mother fixes Dove with a scowl that distorts her face into something monstrous. "You little bitch. Do you think you've won? Don't you think it's funny that he chose *you* when you look exactly like *me*?" Her laughter is manic. "He'll see me every time he looks at you, little girl. Every time you fuck, he'll be thinking of *me*."

Dove stiffens beside me momentarily. Just the thought of my mother's words getting to her, especially knowing that Dove is aware that I *did* see my mother when I looked at her at first, is enough to send me into another blind rage.

I can't bear the thought of Dove having to think that. Ever.

"When I look at her, all I see is a woman you could only dream of being. The woman I fucking love!"

Dove jumps back as I bring the crowbar down on my mother's face in rapid succession like I'm fighting for my life.

And, in a way, I am.

Fighting for my lost innocence.

For the childhood she stole.

For a future free of her sins.

Her jaw unhinges, dripping blood as it dangles grotesquely, like something you'd see in a horror film. I don't know if it's the adrenaline or if it's because I want this monster dead, but my stomach doesn't churn. Instead, my insides are steel as I swing the crowbar like a baseball bat. The force of the blow knocks over the chair, and she hits the concrete with a wet thud and a crunch as her skull explodes.

Blood pools through the sweaty, sticky locks falling from her ponytail. Her body convulses as it bubbles in her throat, spilling from the space where her jaw was, desperate whimpers of pain escaping the open cavity in a wheezy song of death.

Dove crouches, smiling at Mother's rolling eyeball. "Don't worry," she coos. "I'll take great care of him."

Seconds later, Robyn Campbell dies the gruesome death she deserves.

The adrenaline fades, and my stomach turns. I stagger away, vomiting pink bile onto the concrete.

Dove's hands rub my back. "It's okay, baby. I got you."

When I finish, I wipe my mouth and pick her up, burying my face in her neck as I carry her upstairs. She clings to me like a koala, whispering soothing things into my ear, like how I'm safe now and how she's never going to leave me.

I'm covered in blood and bits of body parts I don't

want to think about. When I set Dove down, I see it's on her too. I strip her down, motioning for her to get into my bed before undressing and joining her. She lets me intertwine our limbs as we lie on our sides, staring at each other as the time passes. She knows this is what I need—to surround myself with her presence.

Eventually, I ask, "Does killing her make me a monster?"

Dove smiles somberly. "Do you think *I'm* a monster, Wren?"

"No." I shake my head. "You're the strongest, most beautiful thing I've ever seen. You gave me the strength to face her. I don't think I could have done it without you by my side. You make me a stronger man, Dove."

I draw her impossibly closer, gently cupping her cheek to tilt her head, my lips desperate for hers. "I'm in awe of every part of you, and it terrifies me how much I want to claim all of you—all your strength, your love, your demons." I punctuate each point with another kiss, pouring everything I feel into my touch. "I never want to be without you again. You make me whole, and I love you so damn much I'm scared it's going to drive you away."

"You could never drive me away, Songbird." She smiles, her tears mingling with our lips, the salty taste peppering her words. "I love you so incredibly much, Wrenley Campbell. I never imagined feeling this intensely for anyone, but I promise you have me—body, heart, and soul. No matter what our past holds, our future is together. Okay?"

"Okay, Turtle Dove."

"You know turtle doves mate for life, right?" she asks with a wolfish grin. "That means you're stuck with my pretty, pink palette until the end of time. How do you feel about a pink suit for work?"

Chuckling, I nudge her nose. "Mating for life, I'm okay with. A pink suit? Never gonna happen."

<u>Dove</u>

A loud grumble from my stomach signals my need for the bathroom again. "Okay, usually my stomach is much stronger than this. I'm blaming it on the In-N-Out, Songbird. It wasn't *that* great, by the way."

Wren finishes tying off his side of the rope securing the tarp we wrapped Robyn's body in, then shoots me a look of sheer betrayal. "You went without me? I told you I wanted to take you for your first time!"

His pout is adorable, and now I feel absolutely awful for telling him I went. "We can go again? After we dump this in the giant-ass woods and get cleaned up. Maybe I just ordered wrong?" I offer with a weak shrug.

It took over two hours to clean up his mess. Thank

god Robyn had a Costco-sized bottle of hydrogen peroxide, and the blood was fresh enough to scrub away without too much trouble. Now, all that's left is waiting for nightfall before we haul her out to the deep, dark Redwoods.

By the time anyone finds her, the animals will have picked her clean. She may be well-liked in the community, but Wren says it's the kind of town where no one asks questions and everyone has secrets.

At his silence, I shift from my crouch at the end of the tarp and sink to my knees beside him. "Are you okay?"

He nods, pulling me into his arms, crushing me against his chest. "You can't imagine the terror I felt when I thought she hurt you."

"It's okay. I'm here. I'm alright." I repeat the words as he holds me close. It's been like this since we left his bed—Wren needing to see me, touch me, hold me, just to remind himself that I'm here, that I'm real.

I've never felt fear while doing what I do. Murdering vile men has always been something I feel so passionately about that the adrenaline makes me strong enough to outsmart my victims.

But now, I understand. The sheer panic when I realized it was him, not a dog, making those sounds— it made me sick. I'd never been so scared for someone else in my life. I thought she'd hurt him, and I was going to make her death a long, excruciating one if Wren had let me.

As it is, I worry this will haunt him. That Robyn has found another way to scar my songbird—to leave her mark on his soul.

"I love you, Dove," Wren says, as if he can hear where my thoughts are spiraling. He pulls back, tilting my head up so our eyes meet, his thumbs brushing softly over my cheeks. "*You*. I only see you, baby."

There isn't a shred of doubt or hesitation in his gaze. I smile and pull him to me, sealing our lips together after I whisper, "I know, Songbird. I know."

WRENLEY'S RETCHING does not make a euphonious accompaniment to the screams clawing their way out of Billy Tweely's throat.

"Geez, you'd think I was killing you or something," I tease the man who looks about five seconds away from passing out or joining my songbird in emptying his stomach. "We're not even at the good part yet."

With one final swipe, my dagger severs the last stubborn sinew of Billy's penis, and the man passes out mid-shriek before I can even reach for the soldering iron to cauterize the wound.

"I think it's time to get this sharpened," I mutter, assessing my favorite weapon before spinning to see my boyfriend still bent over, the back of his hand pressed to his mouth.

"Aww, baby. I thought you were jealous when I was

touching it earlier." I dangle the mangled flesh back and forth like a wriggling fish on a hook. Wren looks at me over his shoulder—then promptly throws up again.

"Yup. Nope. Not jealous anymore," he gasps between heaves.

I cauterize the wound before Billy bleeds out, then skip across the room to check on my man. "What did I tell you about doggie bags? Now it's gonna take longer to clean up."

"Turtle Dove, that's the least of my worries at the moment." Wren's weak tone tugs at my heartstrings. Removing my mask, I run a soothing hand up and down his back.

"Baby, I ask this with love—but I watched you bash a head in without flinching. What gives?"

"My dick is experiencing sympathy pains," he rasps before hunching over again.

At this point, he's just dry-heaving. I try to keep my laugh contained, but it bubbles up anyway, escaping as an unladylike snort. "You sound like a cat throwing up a hairball."

"Will you just hurry up already?" He waves me off, straightening as he runs a hand through his hair. "We have someplace to be, and at this rate, we're gonna be late."

Billy stirs, groaning as he teeters on the edge of consciousness. I twirl back toward my present, slipping my mask on with a flourish to remind my songbird exactly whose special day it is. "Hey! You only turn thirty once, and last time I checked, today is *my* birthday. I'll cut off dicks if I want to."

"Dick, Dove. Singular."

"Keep rushing me, Songbird, and it'll be plural."

THE TIPSY TACO is busier than usual, and as soon as Wren and I round the bar, I see why.

Pink sparkly garland ropes off the section around the pool tables, where a giant rose-gold "thirty" balloon floats above a tower of pink-and-white-topped cupcakes. A banner reading Happy Birthday, Dove hangs above a buffet table draped in pink, laden with tiny taco shells and all the fixings.

Most of our coworkers mingle, while Vixey darts between tables, balancing a tray of pink drinks. Everyone gives Bunny and Hunter a wide berth—the two of them clearly in the middle of an argument that has my best friend's face blotchy with frustration.

"Baby." My chest swells, and I grip Wren's arm as he watches our friends with an annoyed expression. "Is this supposed to be a surprise party for me?"

His irritation melts into affection as his gaze slides to mine. "It was. But it looks like those two can't stop bickering long enough to answer their damn phones!" The last part is said loudly and aggressively as we approach them.

Bunny jumps, her eyes widening as Hunter pivots toward us. "Shit! Happy birthday, Love Dove!" she shouts, throwing her arms in the air and waving her hands to get everyone's attention.

A chorus of voices joins in as all eyes turn to me. "Happy birthday, Dove!"

"Aww, you guys shouldn't have. Thank you!" I lean into Bunny while Wren pulls Hunter a few feet away, and everyone resumes whatever they were doing before we arrived.

Given the time it took us to clean up, go home, shower, and get ready, I'd say we're over an hour late.

"Everything okay?" I ask Bunny. "You look like you need a trip to the alley to scream."

"It's fine!" Bunny breathes out, too quickly. "Hunter is just being... Hunter."

"Hot as hell? Big dick energy? Keeps begging to fuck your brains out in the bathroom again?" I waggle my brows.

"I heard that first part, Turtle Dove," Wren calls over his shoulder.

"Me too, doll. I'm flattered," Hunter adds with a smirk.

Bunny levels me with a flat look as I wink at her. "I don't hear a denial from either of you this time."

"You're lucky I love you," she mutters as Vixey bounces over.

And by bounce, I mean she literally trips at the last minute and has to hop a few times to regain her balance.

"Happy birthday, Dove!" she cries, throwing her arms around me. "Here! This is for you!"

Bunny stiffens as Vixey shoves a Baby Doll Killer plushie into my hands. "Isn't it cute?"

My best friend and I exchange a glance before looking back at the tall girl whose honey eyes glow with excitement. "I thought maybe you could put it on your desk! You know, because you write about her!"

A relieved sigh whooshes from my throat. "Thank you, Vixey. That's so thoughtful!"

"You're welcome! Anyway, I gotta get back to work, but happy birthday again!" She flounces off with a whimsical air about her after throwing Bunny a smirk that practically screams *ha, your friend likes me, and there's nothing you can do about it.*

"I hate her," Bunny grumbles.

"Why? She's sweet, and she has killer style." I make a mental note to ask Vixey where she got her hot pink cargo pants before looking at my present.

"No one is *that* nice," Bunny snips. "There's just something *off* about her. I'm telling you."

"Excuse me, ma'am. *I'm* that nice. Now stop being mean to the poor girl and look how cute this is!" I hold up the plushie—a mini version of me, complete with a garter and dagger strapped to its thigh.

There's a card attached to the hand with the Etsy info for the seller. I pull it up in the app and find an entire shop dedicated to Baby Doll Killer merch."Ooh. Maybe I should order a ton and leave them at the scenes like calling cards."

"Oh, good," Bunny deadpans. "Then they can slap a serial killer-endorsed banner on the website. Hashtag licensed merch. And Hunter can link that directly back to you."

"I can link what back to her?" Hunter asks as he and Wren join us.

My boyfriend slips his arms around my shoulders, pulling me back against him just as Bunny snaps, "Mind your own business!"

Hunter slaps his open palm against the edge of the pool table beside us before stepping into her space, pointing a finger at her. "Listen, little rabbit, I've had about enough of your mouth today—"

Bunny snaps her teeth at his outstretched digit and snarls, "Funny, you were singing a different tune last night!"

Wren and I exchange wide-eyed looks before discreetly backing away from the two of them.

"Is it just me, or is she extra pissy lately?" Wren whispers, grabbing two drinks from Vixey's tray as she passes and handing one to me. The liquid shimmers with edible glitter, swirling through the pink alcohol, crisp and fruity on the nose.

"You'd think she'd be happier considering they're sleeping together."

"Did she finally admit it?"

I shake my head, eyeing our best friends. "No. But look at them. He's seconds away from sitting her on that pool table and showing it some very dirty moves."

Wren chuckles and sits at a nearby table, pulling me between his legs. "Speaking of dirty moves, while I did help set up this party, I can't wait to get you home so I can give you *my* present."

"Oooh." I wind my arms around his neck, relishing the way his eyes darken, his thighs flexing as I press into him without fully climbing into his lap. "Is it your gorgeous cock wrapped in a pretty pink bow?"

He laughs, kissing me softly. "No, but I can make that happen."

Wren leans in for a deeper kiss, but a sharp squeal makes us both jump.

"Are you two together?" Cecilia shrieks, nearly shattering my eardrums.

Wren and I exchange baffled glances. "We've been together for a while now, Cecilia," I tell her.

"How long is a while? You'd never know with the way you two carry on at the office," Sharon chimes in, standing beside her friend, who gapes at us like we just murdered her dog.

Wren leans in, voice low against my ear. "I just had you for lunch on my desk Thursday. What do they think we do when we lock the door?"

Giggling, I tell the women, "I guess we're just really good at keeping secrets." I glance back at my man with a knowing smile. "Aren't we, Songbird?"

WREN'S FINGERS tighten in my hair, the prominent veins of his cock sliding against my tongue as he hits the back of my throat. Saliva pools from the corners of my mouth, *"erotic and aesthetically pleasing,"* as Wren once told me.

"Fuck, Turtle Dove. It's your birthday. I should be the one on my knees." His head tips back, another curse falling from his lips as I suck harder, swirling my tongue around him while he pulls out.

I speak against his tip like it's a microphone. "How many times do I have to tell you, Songbird? It's my birthday. I get to do what I want."

Wren moans as I trail my tongue along his shaft until my chin presses against his balls. I suck each one into my mouth, massaging them with my lips before kissing my way back up, savoring every whispered curse.

I love watching him unravel, surrendering to the pleasure I give. Love the way he loses himself to the deep, euphoric bliss that permeates the body when you trust your partner. Our give and take is instinctual—an ebb and flow like rhythmic ocean waves.

This is what pure contentment is.

Wren jackknifes up, momentarily choking me as he lodges deep in my throat, gripping my shoulders to haul me onto him. "Get up here and hold onto the headboard, birthday girl."

I obey, throwing my head back as he lowers me onto his cock. His first thrust is painstakingly slow, but then he picks up his pace, kissing down my throat as he grips my hips, pulling me onto him while propelling his own upward.

"I haven't even started your birthday spankings," he murmurs into my neck before his palm strikes my ass.

Pleasure spikes through my spine. Wren digs his fingers into my flesh, grinding me down on him. My nipples tighten, toes curling as my orgasm coils in my belly.

Another sharp slap. "Are you going to count for me, Turtle Dove?"

"Three," I squeal as his palm lands again.

"You're so fucking good for me." He nips at my nipple, my back arching deeper.

"Four," I cry, fisting his hair and holding him to my chest.

He pulls me forward as he reclines, guiding me to ride him. His hand tangles in my hair, his other striking my ass, building me higher.

"Fuck me, Dove. Ride me until you make a mess all over my cock."

I use the headboard for leverage, bouncing against him, counting every sharp smack until my voice breaks. Sparks detonate under my skin, pleasure coiling tighter, sharper.

"Baby, I'm going to come."

"That's right, Turtle Dove." Wren takes over, pistoning into me, striking that sweet spot over and over until stars explode behind my eyes. "Fuck, you're gripping me so tight. I'm coming, too."

Moans and cries tangle as we chase our release, bodies moving in tandem to stretch the moment longer.

"Fuck, Songbird." My fingers ache as I pry them from the headboard, slumping against his chest. "Best birthday gift ever."

Wren chuckles, tracing lazy patterns down my spine. "That wasn't your gift."

Fang whines outside the door, scratching to be let in, cutting me off before I can ask what else he has planned. Wren slides from bed, tossing on boxer briefs before letting our dog inside.

"Sorry, little rat. I was busy desecrating your mother, and your innocent eyes didn't need to see that." He lifts Fang, nuzzling their noses together before setting him on the bed.

"I prefer the term worship!" I curl onto my side and pull up the sheet, fisting a hand in my hair to prop my head up as I watch him disappear down the hall.

Fang groans and puts a paw over his face and I can hear Wren laughing from down the hall.

"See? This is why we lock you out of the bedroom now," I explain to my pup as I ruffle his head fur.

A few moments later, Wren appears with an elongated pink box. "*This* is your gift, Turtle Dove." He hands it to me and perches on the edge of the bed as I scramble to a sitting position to open the box. "Happy birthday."

"Baby, you didn't have to get me anything!" My tone denotes my excitement as I tear the lid off and rip into the white tissue paper.

As I take in what lies inside, my breath catches. A decorative dagger gleams up at me. It's the full length of my hand, with a glittering onyx blade and a pink shimmering hilt decorated with black and pink charms in the shape of bows and skulls. Hand-painted doves rest at the base of the tang.

"Do you like it?" Wren asks as a tear rolls down my cheek.

"I love it," I whisper, not trusting my voice to not crack if I speak any louder.

"There's an inscription on the back," he says quietly, almost as if he's unsure what my reaction will be.

I turn it over to see silvery words etched into the steel.

For life.

"Just like turtle doves," Wren whispers. "I love you."

"I love you, too. Thank you, Songbird. This is beautiful and I will cherish it always." I launch myself into his arms, sending Fang flying across the mattress.

Wren laughs, holding me while ensuring Fang doesn't fall. "This is what our forever looks like, Turtle Dove."

I push his hair off his forehead as I grin through my happy tears. "Does this mean you're going to keep going on kills with me?"

He smiles before kissing me softly. My body comes alive again as he softly groans against my lips. "I'll go, but only to be your muscle. You can keep being the vengeful vigilante."

The soft thud of Fang getting off the bed is lost as Wren shifts me back against the pillows, pulling the sheet from my naked body. He takes the dagger and places it back in the box, setting it on the nightstand before joining me in bed.

"Hmmm, the Doll and her dagger."

"I like the sound of that, Turtle Dove."

I pull him to me, sealing our lips together as I wrap my legs around his waist.

Though he's much taller than me, I feel like we fit together like a puzzle piece. I accept Wren for who he is and am in awe of all he's overcome, and he treasures all of me—even the darkest parts. We were both missing a part of our soul the other makes whole.

And right now—I've never felt more complete.

Love in the Time of Serial Killers.
By Wrenley Campbell
Senior Investigative Journalist

WHEN I RETURNED to the city after a decade away, it was for one reason and one reason only.

I wanted to meet the Baby Doll Killer.

Not only did I admire her aptitude for seeking out and cleansing the city of the filth that scours it, but I respected her. She had the audacity to film herself, to send the footage to the police along with the evidence of her victims' alleged crimes. It wasn't just vengeance—it was a statement.

The Doll became my obsession. I revered her. I marveled at her. And, if I'm being honest, I wanted to stand before her—to meet her as an ally, of course.

That's why I applied for a job at Metro Media, the city's leading source of information on the notorious masked killer. M.M.'s top journalist, Dove Carroway, always had the inside scoop on the Doll. I assumed—ignorantly, I might add—that I could tag along and reap the benefits simply by existing.

I was entirely wrong.

Not only was I mistaken in thinking I could usurp a colleague's hard-earned position, but I was grossly misguided in assuming that, as a man, I could cultivate a better relationship with the Doll than a woman could. That I could charm my way into her trust, persuading her to pass along information to me instead of to the woman who had rebuilt this firm through sheer determination and relentless hard work.

If you think this article reads like a love letter to my colleague, you'd be absolutely right.

Dove and I didn't start off well. In fact, I'd wager she would have been justified in getting me fired more than once. But the longer we worked together, the more I began to understand exactly the kind of woman she is.

We bonded over our shared respect for the Baby Doll Killer—what she stands for, what she represents. And, with Dove's permission, I'll say this: we connected over a past we both know too well, a deeply rooted trauma that mirrors those the Doll seeks to avenge.

I came to understand why Dove made the Doll her

singular focus. She doesn't just report on her—she under-
stands her. She's lived through it, survived it, and used
her harrowing past to carve out a future. It's why her
readers feel so deeply when they consume her work. She
pours every ounce of herself into it. And, in the midst of
our working relationship, she gave me the strength to do
the same—to face my own past and reclaim my life.

Dove Carroway is the strongest person I've ever met.
It's no wonder I fell for her—because anyone who knows
her does. It's inevitable.

My purpose for returning to New York is no longer
confined to the Doll and my reckless need to meet her.
Some might call my obsession with her a mistake, but
that obsession led me to the greatest "mistake" of my life.

So, to the Doll—whoever you are—thank you.

Thank you for speaking for the children who cannot.

For seeking justice when no one else will.

For giving me the strength I never knew I had.

And for, however unintentionally, introducing me
to the love of my life.

I watch nervously as Dove's eyes turn glossy,
her baby blues skimming each line with careful scrutiny. I know the exact moment she finishes—she
exhales a breath she's been holding since halfway

through the article and sinks back into her plush, pink chair.

She doesn't speak right away, and the silence stretches until I can't take it any longer. "Well? What do you think?"

She smiles. Dove's smile is the most beautiful thing I've ever seen, but this time, it holds something different—something life-changing.

"I love it," her reply is soft.

Without looking at me, she reaches for her mouse and clicks publish. The simple motion tightens my chest before warmth surges through me, flooding every nerve. I can't help myself—I spin her chair around and pull her into my arms.

"I love you," I murmur.

"I love you too. And this?" She pulls back and nods to her computer screen. "This is incredible work. You did good, Songbird."

The simple praise means more to me than she'll ever know.

Dove whips a hand in front of my face and taps a nail to my nose. "But don't think this means you're gonna start writing about the Doll, because that's never happening."

Ah, there it is.

I chuckle, catching her pink-and-white marbled

fingernail in my palm. "Don't worry. I've decided I much prefer keeping the Doll all to myself."

"For life?" she teases, leaning in until her watermelon-painted lips hover just above mine.

I curl our hands together, pressing my forehead to hers as my thumb strokes the bare spot on her ring finger—the one I intend to embellish soon. "For life."

Want to know what happened in the bathroom between Bunny and Hunter?

Sign up for an exclusive bonus chapter and sneak peek into book two of the Serial Killer Book Club.

I think I'm in my dark rom-com era, and I'm loving it.

I got the idea for this story as soon as I returned from a girls' trip last year. I'd planned on coming home and writing a Christmas book, but two weeks later, I had ten thousand words and an outline that was making me laugh so hard that I just knew I had to pursue this project instead.

Dove and Wren came together so perfectly in my head, their trauma, their love, their I-want-to-hate-you-but-I-also-want-to-fuck-you attitudes. If you've read my debut novel, Where the Flowers Bloom, you know I like to explore grief as a significant theme and how everyone experiences it differently. I think the same can be said of traumas.

I've had multiple conversations with people who went through similar experiences since I started the

Angels of Désirer series as well, which also explores these heavier themes of what can happen to children when they've been failed by their families or the system. And each story was similar, yet so vastly different, and that's what I tried to show through Dove and Wren's characters.

It was really important to me to highlight Wren's trauma as well. I think, not only as a man but also as a man who was consistently made to feel like it was his own fault, not just for what happened to him but also for not being able to walk away from his mother—I feel like society doesn't pay as much attention to these stories when they are coming from anyone other than a female and that needs to change.

Both men and women are abused. Both men and women can be abusers.

We can all take back our lives and change our stories. Some of us just need a little more help than others. So, to have Dove be that person for Wren really allowed me to craft a strong female and sort of flip the script where we got to see a woman taking on that role instead of the male.

I'm happy to give a strong voice to all the FMC's for this series.

And I'm excited to see what comes next for them.

Acknowledgments

To my team: I love you. I couldn't do this without you.

Jessica, Cady, Ashley, and Lauren, for all the hours you sat and agonized over these characters with me and all the laughs that we had, I can't thank you enough. For the endless chats and voice messages, the tears, the fears, and all the freaking chickens, I'm just so incredibly thankful for all of you.

My proofreaders, Heather and April.

My editor, Samantha. WWSD. I'm part of the team now. You're never getting rid of me.

Victoria with Cruel Ink Author Services. I'll never be able to craft another blurb without you. Thank you so much for removing the stress and creating a fantastic blurb.

Charly, my cover designer, just... WOW! I went into that intake form with no clue of what I wanted and just a bunch of ideas of what I didn't like, and in ONE take, it was like you reached into my brain and created everything I envisioned. I'm so in love with the cover, the graphics, and the aesthetic of the entire series. You're absolutely amazing.

To my husband, Mr. Darby. Thank you so much for putting up with me and being my turtle dove. This book nearly destroyed me—let's be honest, my impossible timeline is what did me in—but you sat through it all with a smile on your face and understood that I needed to put in the long hours in the office. I appreciate all the support you continue to shower me with.

As always, last but not least, thank you to the readers who continue to take a chance on the Darbyverse. Thank you to the Darby Darlings, the hot chicken hunnies; without you, I'd have drowned a long time ago.

Xo

About the Author

D.L. Darby lives in Anchorage, Alaska. She's a fur momma to her dog and cat and a superwife to her husband.

By day, she's a hairstylist, and by night, she's continuously drafting new ideas on her murder board at home. When she's not working, reading, or writing, you can find her glued to the TV, binging whatever new reality show Netflix has created.